NO EASY ANSWER

VALERIE KEOGH

BLOODHOUND
— BOOKS —

Print ISBN 978-1-913942-46-5

ALSO BY VALERIE KEOGH

THE DUBLIN MURDER MYSTERIES

No Simple Death

No Obvious Cause

No Past Forgiven

No Memory Lost

No Crime Forgotten

PSYCHOLOGICAL THRILLERS

The Three Women

The Perfect Life

The Deadly Truth

The Little Lies

For Gillian... because I promised.

An Garda Síochána: the police service of the Republic of Ireland.
Garda, or gardaí in the plural.
Commonly referred to as the *guards* or the *gardaí*.
Direct translation: "The Guardian of the Peace."

1

Detective Garda Sergeant Mike West was sitting at his desk in Foxrock Garda Station before the day shift officially began. Normally, he used this quiet period to review and assess their active cases and plan for any new ones that had come in overnight. This morning, however, he was faced with a mountain of paperwork pertaining to the case they'd finally closed late the day before.

He switched on his computer, staring into space as he waited for it to power up. The identity of the main perpetrator had come as a shock to them all. But with his solicitor whisking him off to the Central Mental Hospital in Dundrum for an assessment that would probably see him locked up there for many years to come, it was his two accomplices who would serve jail time. It wasn't the best outcome, but at least the victim had had justice served. Sometimes, West knew, that was all they could hope for.

It had been a busy few weeks for the detective unit with two challenging cases coming one after the other. Graphic images from both had stuck in West's brain and in the middle of the night, if he woke, they'd be there in full colour. Little Abasiama curled up in that abandoned suitcase... a body hanging from the beams in St Monica's church. Difficult cases. It had taken perseverance, hard work and a dollop of luck to solve both.

That morning, West was relieved to see there was only one new case logged since the previous evening. They were due a quiet spell. He read the scant details of a hit-and-run which had resulted in the death of an elderly woman.

Hopefully, it wouldn't have such a catastrophic effect as the last hit-and-run they'd dealt with, one whose far-reaching impact had resulted in further crimes, further heartbreak. Ella Parsons... he wondered how she was coping. With Milo Bennet in prison and his wife now living in Cork, West hoped that Ella, her husband, and her son could get on with their lives. He'd been shocked the last time he'd seen her, a pale wraith of a woman wracked with guilt for the death of the boy she'd knocked down and killed in a moment of careless stupidity. Sadly, he guessed, there was never going to be peace for her.

West shook his head and focused on this new hit-and-run. It appeared sad but uncomplicated. An elderly woman, Doris Whitaker, was found lying on the side of Torquay Road. Injuries sustained indicated she'd been hit by a vehicle.

They'd follow procedure; do the usual appeal to the driver to come forward or for any witnesses to the incident. Nearby CCTV might have caught a speeding car, or a slow-moving erratic one. Either was dangerous. They might get lucky, but West didn't think much of their chances.

He closed the report and brought up the paperwork he needed to complete that morning. But instead of starting the process, he sat back with the faint smile that had been there, on and off, since the night before. He'd arrived home, late and weary after closing the case to find Edel Johnson, not in bed asleep as he'd expected, but in the kitchen dishing him up dinner. He'd stared at her... the hair tied back in an untidy ponytail, the well-worn pair of cotton pyjamas, the tip of her tongue between her teeth as she scraped the end of the lasagne onto a plate and before he'd time to think, he'd asked her to marry him.

It was far from romantic; he was surprised she didn't laugh. But she didn't... she'd said *yes*.

He was still daydreaming when Garda Peter Andrews appeared in the doorway. 'Coffee?'

'Yes,' West said and a minute later picked up the mug that was placed before him and took a cautious sip.

Andrews slurped noisily from his mug. 'You need to learn to trust me.'

'I will when you learn not to mix them up and poison me with your sugary slop.' West took a mouthful and put the mug down. 'We did well yesterday.'

'I'd have preferred to have locked all three away, and that Laetitia lassie too, but what we got is okay.'

Neither man had taken to the petite Laetitia Summers, a woman who viewed the world through a self-obsessed lens. 'She's a slippery customer,' West said, 'but even she can't escape what she did. When her case comes up, she'll do time.'

'Good, the longer the better.' Andrews drained his coffee and put the mug down on the floor beside him. 'Inspector Morrison must be pleased too. Another case solved, plus no more priests running around the station or phone calls from the bishop.'

The recent discovery that the inspector had a dislike of the clergy had not made investigating a death in a church any easier. 'He'll be happy for a day or two.'

West and Andrews discussed the case for a few minutes before moving on to the active cases the team was currently investigating. 'Only one new one to add to our workload,' West said. 'You've read the report?'

'The hit-and-run? Yes, I have. Sad. We'll do an appeal for witnesses?'

'Yes, and an appeal for the driver to come forward.' The shock of knocking someone down would last for a few hours, then the brutal reality of what they'd done would kick in. The driver might do the right thing and hand himself in. It happened.

'I'll get Allen to start a check on the CCTV. We might get lucky.' Andrews picked up his mug and got to his feet. 'Okay, time to get on with it.'

'Before you go, I have some news for you.'

There must have been something in the way he said it, or maybe it was the reappearance of that smile but Andrews grinned and approached the desk with his hand extended. 'Well, it's about time!'

West grabbed his hand and shook it. 'Yes, tell Joyce she can go shopping for that hat at last.'

'It's marvellous news, congratulations.' Andrews kept hold of the hand for a moment longer then dropped it and sat back in the chair he'd vacated moments before, all thoughts of work forgotten in the face of this more exciting news. 'I thought you were going to shilly-shally forever. Joyce will be pleased. But as for the hat, she bought one in the sales a few months ago. She was sure it was going to happen.'

'Your wife is a very smart lady.'

'She is that, all right. So, when's the big day?'

West had expected Edel to want a small wedding, but to his surprise she told him she wanted a lavish affair. 'Next spring. Edel wants a big wedding with all the trimmings. It seems her first marriage was a registry office affair–'

'Not surprising since her so-called husband was running a scam.'

How could West forget? It was, after all, how he'd met his

fiancée. Edel had been the chief suspect in the disappearance of her husband. 'We've come a long way since then,' he said.

'A murder attempt, a couple of kidnappings, extortion.' Andrews counted them off on his finger. 'Yes, you certainly have come a long way. I know why you want to marry her, she's both beautiful and smart, but is Edel sure she wants to tie the knot with you?'

Whatever West would have replied was interrupted by Garda Mick Allen peering around the door frame. 'Sorry to butt in,' he said. 'The family of the elderly woman who was the victim of a hit-and-run driver yesterday evening are here and want to talk to the lead investigating officer.' He shrugged. 'I told him he could speak to me but he looked me up and down, obviously found me wanting, and asked to speak to a more senior officer.'

'It looks like we'll have to continue this conversation another time,' West said to Andrews. He tapped his keyboard and brought up the report on the hit-and-run. 'Bring them into whichever interview room is free, Mick, and I'll be there in a minute.'

West read over the report again. The garda on the scene had briefly questioned the woman who'd found the victim. But Lynda Checkley had been so shocked and horrified to have discovered the dead woman to be a relative that she'd little to say.

'They're in the Big One,' Allen said from the doorway. 'I know they're probably in shock but Darragh Checkley strikes me as a difficult customer.'

West had been a solicitor before he joined the Garda Síochána and he'd dealt with more than his share of awkward customers during that period. Truth was, anyone who dealt with the public in any capacity had to learn to deal with sometimes rude and often obnoxious people... it didn't mean they had to like it though.

The Big One... officially Interview Room One... was identical in all but name to the other interview room which was always referred to as the Other One. For reasons West had never managed to pin down, the Big One was the favourite of the two. He opened the door and automatically assessed the two people who sat at the far side of the table. They were a well-dressed middle-aged couple, the man pale and stern-faced, the woman, lower lip trembling, heavily made-up eyes smudged from crying. She held a balled-up tissue in her hand; as she lifted it to dab away tears diamond rings on three of her fingers glittered in the light from the strip of halogen overhead.

'I'm Detective Garda Sergeant Mike West,' he said, coming into the room and extending his hand. It was taken firmly by the man, limply by the woman who swapped the well-used tissue to her other hand to do so.

'Darragh and Lynda Checkley.' The man spoke for both of them.

West took the seat opposite and laced his fingers together on the table. 'My condolences for your loss, Mr and Mrs Checkley. It is terrible to lose someone in such difficult circumstances but please be assured we will do everything we can to catch the perpetrator of this crime.'

'Great words,' Checkley said with a sniff. 'What I'd like is more action. What exactly are you doing to catch the bastard who killed my cousin?'

'Everything within our power,' West said quietly. 'Perhaps, if you feel up to it, Mrs Checkley, you could tell me exactly what occurred yesterday.' He indicated the monitoring device in the corner of the room. 'As a routine, we record conversations. Is that okay with you?'

Lynda Checkley nodded, keeping her eyes on the tissue that

was disintegrating in her hand. 'I was on my way to visit Doris; I go once a week to see that she's okay and if she needs anything.'

'Did you ring her to let her know you were going?' West hoped to be able to pin down the time of the accident but he saw by the shake of her head he wasn't going to get lucky.

'No, but I never did. Doris was ninety, her heart wasn't working so well and she'd get breathless if she went too far. If she ran out of milk or something she might manage as far as the shops in the village or sometimes she went out for a bit of exercise or fresh air. She'd walk up the road a little, then back again. If she wasn't in, I'd just wait in the car until she came home.'

'And yesterday?'

Lynda looked up then with tear-washed eyes. 'I was almost at her house when I spotted something on the side of the road.' She snuffled softly and rubbed her nose with what was left of the tissue. 'I thought it was rubbish at first, that someone had dumped stuff, you know the way people do. I was going to pass by when a flash of colour caught my eye. The distinctive shade of green of Doris's favourite coat. She wore it all the time.' A tear trickled, she brushed it away. 'I stopped the car in the middle of the road and ran to her side. She was curled up and I thought at first she'd maybe fainted or something but when I turned her over, I could see the blood and the bruises.' She began to cry, leaning towards her husband who wrapped an arm around her and looked across the table to West as if her upset was all his doing.

'I think my wife has been through enough, don't you?' Checkley patted her on the back gingerly. 'Stop crying, Lynda, you'll make yourself ill.'

She didn't stop, instead she pulled away and hid her face in her hands.

Checkley looked as if he were going to remonstrate with her

again, but perhaps he knew he'd be wasting his breath. He focused on West instead, stabbing the air between them with a stubby finger. 'I'll be in contact daily, Sergeant West, until we get this bastard put away. Is that clear?'

'Perfectly.' West reached into his jacket pocket and took out a card. 'You can ring me on this number at any time.'

The card was taken without a word of thanks and shoved into a pocket. Checkley reached down to put an arm around his wife. 'Let's go, darling.' Without another word or glance in West's direction, they left the interview room.

West got to his feet. He'd make allowances for grief but he had a feeling that even under normal circumstances Darragh Checkley wouldn't be the most pleasant of characters to deal with. Remembering what had sounded very much like a threat of daily contact, West hoped they'd find the hit-and-run driver quickly.

Back in the main office, he spied Allen on his computer and headed over to have a word. 'I agree with your take on our friend.'

'A bit of a prick, isn't he?' Allen's hands were still flying over his keyboard. 'I've spoken to my contacts in the traffic corps. They had a mobile safety camera in operation on Stillorgan dual carriageway from 5pm till midnight. Nothing of any interest to us, unfortunately, but it was a bit of a stretch anyway. I've contacted the shop owners in Foxrock village... the ones we know that have working CCTV cameras outside, and they'll let us view the footage for the couple of hours in question.' He stopped tapping then and looked at West. 'I'm going back an hour from the time she was found.'

West knew Allen was assuming someone would have walked or driven past and seen the woman within an hour of her being knocked down. But Torquay Road was a quiet street, lined with large, detached homes. Unless you were going to walk to the shops in Foxrock village, there was no reason to be walking along it. And cars may have driven past thinking the poor woman's body was rubbish as had been Lynda's first assumption. 'I don't think the footfall is huge there. I'd expand the time frame by an hour... maybe even two.'

'Okay,' Allen said and went back to tapping the keyboard.

West left him to it and headed back to his office.

2

Darragh Checkley, true to his word, contacted West later that afternoon and the following morning, his tone becoming more irate as the hours passed without an arrest being made.

The post-mortem on Doris Whitaker's body was scheduled for Friday at 10am. West didn't expect to learn anything new but he went along as a matter of routine. It wasn't a great time to battle traffic to Blanchardstown but he pulled into the car park of Connolly Hospital at ten minutes to the hour, paid the extortionate car parking charge and made his way around to the mortuary that was situated in an old flat-roofed building to the rear of the new, extended, modern hospital complex.

He'd come straight from his home in Greystones. With only a few minutes to spare he rang the station and had a word with Andrews. 'I'll be in later,' he explained. 'I'm switching off my mobile so if the delightful Mr Checkley should ring, he's all yours.'

'Thanks for that. Just what I want to make my Friday complete.'

'Yes, well it's your turn to try to remain polite in the face of his rudeness. Anything new in for us?'

'A missing person. An elderly woman, Muriel Hennessy. She was last seen by her daughter on Sunday. Her son called to see her late yesterday afternoon. When she wasn't there, he waited an hour then went out to look for her. He spoke to a few neighbours but nobody could remember when they'd seen her last.'

West frowned. It had been wet and cold the last few nights. If an elderly woman had been caught outdoors, hypothermia might have set in. He remembered well the feeling of confusion that had come with it when he and Edel had been trapped in the cave on Clare Island. Hypothermia was a dangerous enemy.

'He rang it in at 9pm,' Andrews went on. 'Uniforms started a search straight away. Some of the neighbours joined in, too, but so far, no luck.'

'She might have fallen somewhere, got confused and lost her way. Call on the neighbours again and try to pinpoint when she was seen last. You know the drill, Peter. Ask Blunt to get us some extra help too, the more we have looking, the sooner we'll find her.'

The call had delayed him longer than he'd expected and it was two minutes past ten before he took a seat in the viewing area of the mortuary. The state pathologist, Dr Niall Kennedy, had already started but looked up to acknowledge West's arrival with a lift of a bloodstained gloved hand. 'I've finished my initial examination, Mike,' he said. 'There's extensive bruising to the victim's right side with a simple fracture of the right femur all of which are consistent with being hit by a car. There are more injuries to her left side where she hit the pavement – fractured humerus, clavicle, three ribs and, what I think will prove to be the fatal blow, a depressed fracture of her cranium.

'I've looked at the crime-scene photographs. I gather from the reports that the body was moved by the woman who found her but there is blood visible on the kerb, the angle of which matches the depression in her skull. I'd say she was thrown into the air by the car, and her head hit the kerb when she landed.' Kennedy continued to work as he spoke, removing organs, examining, weighing.

The blood and gore didn't bother West although the sound of the saw as Doris Whitaker's head was cut open did set his teeth on edge.

'In general, she was a remarkably healthy ninety-year-old,' Kennedy said finally. 'Some signs of cardiac disease but nothing that would have killed her any time soon. She might even have recovered from her injuries but for the head trauma.' He took off his gloves and fired them into the clinical waste bag. 'That was the kill blow and death would have been instantaneous.'

West raised a hand in thanks and left. Poor Doris, a nasty way to end her life but at least it had been quick. He'd tell Darragh Checkley the next time he spoke to him. Maybe knowing that would make it easier for him.

It was midday by the time West walked into the station. The main office was empty apart from Andrews who was hunched over some reports. He looked up as West opened the door, stretched, and linked his hands behind his head. 'How'd it go?'

'Poor Doris was pretty bashed up,' West said, perching on the side of the desk. 'Looks like her head hit the kerb when she was thrown and she sustained a fatal injury. Death, according to the pathologist, was instantaneous.'

'Well, I hope you're not thinking that will give that Darragh Checkley any comfort. He's been on the phone already, wasn't at all happy that you weren't here to speak to him.'

'It had crossed my mind but not with any real expectation. He's a difficult man.' West grinned at Andrews' expression. 'Yes, I can imagine you had more colourful words to describe him.'

'Just a few.'

'I'll give him a ring, try and sweeten him. I don't suppose we've got anywhere with finding the perp, have we?'

Andrews shook his head. 'No joy with any of the CCTV footage in Foxrock. Allen checked all garages within a five-mile radius to see if any cars had been booked in for repairs for damage consistent with a collision.' He shrugged. 'She was only a little bit of a thing; chances are any damage to the vehicle was minimal and didn't need repair. There has been no response to our appeal for the driver to come forward either but we'll run it again. You never know, we might get lucky.'

Luck. West often wondered if the general public realised how much they depended on it. 'Anything else?'

'Baxter and Edwards are co-ordinating the search for the missing woman, Muriel Hennessy. No sign yet but it's a big area, lots of back lanes, outhouses, and the like. It's going to take time. We have plenty of bodies helping. The daughter's friends arrived to help plus Tom managed to get us some extra uniforms from Dun Laoghaire and Blackrock.'

Tom Blunt, their desk sergeant, had an uncanny knack for conjuring up staff from other stations when needed. In a case like this one where the more eyes on the ground, the better, it was useful. 'They owe me,' was all Blunt would ever say when he asked how he managed it. Since the monosyllabic Blunt commanded huge respect, not only in Foxrock Station, but further afield, nobody ever took the liberty of asking what for.

'Good,' West said. 'Hopefully, we should locate the poor soul before nightfall.'

'I checked the forecast. It's going to be cold and wet so I hope so. Mrs Hennessy is eighty-five. It isn't a good age to be wandering around outside. Plus,' Andrews added, 'we've no idea how long she's been missing.'

West left him to his reports and headed to his office. He'd

cleared his in-tray of outstanding paperwork the previous day so the pile that had grown during the course of the morning made him frown. He flicked through it as he waited for his computer to power up. Mostly it was rubbish that went directly into the bin leaving him with only a few reports to read that he scanned with little enthusiasm.

The same reports came through online and he shook his head at the stupidity of the duplication which he knew was done simply for Sergeant Clark's benefit. Clark, in charge of the robbery division, had been known to state categorically that he'd never received an email if it suited him. West had no time for the lazy, boorish detective.

He'd not much regard for the boorish Darragh Checkley either, but he picked up the phone to ring him anyway in the interest of maintaining a relationship with the man. The phone was answered almost immediately.

'I was at your cousin's post-mortem this morning. Dr Kennedy, the state pathologist, said her death would have been instantaneous. I wanted to let you know that she wouldn't have suffered.'

West didn't expect thanks so wasn't disappointed at Checkley's sharp reply. 'That's all well and good but I gather you are no nearer to catching the bastard who ran her down.'

It seemed easier to stick to the standard reply. With someone like Checkley, you were never going to win. 'The case is ongoing, Mr Checkley, and we're following up several lines of enquiry.'

A gruff laugh came down the line. 'Sure you are. Right, I'll ring back tomorrow and we'll see how far along those lines you've managed to get.'

The phone went dead and West hung it up with a grunt of irritation just as Andrews came through the door. 'Checkley?' he said, with a grin.

'Who else?'

'Well, you'll be glad to get out of here then.'

West raised an eyebrow. 'Something interesting?'

'Maybe.' Andrew wagged his head side to side. 'A call came in from the recycling centre. They think they've found something suspicious. I didn't want to pull gardaí from the search for the Hennessy woman so I thought we could go. Get some fresh air.'

'Good idea.' West jumped to his feet. 'We could get lunch somewhere while we're at it.'

The recycling centre wasn't far from the station. As Andrews drove, he kept up a running commentary of the weird, wonderful and downright bizarre things he'd been called to over the course of his career.

West wasn't listening. His mind was on the following day when he was taking Edel to buy an engagement ring. 'Debeerds.' He hadn't realised he'd spoken aloud until Andrews turned to look at him.

'That's what I said! Downright weird!'

'Right.' West didn't think there was any point in enlightening him. He tried to put the following day from his mind and concentrate on what Andrews was saying.

A few minutes later, they pulled into the recycling centre. Whatever the staff had found that warranted calling out the gardaí obviously wasn't considered serious enough to shut down the business. Cars and vans continued to arrive; each parking space quickly taken by the next vehicle. Boots yawned open to disgorge the unwanted, the broken and the rubbish. Up the metal steps the customers went, laden down, then a quick toss and it was gone.

Andrew pulled up outside the site office and both men got out. A thin man wearing neon-bright overalls stood in the doorway and lifted a hand in greeting as the two men approached. 'I was hoping you'd be here soon.'

'Mr Todd?'

'Yea, that's me. Clem Todd.'

West introduced himself and Andrews. 'You reported something suspicious in one of your containers?'

Todd waved to the far end of the site. 'It's the household domestic waste container. It's due to be emptied later today so it's quite full. A customer came running down the steps shouting that he'd seen a leg sticking out of a bag. A leg is a bit suspicious, isn't it?' When that didn't get the reaction he wanted, he jerked his thumb into the office behind. 'He's sitting inside.'

The office door was open, West could see a man sitting cross-legged, eyes wide in excitement or shock. 'We'll speak to him in a moment. I assume you've closed off access to that container?'

'As soon as your man there said what he'd seen we shut it off with a chain.' Todd folded his arms across his chest. 'We have a second container for domestic waste but this is a big site. Only having the one is slowing things down and our customers are a bit pissed off. As soon as you can let us get back to using it, I'd appreciate it.'

West didn't have the heart to tell the man that if there really was a leg in the container, it would be shut for a long time. 'Okay. We'll go have a look.'

'I bet it's a doll or a mannequin,' Andrews said as they crossed between parked cars to the container in question.

Todd had been true to his word. A chain had been hung across the stairway that gave access to the container, a battered sign hanging from it proclaiming that it was not in use. West unhooked the end of the chain and he and Andrews set foot on the first step. 'Right,' West said, hooking the chain back in place. 'Let's see what we've got.'

The stairway rattled ominously as they climbed. On the broad top step, the container edge was about chest high. Anyone bringing a bag of household waste would have to heft it up to throw it in.

'There,' Andrew said, pointing to a black plastic bag almost in the centre of the mass of rubbish and out of their reach.

West looked to where he pointed. 'Yes, I see it. It's not a mannequin or a doll though.' If it were it would have been a garish pink, pseudo-healthy shade. Not the mottled, greyish foot that extended at an angle from the bag. 'There must be 500 bags here, maybe more, along with other unbagged rubbish. This isn't going to be easy.'

'Forensics are going to love us. Maybe we should throw another bag on top, tell Todd it was a mistake, and run away.'

'I could see the headline now,' West said as he turned to take the steps down. '*Cops cop out on container corpse.*'

Andrews snorted. 'I can better that. How about, *Gardaí don't have a leg to stand on!*'

'In lieu of those scary headlines, perhaps we'd better investigate.' West put the chain back over the steps and together they crossed to the site office.

The man who'd made the grim discovery stood as they entered. 'I was right, wasn't I?'

'We'll get our forensic people out and they'll make that determination,' West said, giving nothing away. 'Can you tell me exactly what happened?'

The man rubbed his hands together. 'Nothing much to tell. We're moving house and wanted to get rid of a pile of stuff. I'd put loads of things in the recycling containers and was getting rid of the final two bags of rubbish. I took them up the steps and had to put one down to heave the other up to throw it on top. The container is quite full.' He looked accusingly at the site manager as he said this.

'And then?' Andrews nudged him.

'There was a mound of bags, when I threw my second bag in,

it hit it and made it sort of tumble down... well, not tumble really, more fell apart.' He held his hands up. 'It all happened so quickly. Anyway, I was turning away when I noticed something sticking out of one of the bags.' He looked from Andrews to West and gulped. 'I love zombie movies and TV series, that's how I knew what it was.'

'A zombie.' Todd gave an uncertain laugh.

'No–' the man glared at him, '–a dead body.'

'Okay, thank you,' West said. 'If you'd leave us your name and address, we won't need to keep you any further but, at your convenience, you need to come to the station and write a statement.' West saw doubt in the man's eyes. 'Or we could arrange for a garda to call to your house.'

The man shrugged. 'No, that's fine I can call into the station.' He left his details and strode away, his shoulders hunched around his ears telling the world he was not a happy man.

West turned to the manager. 'We're going to have to keep that container shut down for a while, I'm afraid.' He saw resignation in the man's weather-worn face. 'We also need an area for the forensic team to use. All the bags in that container will need to be removed and opened.'

Todd ran a hand over his face. 'You're talking about nearly 500 bags!'

West looked back to the container and nodded. 'Yes, that's what I estimated.'

3

An hour later, the garda technical team arrived. Todd, proving himself to be a competent site manager, quickly rearranged the parking to free up a large area close to the container in question and directed the team's vehicles into the space with a wave of his hand.

West walked out to meet them, pleased to see Detective Sergeant Maddison in charge.

'Afternoon, David,' he said.

Maddison's weathered face was topped with a grey buzz cut that never seemed to grow. He ran his hand over it and looked towards the container with a sigh. 'Body dump?'

There was no time for small talk when faced with clearing a full container of rubbish. 'I'm afraid that's what it looks like. There's a foot and part of a leg poking out of a burst refuse bag at the top. The man who alerted the staff was throwing his own bag in. He says he disturbed a mound of bags which toppled, so it may be that the bag was there for a few hours.'

'Or days. Bags get moved around by the weight of others.' Maddison glanced back to the container. 'Did the manager say when it was emptied last?'

'Wednesday.'

'Okay. We'll start with the bag with the body part and see what it contains. Best-case scenario, the bag contains one complete body.' He didn't say anything more, leaving to join his team and start what was going to be a difficult job.

He didn't have to say more, anyway. West knew what the worst-case scenario would be. One body part that would send them searching for the remainder of the corpse, or multiple body parts from more than one victim that would start warning bells clanging loudly.

'Todd's going to have the CCTV footage sent to us,' Andrews said, joining him. 'It shows vehicles entering and leaving, and the area in front of the office, but unfortunately doesn't show the access stair to the container.'

'I was hoping we'd get a shot of someone hauling an unusually heavy bag up the steps.'

'That's you being sarcastic,' Andrews said with a grin.

They stepped back as more of the team headed for the container. 'Maddison is going to remove the obvious body-part bag first, so we should know pretty quickly what we're dealing with.'

There was nothing to do but wait. They knew better than to hang around and get in the way of the technical team so they walked back to the car and sat inside.

Andrews yawned. 'You going to ring the inspector?'

West was debating that very idea. 'No, we may as well wait till we have the full story.'

'A serial killer on our patch disposing of bits of bodies wherever they fancy.' Andrews' voice was almost cheerful.

'You've been watching too much TV again. It'll turn out to be something less exciting... skulduggery from whatever company oversees the disposal of body parts from a hospital or something.' It was a far preferable outcome than Andrews' prediction. They could do with a simple case to investigate for a change.

Less than twenty minutes later, they saw one of the technical team approach the car and got out to meet him.

'News?' West said.

'Sergeant Maddison said to come and get you,' the man said, giving nothing away.

The technical team had screened off a section of their allocated area. It gave them some privacy from the members of the public who strained to see what was going on. Maddison stood at the entrance waiting for them. 'You are not going to like this.'

Seven words that were guaranteed to make the hair on the back of West's neck stand on end. He met Andrews' eyes and knew he felt the same. They followed Maddison through the narrow opening into the small, enclosed area. The smell here was rank, a foetid stink of decay that had West automatically screwing up his nose.

The contents of the large, black plastic bag were carefully laid out on a white plastic sheet. At first glance, it didn't seem too bad. One body. It only took a second to see that West's first estimation was wrong and he bit back a groan. 'There's two left hands.'

'Yes, but unfortunately–' Maddison pointed to the torso, '– neither arm belongs to that.'

West looked at him, startled. 'Three bodies?'

Maddison shook his head slowly. 'Hard to say at this stage but I think there might be four, at least.' He pointed to the only leg. 'It doesn't match the torso or the arms.'

Four bodies. West hunkered down to take a closer look, fascinated despite the choking stink. 'All of the parts look to be at a similar state of decomposition.'

'There's something odd about them, but I'm puzzled as to

what. I've contacted the state pathologist, Dr Kennedy, and we're sending everything in to him now. I wanted you to see it all before we did.'

West took a final look around the ghoulish display. 'Thanks. Dr Kennedy will no doubt be able to enlighten us.'

Maddison jerked a thumb to the opening. 'We'll keep on here, hopefully we'll find the rest.' He took a final look at the body parts on the ground. 'It's odd though...'

West looked at the macabre collection. 'Odder than that?'

'I'd go for equally as odd. Somebody kept at least four bodies until they were dead a considerable amount of time, then they chopped them up. But instead of putting one body into one bag, they just shoved the parts in any old way. As if they'd piled the body parts up and took whatever was nearest.'

'Four bodies!' Inspector Morrison looked understandably appalled; his frown so deep that his hairy eyebrows formed one line across his forehead.

West propped a shoulder against the wall of his office. 'At least four. They'd only opened one bag, inspector, there's around 499 more to go through. They may find more remains, hopefully enough to make four complete bodies and no more. It would be convenient if they could find the heads, too, of course–'

'Convenient?' Morrison looked even more horrified and gave an audible gulp.

'Well, yes, to enable us to identify the victims.'

'It's a sad situation when we speak about finding a bag of heads as being convenient, Sergeant West.'

'I wasn't thinking about a bag of heads,' West said. That thought made him grimace. 'But unless DNA or fingerprints work in our favour, it may be difficult to identify the bodies without a face.'

Morrison looked as if he wanted to say more but then swatted the idea away with the back of his hand and sat in his chair, his eyebrows separating into their individual components again. 'Dr Kennedy will be able to provide the Missing Persons Bureau with DNA from each victim.'

West knew the bureau had a vast database. It would be a start. 'It's going to take a few days for the technical team to work through that container.'

'Meanwhile, we've got to find out who is killing people, chopping them into pieces and disposing of them on our patch.'

'Four people.' West didn't want to state the obvious, he knew the inspector would be thinking the same thing.

'Don't say it,' Morrison replied sharply. 'Let's get all the facts before we jump to conclusions.'

West took the back stairs down to the detective unit. Okay, they hadn't said the words, but he knew Morrison would be sitting at his desk thinking about them all the same.

Serial killer.

4

W est was sitting behind his desk when Detective Garda Seamus Baxter walked in, his round freckled face set into grim lines.

It was an expression West knew well. It said they'd reached an outcome in an investigation that wasn't a happy one. 'You found Mrs Hennessy.'

'We've found the body of an elderly woman.' Baxter dropped onto the chair and ran a hand through his ginger hair. 'It was found behind the refuse bins in the laneway at the back of O'Dea's Takeaway.'

West knew the place. He frowned. 'She'd wandered a bit further than we thought, then. What on earth took her around there?'

'There's what looks like vomit near the body. Maybe she was feeling sick, didn't want to embarrass herself by puking in public so took herself out of sight.'

'Perhaps,' West agreed. 'And it's definitely her?'

Baxter shrugged. 'It looks like her body has been there a couple of days at least. The bins were emptied by the council on Monday so her body could have been there any time since then.

Staff in the takeaway empty their rubbish into the bins in the evening but the area is poorly lit and her body was tucked up almost behind so she wouldn't have been seen.

'Apart from the council, nobody else uses the laneway so it's quiet but there's enough food remnants around and enough open spaces in the vicinity for it to have a sizeable population of rodents.'

Rats and mice. West grimaced. 'Bad?'

'A lot of damage to the exposed bits, her face and hands especially. She was wearing a heavy coat, buttoned up to her chin which prevented more damage to her torso.' Baxter shook his head. 'The family won't want to see her like that but at least the rodents left her wedding ring and a pretty ugly engagement ring. They'll suffice for identification.' He got to his feet. 'The daughter is on her way in now. She was out with one of the search parties.'

'She'll know it's bad news.'

'Yes, but it won't make the telling any easier.' Baxter nodded towards the main office. 'Edwards is calling all the search teams in and the body is on the way to the mortuary.' Straightening his shoulders, he left to wait for the arrival of Muriel Hennessy's daughter.

Andrews entered as Baxter left. 'Sad end to that case.' He sat on the seat the younger man had vacated, folded his arms and looked across the desk. 'Well?'

West didn't have to ask what he meant. He and Andrews were on the same wavelength, they knew each other's thoughts. Sometimes it was eerie, mostly it saved a lot of work. 'The inspector doesn't want to hear the words *serial killer* until we have something more to go on.' He shrugged. 'He's right, you know, there was something odd about those body parts, did you notice?'

Andrews had, of course. 'Any body parts I've seen before

were–' he searched for an appropriate word, then untucked a hand and waved it, '–wetter, if you know what I mean.'

West did. Decomposing body parts tended to stick in your mind long after a case was resolved. 'I do, and I agree, these looked dried out and it was odd that there was no blood. Maybe they'll turn out to be man-made, you know, tossed out by some drama society or something.'

'Maybe.' Andrews checked his watch. 'No point in worrying about it till we hear and that's going to be Monday at this rate.' He jerked a thumb back to the main office. 'Jarvis is having a look at the CCTV footage from the two cameras but it's going to take a few hours. He said he's going to stay till he's done.'

'Looking for someone carrying unusually heavy bags and seeming furtive?'

'Now that would be something. Unfortunately, he's likely to see nothing. The cameras were obvious and it would be easy for someone to avoid them by parking a little further along. They wouldn't be able to avoid being picked up by the camera on entering though. On Monday we can start identifying ownership of each vehicle, see if anything comes up that way.'

'Monday,' West said, getting to his feet. 'Until then, let's enjoy the weekend.'

Music was blaring as West opened the door of his home in Greystones. It brought instant relaxation to his tense shoulders. Edel Johnson, his fiancée, the woman who had led him a merry dance over the last year. She filled his home with life and love.

He stood in the kitchen doorway and watched her in amusement. Her fingers were flying over the keyboard, her head down, focused, hair loose and wild as if she'd run her fingers through it several times during the day. How she could write with that music blaring he didn't know. It was Tyler, the chihuahua, who noticed his arrival and ran forward to say hello and drew Edel's attention from her writing.

'Mike,' she said, looking at him, then at the time displayed on the corner of her screen. 'Oh no, is that the time.' She got to her feet and stretched her arms up, closing the distance between them as she did and bringing her arms down around his shoulders. 'I've had a really productive writing day. The words were jumping from my fingers.' She rested her head on his shoulder. 'I came down to make something for dinner about an hour ago but made the mistake of bringing my laptop with me. Honestly,' she said, pulling back to look at him. 'I only sat to write a couple of words.'

West tightened the arms he'd slid around her waist. 'I'm glad it's going well for you,' he said, kissing her before taking a step back. 'Now how about you get out of your writing clothes and we go out for something to eat?'

Edel laughed and pulled at the fabric of her T-shirt. 'You mean you don't think a scruffy T and baggy bottoms are a good look?'

'I love you in anything but I bet you a hundred euro you won't go out like that.'

'You could have made it interesting and bet me a thousand, then I might have given it some consideration! Okay, give me ten minutes and I'll be ready. Why don't you ring the Italian and see if they have a table free?'

The Italian restaurant overlooking the marina in Greystones, half an hour's walk away, was one of their favourites. With Edel's hand clasped in his, West listened as she told him about the direction the crime novel she was writing was going. 'It'll be finished on schedule,' she said. 'Then I'm going to dive straight into the next.'

A few months previously, Edel had a contract with a

publisher to write family sagas. Thanks to a conniving, manipulative woman who'd crossed their paths, that contract was torn up. Edel had been devastated. Self-publishing hadn't worked for her so when her agent Owen Grady came up with a plan to re-establish her, she'd jumped at it. By then, however, she'd decided to write crime novels rather than family sagas. It was a change West was still adjusting to.

'No regrets,' he asked her now as they approached the restaurant. When she looked puzzled, he clarified. 'About switching to crime?'

Her laugh pealed out, drawing an echoing smile. 'You really need to be careful when you say that: people could misinterpret.'

It wasn't until the waiter had taken their order and they were sitting with glasses of wine in their hands that she answered his question. 'No regrets at all. I'm really enjoying writing this book and I know it's going to be a great series.'

'Good,' he said, reaching for her hand. 'I'm glad you're happy.'

'I am. Now why don't you tell me about this new case that's clouding your eyes.'

He looked at her in surprise.

Edel raised her glass to him and smiled. 'I can't read your mind but you'd relaxed after the church murder was solved and today, you're distracted again.'

'Maybe it's the thought of finally marrying the woman I love that has me distracted?'

'Hmm, nice try. I like to hear about your cases. Why don't you tell me about it?'

The arrival of their food claimed their attention for a few minutes. West looked across the table as Edel picked up her first slice of pizza. A discussion of the provenance of body parts wasn't the usual romantic dinner conversation but perhaps their relationship was never destined to be typical. 'Okay, let me tell you about my day.'

∼

'An interesting one,' Edel said, manoeuvring another slice of pizza into her mouth. 'And all the parts were in the same condition?'

'Looked to be so anyway.' He shrugged. 'They might yet turn out to be man-made.'

'Or fallen off zombies,' she said with a chuckle.

'That's what the guy who found them said.'

'A new type of criminal fraternity?' She reached for another slice. 'Might be an idea for a novel there.'

'Okay, how about we change the topic to something more romantic.' West reached for her left hand and tapped her ring finger. 'Tomorrow, we'll go shopping for that ring I promised you.' He watched the crime writer immediately drop away and his fiancée return. 'I thought we'd go to Debeerds,' he said, naming an iconic Grafton Street jewellers that made Edel's eyes sparkle. 'I want to get you something special.'

'I have something special,' she said, returning the pressure of his hand.

'Something more special then,' he insisted with a laugh. And the conversation for the rest of the evening centred around the next day, and the days after that.

∼

Edel was amused and touched by the fuss Mike was making. She assumed they'd drive to Greystones and take a DART into the city from there so was taken aback when he told her to hurry, that a taxi was picking them up at 10am.

'Honestly, we could have gone by DART, Mike,' she remonstrated.

He shook his head. 'I was thinking about hiring a limo but thought that might be a bit OTT.'

She laughed. 'God, yes, maybe a bit. Okay, a taxi it is then but you'd better go downstairs and leave me to get ready.'

A glance at the clock told her she had fifteen minutes to spare. She'd planned to wear trousers, a warm jacket and comfortable shoes for walking around the shops. With a sigh, she decided more of an effort was required and looked through her wardrobe for something to suit.

When she heard Mike call up the stairs that it was almost ten, she was nearly ready. The black jersey dress clung in all the right places and wasn't something she would normally wear during the day, but it looked right for the occasion. She added a plain gold neck chain and earrings, slipped her feet into black high heels that would be murder by the end of the day, picked up her coat and bag and headed down the stairs just as she heard the sound of the taxi pulling up outside.

She knew she'd chosen the right outfit when Mike's eyes lit up.

'You look stunning.'

'You don't look so bad yourself,' she said, reaching his side and slipping her hand into his. And suddenly, she knew there'd be no problem with her high heels, she was going to float through the day.

The taxi left them near the main entrance to Stephen's Green.

'Maybe we could go for a walk around the park later,' West said, taking her hand as they crossed the road and headed down Grafton Street.

The pedestrianised street was, as usual, thronged with people. Several street performers, musicians, singers and mime artists, competed for attention and money. Edel and West stopped to listen and watch. It was sunny, the weather unseasonably warm, they had a day to themselves and they were determined to enjoy every moment.

Finally, they arrived at Debeerds, its double-fronted windows glittering with a dazzling display of jewels. Edel tightened her grip on Mike's hand as excitement fizzed. For a second, it was dampened by memories of her first engagement to the charming Simon Johnson, the lying, cheating bigamist who had caused her so much pain and grief. She turned to look at the man beside her and said a final goodbye to the memory. 'I love you, you know,' she said to Mike.

'And I, you.' He kissed her quickly, then pressed the doorbell to gain admission to Debeerds.

The upmarket, traditional jewellery shop was synonymous with expensive luxury and West and Edel were greeted like valuable returning customers. The shop was spacious and well designed with a counter directly opposite the door and one to each side. Upholstered red velvet chairs were set in pairs at discrete intervals in front of the counters, only two of which were occupied.

An assistant crossed the shop floor to greet them. 'Good morning. And what can we help you with today?' He looked from one to the other. 'No, don't answer that, I can tell from your wonderful expressions.' And without another word, he led them to chairs set in front of counters that dazzled with diamonds.

Edel gasped and sank onto a chair, her eyes fixated by the array of gems on display. How on earth was she going to decide? And, goodness, how much did they cost?

The assistant joined them from the other side. 'Now, did you have something in mind?'

She felt Mike's eyes on her and turned to meet them. 'Wow,' she said, then turned back to the assistant. 'Something very simple.'

'I like that one,' Mike said, pointing to one of the rings.

'You have excellent taste,' the assistant said, reaching for it. He placed it on a velvet cushion in front of Edel. 'This is platinum and rose gold set with a square princess-cut diamond.' He nudged the cushion towards her. 'Please, try it on, I think it might actually be your size.'

It was. Edel slipped it on her finger and gulped. It was magnificent. 'Very nice,' she said, taking it off. 'Now, perhaps something simpler.'

'Of course.'

A selection of rings were placed in front of her, but the experienced assistant left the first ring sitting on the cushion. It threw all the other rings into shade. 'Maybe this one,' Edel said, holding her hand up. The tiny solitaire twinkled once.

'You really prefer that to this?' Mike picked up the first ring and held it beside the one she wore. 'There's no comparison.'

'Perhaps I'll leave you for a moment to discuss it,' the assistant said before vanishing.

'Look,' Mike said, pulling the small solitaire from her hand and slipping the other one on. 'It suits you so much better. Strong and beautiful.'

Edel couldn't take her eyes from it. 'It's lovely... but it must cost a fortune.'

'So, I'll sell the house.' He laughed when he saw her face. 'I'm kidding! Seriously, I can afford whatever it costs.'

'It could be several thousand euro,' she said, annoyed with herself for weakening. But it was so beautiful.

'I tell you what,' Mike said, taking her hand in his. 'How about we reach a compromise. If it's more than ten K, you choose something else. Less than that and we get it.'

Edel narrowed her eyes. She wasn't sure where the compromise was there. She looked at the ring on her hand, held it up to the light and knew she wanted it.

The assistant sidled along the counter. 'I see you've decided.'

'Not quite,' Edel said firmly.

'My fiancée is concerned about the cost,' West said. 'So we've come to a compromise.'

'Excellent.' The assistant took it in his stride and without asking what the compromise was, reached behind him for a notebook. He took a pen from his pocket, scribbled a figure on the page and with dramatic flair tore the sheet from the pad, folded it and slid it across towards West.

Edel watched with a wary eye as Mike unfolded the page. It would have been simpler, surely, for the assistant to tell them but she bit her tongue and played the game the way she supposed it was usually played.

'That's fine,' West said.

'Not quite,' Edel said, reaching for the paper. There was a moment's duelling before Mike handed it over. She unfolded it and swallowed the gasp. Eight thousand euro. For a ring. She opened her mouth to argue but caught Mike's eyes and shut it again. They had agreed on a compromise. It was less than ten K. 'Yes, thank you, it is stunning.'

Since it fit perfectly, all that was needed was for Mike to hand over his credit card.

'Now, if you'll allow me,' the assistant said, when that was done and the card returned, 'I'll take the ring back for a final polish.'

'It looks perfect,' Edel said, reluctant now to remove it.

'I will make it sparkle even better; I promise you.'

There seemed no point in arguing so she slipped the ring from her finger and handed it to him.

'It's the most beautiful ring I've ever seen,' she whispered to Mike as they waited for him to return.

'Perfectly matched then.' He leaned forward and planted a kiss on her cheek.

A few minutes later the assistant returned. 'Now, see, more beautiful!'

Edel didn't notice any difference but for politeness agreed that it was as he slipped the ring back onto her finger. 'Thank you.'

The assistant shook hands with them both and wished them well before hurrying around the counter to see them to the door. He was delayed momentarily by one of his colleagues, leaving Edel and West standing in the middle of the shop.

Edel was surprised when Mike nodded to the person sitting in the chair behind and saw a middle-aged man staring bad-temperedly at them. Her faint smile didn't have any effect and she looked away, unwilling to have anything spoil her pleasure.

'My apologies,' the assistant said, hurrying toward them. He opened the door, thanked them for their custom and wished them a happy future.

'We're going to have a very happy future,' Edel said, linking her arm through Mike's, flicking her hand backwards and forwards to make the diamond sparkle. 'It's so beautiful.'

They strolled back up Grafton Street and had time for a walk around Stephen's Green before heading for the Shelbourne Hotel where Mike had booked a table for lunch. Edel mentally congratulated herself on dressing for the part as the maître d' led them to their table where a bottle of champagne sat in an ice bucket waiting to be popped. It was all so perfect; she couldn't stop smiling.

Conversation was light and cheerful and frequently touched on how stunning the engagement ring was. 'It was crazily expensive, Mike.' Edel held out her hand, admiring how the diamond glinted under the Shelbourne's huge chandeliers.

'It's worth it to see you happy.'

'I'd have been happy with a brass ring as long as I'm marrying you.'

'Now she tells me,' Mike said, raising his eyes to the ceiling.

It wasn't until the coffee was served that Edel remembered the man in the jewellers. 'Who was the man you nodded hello to? Not one of the criminal fraternity, I hope.'

'No, a man whose elderly cousin was killed in a hit-and-run recently. He's been pressurising us to find the person responsible.'

'Ah, I see now. He was giving you a terrible look. I suppose he was thinking you should be out finding the driver rather than cavorting with me.'

'Probably. He's not a particularly pleasant man to deal with.'

'He certainly seemed unfriendly,' Edel said. 'He's got expensive taste though.' She saw a spark of interest on Mike's face. 'I was doing some research for one of my characters the other day. I wanted to know what kind of watch he'd wear so I was looking up Rolex. I heard your friend say he'd take the watch he was trying on as we were leaving.' She raised an eyebrow. 'It caught my attention because it was exactly the one that I decided my over-the-top character would wear. You're talking around eighteen K for that, Mike.'

'Eighteen thousand euro for a watch!'

Edel laughed, held out her hand and wiggled her ring finger. 'Well, you paid eight thousand for a ring.'

'And it was worth it.' He reached for her hand and held it tightly, his thumb brushing over the ring.

'Maybe he thinks the watch is. What's worrying you about it? And don't say nothing, I can see it in your eyes.'

West shrugged. 'It's probably nothing but his cousin was

killed on Wednesday, and now he's in buying an expensive watch. Just seems a bit off to me.'

'Maybe it's his birthday and it had been planned for a while.' She squeezed his hand. 'Time enough to go back to being crime writer and detective garda tomorrow night. Let's stay in fiancée/ fiancé mode a little longer, okay?'

And for the rest of the weekend, that's what they did.

5

W est might have given the impression that he'd forgotten about Darragh Checkley's purchase of an expensive Rolex, but he hadn't. It bothered him and he wasn't sure if it was simply because the man was an obnoxious boor or whether it was something else.

He toyed with the idea of looking into the man's finances but he had no justifiable reason for doing such a thing and he wasn't a man who bent the rules for his own purposes. Anyway, on Monday morning he had more important things to do. First thing was to return a call from Detective Garda Sergeant Maddison. He hoped the garda technical team leader was going to have good news for him.

His call was answered straight away but that was the last of the good news.

'Four bodies. Complete apart from the heads,' Maddison said. 'At a guess, I'd say an older male and female and two younger, also male and female. We finished emptying the container late yesterday and that was it.'

'No damn heads,' West said. 'That's great. So, they might turn up somewhere else.'

'Or maybe the killer kept them.'

'Like trophies?'

'Both Ted Bundy and Jeffrey Dahmer did, so it's not unheard of,' Maddison said. 'Four dead bodies, Mike, it looks to me like you've a serial killer to find.'

West hung up and sat back. Four bodies. He supposed he should be grateful they hadn't found more. He checked his watch and reached for the phone. It was answered almost immediately by the efficient administrator in the Office of the State Pathologist. 'May I speak to Dr Kennedy, please?'

He was left listening to music that would have appealed to Andrews but which set his teeth on edge. 'They're playing your song,' he said, holding the phone out when Andrews walked through the door seconds later.

'"Ring of Fire', one of Johnny Cash's best.'

West grunted then waved his hand at him to be quiet. 'Good morning, Niall.'

'Whatever it is, the answer is no,' the gruff voice replied. 'The post-mortem of that poor soul Muriel Hennessy will be at eleven tomorrow if that's what you're ringing for.'

'No, I hadn't planned to attend,' West said. It was a cut-and-dried case with no crime element to involve the detective unit; he didn't feel an obligation to go. 'I'm ringing about the body parts that were found in the recycling container. I was speaking to Maddison; he tells me they're finished on site.'

'Yes, he was kind enough to leave me a message to say they'd not found any further parts.' A long sigh came down the phone. 'The skulls are missing, though, so I suppose you're thinking about a serial killer keeping trophies à la Ted Bundy and Jeffrey Dahmer?'

Everyone knew the stories. West guessed he'd be tired hearing those two infamous names before this case was done. 'Yes, but we don't want to jump the gun. Both Andrews and I thought there was something odd about those body parts. Maddison seems convinced they're real, but I'm not so sure so until we have confirmation from you we're keeping a lid on it.'

'Fine, no pressure then,' Kennedy said with heavy sarcasm. 'Okay.' He sighed, relenting as he often did. 'I'll get onto them as soon as I have the post done.'

'Good, well I might drop over to Drumcondra this afternoon and see what's what. If that's okay with you?'

'Sure. Stop in Thunders on your way. I like their meringues.'

With a promise to arrive with supplies, West hung up. 'If I hear Ted Bundy or Jeffrey Dahmer's name mentioned again today, I'll scream.'

'Ah,' said Andrews, sitting on the chair opposite and crossing his ankle over his knee. 'They didn't find the heads then, I take it.'

'No. Hence the trophy idea from Maddison and Kennedy.' West ran a hand over his hair. 'I know we have more to be doing than going out looking for problems–'

'But?' Andrews interrupted. 'What maggot have you got in your head now?'

'Checkley.'

The name made Andrews grimace. 'Apart from being a troublesome git, what's he done to you.'

'It's probably nothing. But he is making such a fuss with his demands that we find his cousin's killer that I didn't expect to see him in Debeerds on Saturday.'

'Debeerds. Well now, I suppose we'll be seeing a big sparkler on Edel's hand when she's in next.' Andrews folded his arms across his chest. 'So what was the charming Checkley doing in there?'

'Paying eighteen grand for a Rolex.'

Andrews whistled softly. 'That's a hefty sum.'

'Less than three days after his beloved cousin was killed so tragically.'

'Do I hear a tinge of sarcasm there?'

'More than a trace,' West said with a grin that faded. 'Something about him is off.' He tapped his hand on the desk. 'You're going to think this is odd but–'

'I knew it!' Andrews threw his hands in the air. 'You've got a maggot in your brain.'

'Hear me out.' West tried to put the idea that had come to him when he woke that morning into words that would convince his sceptical partner. 'Checkley has gone out of his way to be particularly obnoxious. So much so that we've had little time for him and would be delighted to shut the hit-and-run case down as soon as possible by either solving it or having it slide into the cold-case pile. True?'

'Maybe. The hit-and-run isn't going anywhere. The lads have followed up every angle. We have notifications with every garage within a thirty-mile radius on the off chance some damage was sustained.' Andrews held his hands up again, this time in defeat. 'Unless someone knows something and comes forward–'

'Exactly,' West said, leaning towards him. 'It'll get shelved and we'll all be relieved not to have to deal with Darragh Checkley again.'

Andrews frowned. 'So what are you saying? That he's being particularly rude and offensive so that we give up more easily?'

'It's human nature to try more for people we like and less for people we don't.'

'We'd do our job regardless.'

'Yes, but not necessarily go that extra mile.'

'Perhaps,' Andrews conceded. 'But I'm still not sure what you're getting at.'

West sat back and linked his hands on his head. 'There's something. Maybe there's a reason he wants to keep us at a distance.' He blinked as a thought came to him. 'Maybe there's a good reason why we haven't found that hit-and-run driver, Peter.' His hands dropped to the desk, fingers drumming the table as he tried to make sense of the ideas that were spinning in his head. 'Lynda Checkley says she saw Doris lying on the side of the road, stopped her car and ran to help.'

'Yes.'

'What if she saw her before that... what if she saw her crossing the road and took advantage of an opportunity to get rid of her?'

Andrews said nothing for a moment, his eyes narrowed in thought. 'Nobody questioned her story so nobody checked her car and there wasn't likely to be obvious damage to draw attention. By all accounts, the old lady was frail. It wouldn't have taken much to have sent her flying.' He nodded slowly. 'I know the house Doris Whitaker lived in. One of those huge, detached houses on Torquay Road. Worth a few million I'd say. And I'm guessing Darragh Checkley is her next of kin.'

'Money as motive. It's always a good one.' West slapped the table with the palm of his hand. 'I think we're on to something. It's certainly enough to justify looking closer at the Checkleys.'

They'd look closer, and they'd find something. West was convinced of it.

6

West managed to get parking directly outside Thunder's cake shop in Drumcondra. He pushed open the door into the small shop and took a deep breath. The combination of aromas had the usual effect, his mouth watered and he wanted to buy everything in the shop.

He settled for two huge meringues, each sandwiched to its equally large partner by a mass of thick cream that oozed as the shop assistant picked them up. Then, because West couldn't resist, he added a loaf of bread and a fruit cake for home, and a box of small cakes that would be devoured by the team when he got back to Foxrock.

With the neatly tied boxes dangling from his fingers and the bread and fruit cake under one arm, he opened the car door with difficulty and slid inside.

The Office of the State Pathologist was situated in a red-brick building on the corner of Griffith Avenue and the Swords Road. For decades, it had been Whitehall Garda Station and even to this day, Kennedy had told him, they had people knocking on their door looking for the gardaí.

There was a car park at the rear but there was rarely space. West didn't bother trying, instead he drove along Griffith Avenue and found a space near Corpus Christi Church. He parked his car and walked back.

Kennedy was hammering the keys of his laptop when West knocked on his office door.

'Come in as long as you're carrying something from Thunders,' Kennedy sang out without raising his eyes or stopping his fingers. 'Just let me finish this damn report and I'll be with you.'

A coffee machine gurgled in the corner filling the room with the aroma. West cleared a corner of the desk for the cake box. He'd been in the office enough times to know where everything was kept and opened the cupboard to take down a couple of mugs.

'That's it,' Kennedy said. 'Grab a couple of plates, too, Mike. I don't want meringue all over the place.'

They sat in companionable silence while they worked their way through the huge meringues. 'Lordy, I never get tired of eating them.' Kennedy pulled a tissue from a box behind him to wipe his fingers, then threw the box to West who caught it in one hand.

'Okay, now that you've eaten your payment, tell me what you found.'

Kennedy picked up his mug and took a mouthful before putting it down and sitting back. 'Well, the bad news is that they are human remains, Mike.'

West shrugged. It was only ever a slim hope. 'Give me the good news then.'

'I'm still waiting for some results but I'm fairly confident I'm right.' Kennedy stood and reached for the coffee pot, filling both their mugs. 'I hope you didn't want a simple case.'

'Chance would be a fine thing but we could have done with a break.' West sighed. 'Come on, put me out of my misery.'

'Maybe I can offer you a little break,' Kennedy said. 'If you were worrying about a serial killer on the loose, that is?'

'It was something we were considering. Four dead bodies. What else were we to think?'

'Mass murder.' Kennedy held a hand up. 'I don't have all the results back but it is my considered opinion that these four people were killed within a few hours of each other. I'm also going to stick my neck out and say it's familicide.'

'Four bodies. Parents and two children?'

'All I can confirm at the moment is that they're two older and two younger adults. DNA will confirm whether they're related or not.'

'Familicide.' West groaned. 'I think I'd have preferred a serial killer.'

'I haven't told you the best bit yet.'

'You mean there's more?'

'You mentioned you thought the body parts looked almost man-made,' Kennedy said. 'There was a reason for your confusion. I'm estimating that they are around–' he see-sawed his hand, '–maybe fifty years old.'

'What!'

'I had a long conversation with a forensic anthropologist colleague in London and she agrees with my findings. The discolouration, the rather wizened appearance gave me a hint.' He shook his head. 'Honestly, Mike, you do seem to get embroiled in the weirdest cases but I think this one will be your best yet.' He waited a beat for effect. 'They were mummified.'

Andrews' jaw dropped. 'Mummified!'

'That's what he said,' West answered, sitting back behind his desk over an hour and a half later. 'It isn't, it seems, that difficult. The bodies just needed to be kept in a warm, dry atmosphere for anything from a few weeks to a few months and natural mummification would take place.'

'Mummified!' Andrews said again, trying to take it in, his eyes wide in disbelief. 'And that's what happened here?'

'Partially. But someone had done their research in how the Egyptians did it too.' West had felt his stomach do a gentle flip-flop when Kennedy had told him the details. 'It's pretty gruesome stuff.' He ran a finger down his side. 'The torsos had been slit open down one side and all the organs removed. Then the bodies were stuffed with a mix of rags and straw and sewn up again.'

'But... but...' Andrews held a hand up. 'Okay, sorry, this is something else. So this person or persons, killed these people and turned them into mummies. So why chop them up, and why remove the head?'

'Kennedy said... and he sounded like he knew what he was talking about... that the hardest part of the mummification process is removing the brain from inside the skull. Egyptians, it seems, used to remove it through the nose.'

'No,' Andrews begged, 'don't go into detail.' He was munching on one of the cakes West had brought back. He looked at the remainder in his hand and lobbed it into the bin.

West looked at him in amusement. 'All the blood and guts we've seen over the years and this is what makes you squeamish?'

'Yes, well pardon me if the thoughts of some Egyptian sucking a brain out of someone's nose through a straw gives me the collywobbles.'

'I don't think they actually sucked it out, I think they pushed–' He saw Andrews face twist and relented. 'Okay, okay,

I'll stop! But your reaction probably proves Kennedy's theory on why the head is missing. The perpetrator of this bizarre mummification found it to be one step too far and instead decided to remove the heads completely.'

'Bloody marvellous. So we've got to search for four missing heads.'

'No, that's the good news. This all happened around fifty years ago. At least the mummification bit did. According to Kennedy, the dissection into separate body parts occurred only recently and was probably done simply to facilitate removal and disposal.'

'Okay.' Andrews dragged the word out as he grappled with this idea. 'Four dead bodies, killed and mummified around fifty years ago, and now the killer decides to get rid of them.'

'It's unlikely to be the killer. They'd have to be around seventy at least. No, someone else is guilty of dissecting the bodies and dumping them.'

That remark had Andrews' eyebrows shooting up. 'Right, so some toerag comes upon four headless bodies and instead of phoning us, they decide to chop them into pieces and get rid... doesn't make sense.'

'It makes no sense but it's what we've got. There are two older adults and two younger. Kennedy says it's likely they are a family so let's start with looking back...' He thought a moment. 'Sixty years to be on the safe side. Any reports of a missing family. Also get someone to check the same time frame for any heads or skulls that have turned up, either singly or, if we should be so lucky, in a bag of four.'

'A bag of four heads.' Andrews laughed. 'Now wouldn't that be so convenient!'

'One of these days, things are going to go in our favour. Speaking of which,' West said with a frown, 'anything yet on the delightful Mr Checkley?'

'Baxter is digging as we speak.' Andrews got to his feet and checked his watch. 'I'll get Jarvis to look into missing persons in the morning and I'll look into the case of the missing heads myself.'

The case of the missing heads. West would tell that one to Edel when he got home: it would make her laugh.

7

Although West didn't know it, Edel could do with a reason to be cheerful. She was having a bad day.

That morning, instead of her story flowing from her fingers in a steady stream of words, she had hit a wall, unsure of her character's next step. She had sat tapping her fingers on the front of her keyboard staring at the screen, willing the words to pop into her brain but they seemed to be stuck fast.

Light from the window caught her engagement ring and she lifted her hand, tilting it back and forward. Diamonds never shone as beautifully as they did in the jeweller's shop. She'd read somewhere that their lights were specially designed to make everything sparkle better. Still, even on this dull day, it was a beautiful ring.

She stared at the screen once more but she knew the only way to get past the wall was to take a step away. Maybe go for a walk. Or, she stared at her ring again, she could do what she'd planned to do for months and take her old engagement and wedding ring into a jewellers to sell. The proceeds would go to charity. The Samaritans, to be exact. Maybe getting that out of the way would free up space in her brain to work out her storyline.

Less than an hour later, Edel was pulling into the car park of the Meridian Point shopping centre in Greystones. She wasn't in a hurry and window-shopped as she made her way through the centre, letting her mind relax as she filled it with colour. It was almost twenty minutes later when she found herself outside Cunningham's Jewellers.

It had been their advert in a local newspaper that had caught her eye the week before. *Quality jewellery bought and sold.* She'd immediately resolved to sell her old wedding and engagement ring and put that part of her life firmly into the drawer marked *past.*

The door opened into a small but well-laid-out space. Walls were lined with cabinets holding an array of jewellery. Gold gleamed and precious stones glinted in the shop's LED lights. There was only one customer but she was smiling and saying her goodbyes as Edel entered. Relieved to have the place to herself, she bypassed the displays and headed straight to the one counter at the back.

'Good morning,' the sales assistant said. 'What can I help you with today?'

Edel took her hand from her pocket and dropped the two rings on the counter. 'I want to sell these, please.' She looked down at the engagement ring – the diamond and sapphire cluster that her late husband had surprised her with. It sparkled in the light as she nudged it slightly. And the plain gold band – the wedding ring Simon had slipped onto her finger with so many promises. Promises that had all been built on lies. The fingers of her right hand closed over the engagement ring that Mike had given her, rubbing it as if it were a talisman.

The assistant picked up the gold band and gave it a cursory check before putting it down to pick up the other ring. This time he put his hand under the counter and pulled out a jeweller's loupe, sliding back the cover and holding the lens over the stones. 'Very nice,' he said. 'Good quality diamonds and sapphires.'

He put the loupe down. 'It looks good but I can't give you an evaluation, I'm afraid. Mr Cunningham prefers to do that himself and he's not here today. If you'd like to bring them back next week?'

Edel huffed. Now that she'd taken the decision to bring them in, she wanted it done with, wanted these last memories of that disastrous marriage gone.

The assistant must have seen the debate wash over her face. 'You could leave them and Mr Cunningham could give you the valuation by phone, if that would help?'

'It would indeed,' she said, relieved. 'Plus, the proceeds are going to charity so could it be arranged that it goes to the Samaritans directly?'

A raised eyebrow was the immediate reaction. 'How very generous. I'm sure that won't be a problem.'

'Good.' Edel picked up the engagement ring for a final look. It certainly sparkled so beautifully. She frowned then; her new ring was put into the shade by it. 'It's odd,' she said, looking at the assistant. 'I don't know how much it cost but I'm sure it didn't cost as much as this one.' She lifted her ring finger to show him. 'And yet this doesn't seem to sparkle in the same way.'

The assistant caught her hand and pulled it closer. 'A lovely design,' he said, reaching for his loupe. He held it to his eye and bent to look at her ring through it.

Edel saw a frown appear as he straightened and dropped her hand. He held the loupe for a second before snapping it shut. 'The lights we use, these LED lights,' he waved a hand around the shop, 'are chosen to reflect the light from diamonds. *Real* diamonds,' he said. 'Not simulated ones.'

'Simulated?' Edel looked at the ring on her finger and wanted to cry. How could this be? 'You mean like cubic zirconia, or something?'

'No.' The assistant pursed his lips. 'I can't be one hundred per cent sure, but I think it's more likely to be moissanite.' He reached for her hand, pulling it forward so that it was close to the light cast by the illuminated display cabinet beside him. 'See. The sparkle. It's not clear like a diamond, it has a lot of blue and green in it. Moissanite can be found naturally but mostly it's man-made.'

'It's cheap?'

He shrugged. 'Yes. A little more expensive than cubic zirconia because it's harder so doesn't scratch the way zirconia does. But a lot cheaper than a diamond.'

Edel took her hand back and stared at the ring. 'If I told you this cost eight thousand euro?'

'I'd say you've been had.' He frowned again. 'You didn't buy this in a reputable jewellers for that kind of money.' When she said they had and mentioned the name, his frown deepened. 'Okay. Then someone pulled a switch.'

It was Edel's turn to frown. 'The man who sold it to us, he insisted that he take it away to give it a final polish before we left. I didn't think it needed it but didn't want to argue so I slipped it off and gave it to him.'

'He left your sight?'

'Yes, he was gone a minute, maybe two.'

The assistant shrugged but said nothing.

He didn't have to. Edel looked down at the ring again and felt a sharp sting of tears. She and Mike had been so excited, so delighted, they wouldn't have noticed a switch.

'What are you going to do?'

Edel met the sympathetic gaze. 'Do?' She shook her head. 'If I bought a diamond ring in here, then came back a few days later and said I'd been sold a fake, what would you do?'

The assistant considered her question, then sighed. 'I'd assume you were trying to pull a fast one. So, I'd show you a copy of the sales receipt that indicated the carat of the diamond and the overall value of the ring. If you persisted in your claim, I'd call the guards, and let them deal with it. Mr Cunningham would insist on your being prosecuted for what he would see as extortion.'

'Exactly!' She fiddled with the ring. 'It's still a beautiful ring and my fiancé will never know that it's not worth what he paid.'

'You're going to let the man who pulled the switch get away with it?' The assistant sounded horrified at the thought.

'If I hadn't come in here, I might never have known. Sometimes, it's best to be in the dark. Now, if you'd give me a receipt for the rings I'm leaving for valuation, I'll be on my way.'

Any desire to go shopping had faded. Instead, Edel trudged past the shop windows and through the car park. Head down and deep in thought, the blare of a horn startled her. She jumped out of the way of an oncoming car, waving a hand in apology to the scowling driver who raised a middle finger in reply.

She sat into her car, her eyes dropping to the hand that rested on the steering wheel. Man-made or not... the ring looked so lovely and fit her so perfectly. The assistant in Debeerds must have been waiting for someone to choose that particular ring to set his plan in action. He took her beautiful ring, exchanged it, and brought this fake back to her – all done so smoothly, so slickly they'd never noticed.

What was it the assistant had said about the engagement ring she'd left in to sell? *Good quality diamonds and sapphires.* The thought made her eyes sting. A genuine ring for a fake relationship. And now this disaster!

A disaster – if she let it be one. She held the ring up again. It *was* pretty; only she would know it wasn't a diamond. They had the certificate from Debeerds for the insurance so there was no reason to take it in for valuation.

She'd keep the secret and if that meant letting that thief get away with it, well so be it. Mike had wanted to buy her a special ring, to emphasise his commitment to her and to their relationship. She wasn't willing to tell him it was a fake.

Nor was she willing to consider the worry that flitted through her mind. That perhaps it was a bad omen.

8

'I thought you'd find that amusing,' West said that evening. Edel had rung to ask him to pick up a takeaway from the local Indian restaurant on the way and the containers lay between them, the aroma tantalising. Despite having already eaten too much, he reached for the spoon and had another spoonful of the lamb balti.

Edel was pushing a piece of chicken around her plate. She looked up, a puzzled frown between her eyes. 'What?'

'The case of the missing heads.' His eyes watering, he reached for his beer to wash down what appeared to be a whole chilli. It was a few seconds before he could speak. 'Sounded like an Agatha Christie title to me.'

'Oh, yes, it does.'

He looked at her more closely, surprised at her obvious lack of interest. Maybe Agatha Christie was the wrong reference to make or maybe it was something else. He hadn't noticed till now, but she was looking a little pale. 'You're very distracted this evening. Is everything okay?'

'My characters are causing me a little grief,' she said. 'I'll be fine once I can untangle the tale.' She finally speared the chicken with the fork and put it into her mouth. A few minutes of companionable silence later, she asked, 'You really think that Checkley guy is involved in his cousin's death?'

West put his fork down and pushed the plate away. 'That was good.' He sighed and picked up his beer. 'It's a line we're following but I don't know, to be honest. I want it to be. He's an unlikeable man.'

She laughed. 'You've met unlikeable men before, they've not all been guilty of something.'

'True, but ever since I saw him in Debeerds I've had a feeling that we're missing something with him.'

'Gut instinct,' she said. 'That old detective favourite.'

'Something like that.' It was as good a way as any of explaining the inexplicable... the feeling that what you were seeing wasn't the full story, that there was something nasty hiding behind a polished, expensive exterior. He'd seen it too many times to be surprised. 'We'll look into him anyway, see what happens.'

'Dig for some dirt, you mean.'

West frowned at a tone he took to be critical. 'If that's the way you want to look at it. I prefer to think of it as doing my job.' He finished his beer and got to his feet. In silence he took his plate to the dishwasher, put the lids on the half-empty containers and found a space for them in the fridge. He could feel her eyes on him but wasn't in the mood for whatever it was she wanted to say. Possibly he was being overly sensitive but the *dig for dirt* comment had taken him by surprise. Was that what she thought of his work?

It was only when he reached for her plate that he noticed something he should have seen before. She wasn't wearing her engagement ring.

'You haven't lost it, have you?' he said, pointing to her hand. Was that it? She was upset because she'd lost it?

But she shook her head quickly. 'It's up beside my computer. I'm not used to it on my finger yet and when I'm typing it feels awkward so I took it off and forgot to put it back on.'

He should have been relieved but he wasn't because he knew, without a doubt, she was lying. Maybe it was his wary heart.

Or a gut instinct. Edel had been right, after all, about it being an old detective favourite.

Whichever it was, it was shouting that there was something not quite right about her story.

9

The sense that something was wrong didn't fade and West arrived at the station the next morning, grim-faced and tired from a night spent tossing and turning. It was a day he'd have happily buried himself in paperwork. He'd even have welcomed one of Morrison's unending audits rather than have a conversation with anyone. Especially with the man who was heading towards his office door. Andrews saw everything.

'Morning,' West said, keeping his fingers moving on the keyboard.

'Grab your jacket. We've an appointment with the sacristan of Whitefriar Street Church at ten.'

West kept his eyes on the computer screen but his fingers slowed to a halt. *Whitefriar Street Church.* 'Okay,' he said, turning to look at Andrews who was grinning from ear to ear. 'I give in, why are we going there?'

'Because forty-eight years ago, four skulls were found there.'

It was enough to push West's personal problems to the back of his mind. 'You are kidding me!'

'I know, it is so unbelievable that I had to read the report twice.' Andrews sat on the spare chair and folded his arms across his chest. 'Forty-eight years ago, four skulls were found in the side chapel of the church, near the statue and relics of St Valentine. At first, according to the report, they were deemed to be someone's idea of a joke until they decided to test them and discovered they were human skulls. An investigation didn't get far. Nobody was reported missing and it was never solved.'

'Okay, good, so we can get the skulls sent to Kennedy. He can get DNA from them and compare it to the bodies to confirm a match.' He looked back to the computer screen as if there was something important there instead of a routine reply to the supplies department. 'I'm in the middle of this, we don't need to go there, do we?'

'I think it's probably best.' Seeing West open his mouth to argue, Andrews held up a hand to stop him. 'Almost fifty years ago, you didn't argue with the church and I'm not sure that much has changed. Whitefriar Street, as I'm sure you know, is run by the Carmelites. When the skulls were found, they refused to release them to police custody and wanted to give them a Christian burial. They reached a compromise in the end and the skulls are stored in the cellars under the church. It might take a bit of your best persuasive patter to get them to release them.'

'Just when I think I've heard everything,' West said. He reached for the desk phone, dialled a number and put the phone on speaker. 'Niall, how would you like four skulls to go with those bodies?'

'You found them?'

'No, we thought we'd pick some up in Brown Thomas,' Andrews said, referencing the large upmarket department store on Grafton Street.

'Ignore my sarcastic partner, Niall, no, it seems St Valentine is looking after them for us.'

Niall Kennedy's sigh came loudly down the line. 'Are you two on something? Or don't you have anything better to be doing?'

'I'm serious. There are four skulls in the cellars of Whitefriar Street Church.'

'Where St Valentine's remains are stored in a casket. Okay, I get you now. Sorry, maybe I'd find your combined witty repartee amusing if I hadn't been awake half the night.'

'Betsy still teething?'

'I'm just relieved she's not a crocodile,' Kennedy said. 'Right, are you bringing the skulls in? I assume you want me to confirm they belong to the bodies we have, although I'd say it's a given.'

'We're on our way to fetch them now. We should make it over to you late morning or early afternoon.'

'Fine, give me a heads-up when you're on your way.' Kennedy cackled at his own joke and hung up.

'He always has to have the last word,' Andrews said with a shake of his head.

'That's a definite case of the kettle calling the pot black.' West got to his feet and took his jacket from the back of the door. 'Let's get going.'

They were stopped in the doorway by Sam Jarvis. With his jacket off, shirtsleeves rolled up, tie slightly askew, a serious expression on his almost too-handsome face... he looked as if he was posing for a fashion shoot. 'Can I have a word?'

'A quick one if it can't wait till later.' West stepped back into his office and sat on the edge of the desk.

'It'll just take a sec.' Jarvis stuffed his hands into his trouser pockets. Now that he had West's attention, he seemed unsure what to do with it. Finally, he blurted out, 'It's about Muriel Hennessy, the missing woman who turned up in that laneway on Friday.'

'Yes, what about her?'

'She was found almost a mile from her home. Because there

was a pool of vomit found nearby, we'd been running with the idea that she was feeling sick and went off the main road for a bit of privacy to throw up. The post-mortem is being done today so we should have a cause of death.' He hesitated and shuffled from foot to foot.

West wanted to tell him to get on with it, but he recognised the hesitation as the young detective working things out in his head before he spoke. He might have wished that Jarvis had worked it out before he came to speak to him but he wasn't going to criticise one of his team for doing their job well. Andrews, standing behind, raised his eyes to the ceiling.

'It's just that we haven't been treating it as suspicious and I wonder...' Jarvis took a deep breath and lifted his chin as if he knew what he was about to say was going to be challenged. He was the newest member of the team, still finding his feet and slightly in awe of both West and Andrews. 'I wonder if we might be making a mistake.'

'Go on,' West said encouragingly.

Jarvis relaxed a little and took a step closer. 'I was looking through her medical records. It says her mobility was limited due to arthritis in her hips. But she was found a mile from her home... would she have walked that far? And what was she doing in that area, anyway? Neighbours said that the only time they've seen her out in the last few months was when she walked to the local shops which she did about once a week. They're only a five-minute walk away but in the opposite direction.'

West looked at Jarvis's eager face. 'We've still no indication of when she was seen last, do we?'

'No. The son and daughter called around to see her regularly, the daughter at the weekend, the son usually on a weekday after work. He said he'd called to her on the Friday, the daughter saw her on the Sunday, then nobody saw her again.'

'Five days,' West muttered. 'It's a long time frame to cover. Right, so what's your plan?'

Jarvis grinned and pushed his hands deeper into his pockets. 'We need to narrow down that time frame, if we can. I've already checked and, unfortunately, there is no CCTV along that route but I want to canvass the neighbourhood. Someone must have seen her in the last week. I also want to speak to her son and daughter again, find out more about her. And,' he finished, 'I'd like to check her finances. See if her death leaves anyone the richer.'

'Good.' West got to his feet. 'Get Allen to give you a hand and keep me informed.'

'Jarvis and Allen make a good team,' Andrews said as they drove out of the car park. 'But do you really think the Hennessy woman's death is suspicious?'

West turned onto the main road and it wasn't until they were stopped at lights that he turned to Andrews and shrugged. 'Jarvis does. I'm happy enough to go along with that, see what happens. For a couple of days anyway. Much the same as we're doing with Checkley.'

'Baxter is digging. If there's anything to find, he'll find it.'

Andrews' choice of word was an unfortunate one. It immediately brought West back to the night before. It was what Edel had said. Was the reality of being married to a garda hitting her now that he'd put a ring on her finger. He thought they'd been together long enough, that she understood. Maybe he was wrong. Maybe she'd decided she wanted her crime to be limited to what happened between the pages of a book.

'It's Brother Lonergan we'll be meeting,' Andrews said, breaking into his thoughts and dragging him back to the case. 'Seems to be a helpful, friendly man.'

'I hope he stays like that when we tell him we have to take the skulls away.'

'That's why I wanted you to come along. I have great faith in your persuasive powers. I'm sure then he'll be happy to be co-operative.' Andrews spoke like it was a fait accompli.

'I wish I had half your faith.' West took the turn that would lead them to the small car park behind the church. He parked and peered through the window. 'It looks better from the front.'

PRIVATE was painted in white on the only door visible to the rear of the building. Andrews rapped his knuckles against it, waited a moment and tried again, louder. If anyone heard, they weren't rushing to answer.

West pointed to a narrow passageway to one side of the building. 'I bet that goes around to the main entrance.'

The rather dull grey frontage of Whitefriar Street Church was made memorable by its imposing entrance where gold-painted statues on pedestals stood as sentinels. West knew one to be Mary but couldn't put a name to the other. He guessed Andrews would know, and he was right.

'It's St John.'

Why those two were chosen was a conversation for another day. West and Andrews moved into the body of the church and looked around. It wasn't a church West had been in before and he gazed curiously towards the side chapel where he knew the remains of St Valentine were kept. 'You know they've never opened the casket to see if there are remains inside or not,' he said, his voice hushed.

Andrews looked at him. 'You know such odd things. How do they know there's anything inside then, if they've never looked?'

West had read about it, years before, and it had stuck in his head. 'The casket was sent from Rome with a letter from Pope Gregory so they took it on faith.'

'Ah faith, it's a wonderful thing.' Andrews headed down the central aisle of the church as if he knew exactly where to go. West lagged behind. Maybe he should have a bit of faith and stop worrying about stupid things like Edel leaving her ring off and being a bit distant. What was it both she and Andrews were always telling him – that he took himself far too seriously? Maybe. He lengthened his stride to catch up with his partner.

A man dressed in the traditional brown habit of a Carmelite monk stood to one side of the altar. He was engrossed in what he was doing, his fingers splayed around a large, floor-standing, brass candleholder.

'Brother Lonergan?'

Large eyes, the same colour as his habit, turned to look at the two detectives. The monk made a final attempt to finish what he was doing, then took the top part of the stand with him as he walked across to join them. 'Kaput,' he said, waving the piece of metal in his hand. 'Or perhaps I should simply admit it's beyond my capability to fix, which for a DIY fiend, as I am, is never an easy admission to make.' He waved a hand to a doorway behind the altar. 'We can chat in my office.'

It was a fancy name for a small room that appeared to serve a variety of functions. Storage being a main one, there was little room for three men. 'It's a bit of a squash,' Brother Lonergan said, easing a headless statue back to allow access. By dint of moving a few piles of books, and a stack of dusty files, he made space for West and Andrews to sit. Then he sat behind the cluttered desk and folded his arms, his hands vanishing into the cavernous sleeves of his habit. 'You've come for the Four Marys, I gather.'

West saw the smile in Brother Lonergan's eyes so guessed the reference was supposed to amuse. Unfortunately, he had no idea what he was talking about and waited for enlightenment.

It came, as it often did, from Andrews. 'I wouldn't have thought the Carmelites were big *Bunty* fans,' he said.

Brother Lonergan laughed. 'It was a young Carmelite novitiate who found the skulls. She had been a *Bunty* fan before joining the order and it was she who named them Simpson, Field, Cotter and Radleigh after the comic strip, *Four Marys*. You're talking about almost fifty years ago, gentlemen, they got their entertainment where they could.' He shrugged. 'The names stuck.'

'We may be able to give them their proper names,' West said. 'Recently, four headless bodies were discovered. The state pathologist estimates the bodies to be up to fifty years old so it is highly probable that the skulls that were discovered here belong to them.'

Brother Lonergan inclined his head but said nothing.

'I know some of the argument for keeping the skulls in Whitefriar Street Church was to keep them somewhere sanctified rather than having them kept in boxes in garda stores, but this time we hope to reunite the body parts and give each of the four a proper, dignified funeral.'

'That would be a fitting end for them,' the monk said. 'Leaving the skulls was a strange thing for someone to have done. The garda investigation at the time, as I'm sure you know, turned up nothing. Nowadays, thanks to the CCTV cameras we've had installed it would be impossible for someone to get away with leaving them as they were found.'

West frowned. He'd read the report but it didn't specify how or where the skulls had been left. 'I assumed they'd been left in a box in the church.'

'No, not at all. They were displayed.' Lonergan got to his feet. 'It's probably easier to show you, then I can take you down to the cellars.'

They negotiated the passage from the office and retraced their steps to the church and across to the side chapel of St Valentine.

'Have you been before?' Brother Lonergan said, stopping in

front of the pews. When both detectives shook their heads, he pointed to the altar.

West moved closer for a better look. The body of the hollow structure was formed of three different coloured marbles, the top a slab of solid black. A metal and glass grill covered a window cut into the front section of marble and behind this was a casket.

'That's it?' West turned to look at Brother Lonergan.

'Not exactly. The casket containing the relics and blood of St Valentine are in another casket inside.' He turned and pointed to the cameras that were set high above. 'A necessity, I'm afraid. It's a popular tourist destination because of the whole St Valentine's Day rigmarole. We try to encourage people to remember he is a saint, and not a social media celebrity but sometimes...' He shrugged and left it at that. 'Up there.' He pointed to where a life-size statue of St Valentine stood in a mosaic-lined alcove set above and behind the altar. 'That's where the skulls were left. Neatly placed around the base of the statue.'

'I'm surprised nobody saw anything,' West said.

'Almost fifty years ago we didn't get as many sightseeing visitors. Churches were where people came to pray. It is possible, too, that the skulls were there for a number of days before anyone thought them out of the ordinary.' He pointed to the far side of the church. 'The door to the cellar is over there. If you think my office is cluttered, wait till you see down below.'

The cellar was accessed down a narrow, damp, tortuous stairway that brought West unsettling memories of Clare Island. At the bottom, a single light on a side wall did little to dispel the darkness and even the torch that Brother Lonergan took from a shelf provided little light. The ceiling was low, barely high enough for the six-foot West and Andrews to walk without stooping. Every available space was jam-packed with old statues, light fittings, huge candleholders, urns, and other items removed from the church over the years but never thrown away. It would have been the ideal place to have filmed a horror movie.

'The skulls would have been better housed with us,' Andrews whispered to West.

'Through here.' Brother Lonergan pushed open a worn wooden door. Inside, the space was small but it appeared to be free from clutter. There was no light and it wasn't until the monk shone the torch around that they could see what it was.

West was first to understand. 'It's a mausoleum.'

'It is... or should I say it was.' Brother Lonergan moved the torch along the walls. 'It was used when the church was first built but within a few years it was full and it wasn't used again after 1835. Now and then, somebody suggests moving the remains and putting this space to better use but each time, the dead have been allowed to remain.' He focused the beam of the torch onto a shelf on the back wall. 'There you are. Meet the Four Marys.'

10

With the four skulls packed carefully in a box in the boot of West's car, he and Andrews set off for the Office of the State Pathologist. In Drumcondra, West indicated to pull across the road and parked outside Thunders.

'Kennedy has you well trained,' Andrews said.

'You don't want anything?'

An eyebrow went up. 'Silly question. I'll have an éclair.'

It was a few minutes before West returned to the car. He opened the back door to drop the box of pastries on the seat and was almost deafened by Johnny Cash. Andrews, humming along to the radio, eyes shut, was oblivious to his muttered 'For goodness' sake!'

Back in the driver's seat, West reached for the volume control and turned it down.

'You've no soul,' Andrews said without opening his eyes.

Ignoring him, West started the engine and resumed the journey.

They were in luck and found a parking space close by. Five minutes later they were standing in Niall Kennedy's office. 'You'll want this one here,' West said, putting the cake box on top of a pile of folders where it wobbled precariously before settling. 'I think that one needs to go elsewhere.'

'The Four Marys.' Andrews lifted the lid of the box to show the contents. 'Meet Simpson, Radleigh, Cotter and Field.'

To his surprise, Kennedy grinned and took the box from him. 'I didn't take you for a *Bunty* fan. My older sister was though. She had four hideous dolls named after them, used to take them everywhere with her.' He kicked the door open. 'The lab is free, let's bring them in there and have a look.'

Kennedy put the box down on a stainless-steel trolley, pulled on a pair of disposable gloves and opened the box. He whistled softly under his breath as he took out each skull and looked at it closely. A few minutes later, all four were lined up, their empty eye sockets staring at the three men.

'Very interesting,' Kennedy said, peeling off the gloves. He pressed the foot pedal of a bin and dropped them inside. 'I assume that other box contained something equally exciting?'

'Sugar and cream in perfect proportion,' West said as they walked back to Kennedy's office.

Andrews perched on the side of the desk eating his éclair while West and Kennedy with their meringues on plates, took the two chairs.

With his pastry gone in three bites, Andrews' focus was back on the skulls. 'What do you think?'

'That these meringues are the best,' Kennedy said, then shrugged. 'I need to take some measurements, do a DNA comparison but I'd be surprised if they weren't a match to our headless bodies. On a purely visual examination, two are marginally smaller indicating female skulls.'

'Or younger victims?'

Kennedy shook his head. 'I've put the ages of the older corpses to be between thirty-five to forty-five and the younger between twenty and thirty.'

'That's a big margin for error,' West said, putting his plate down and brushing meringue crumbs from his hands.

'Bone morphology – symphyseal and auricular changes – doesn't get more accurate than a ten-year plus or minus, I'm afraid,' Kennedy said.

'Their joints?' West guessed.

'That's it. It's as reliable as we can get without a skull. If the DNA proves the skulls belong to the bodies, I might be able to narrow the margin a little but it's always going to be a fairly wide estimate.'

'What about the relationship between them,' Andrews asked. 'Will the DNA give us that?'

'Yes, we've been assuming they are parents and children. It'll prove if we're correct.'

'Anything that will help us to find out who they are will be good,' West said. 'Right, we'll let you get on with it.'

Kennedy held up his hand. 'Hang on a sec, there's something else I wanted to speak to you about. I did the post on Muriel Hennessy this morning. I'd anticipated a quick one based on the report of her death, the usual stroke or heart attack, so I was mildly irritated to get a call from one of your team, Detective Garda Jarvis, to tell me they were now treating it as a suspicious death.'

'It would be routine to inform you,' West said, always ready to defend his team when they were in the right.

'Oh, I'm not complaining, in fact I'm grateful.'

'He was right?' Andrews said, surprised.

'He was indeed. And I think I'd have missed it if he hadn't alerted me. I'd have made the lazy assumption that she was an elderly woman with existing cardiac disease who overdid it and suffered a heart attack as a result.'

'But she didn't?'

'No, she did. A massive coronary. Death would have been

instantaneous. Had I not spoken to Detective Garda Jarvis only moments before, I might have left it at that but he sounded so convinced there was something iffy about her death, it made me look a little deeper and then...' Kennedy shook his head, a look of amusement crossing his face. 'Seriously, you two, you have the weirdest habit of attracting the oddest cases.'

West shut his eyes and groaned. 'Please, tell me you're joking!'

'I'm afraid not.'

Andrews shifted his position on the desk all the better to stare at Kennedy. 'The heart attack wasn't natural?'

'I'm still waiting for toxicology reports and they may, of course, show something unusual.' Kennedy shook his head slowly. 'I doubt it though. Muriel Hennessy did have advanced coronary heart disease. I'd guess she'd been having chest pains for a while.' He tapped the file on the desk beside him. 'Her medical records are scanty. The only GP visit in the last year was related to increased arthritic pains which reduced her mobility. There is a reference to her having an irregular heartbeat but she refused to have it checked out. She should have done.'

West was puzzled. 'So, this elderly woman with a bad heart, had a heart attack and died. That sounds straightforward.'

'Yes, it does, doesn't it?' Kennedy sat back and folded his arms. 'Except for one tiny detail.'

West glanced at Andrews who shrugged. 'Let him have his moment of fun.'

'Thank you, Peter. I have little opportunity for it in here.'

'Well, if you're finished enjoying yourself,' West said, 'would you tell us what is going on?'

'Muriel Hennessy died of a massive heart attack... that's the straightforward bit. The complicated, puzzling bit is, I'm not sure when she died.'

'Her body was found on Friday, five days after she was last

seen by her family. It had to have been somewhere in that time period.' West frowned when he saw the pathologist shake his head. 'Explain.'

'Yes, okay.' Kennedy's expression turned serious. 'I won't bore you with the science bit but with Jarvis's enthusiastic words ringing in my ears, I looked more carefully at Muriel Hennessy and that's when I noticed it. Ruptured blood cells and intracellular fluid.' He looked at each of the detectives expectantly, shaking his head as they looked back blankly. 'It explained something else that was puzzling me... a slightly more advanced deterioration in the peripheral tissues than in the internal organs.'

'She'd been frozen?' West said, remembering an article he'd read years before. 'Frozen and thawed too quickly so that decomposition began in the peripheries while the internal organs were still frozen.'

Kennedy looked impressed. 'Very good. That's it exactly.'

Andrews looked from one to the other. 'We're not, I assume, talking about a bit of frostbite from lying outside for a few nights.'

'No.' Kennedy shook his head. 'For this level of cellular damage, the body would have had to be frozen solid. Think frozen-turkey frozen.'

'But the cause of death is still a heart attack?' Andrews tried to get the facts sorted in his head.

'Yes, but whether she had it before she was frozen... or while she was being frozen... it's impossible to tell, I'm afraid.'

West shut his eyes briefly and rubbed a hand over his face. 'Okay,' he said, dragging the word out. 'How long would it take to freeze a body?'

'Depending on the freezer... two, maybe three days.'

'And how long to defrost?'

'I think the reason that there was a discrepancy in the level of the decomposition of peripheries compared to internal organs is that they did it too quickly. The optimum way would have been to defrost in a refrigerator for at least a week.'

'But they hurried the process?'

'Yes, or they may not have had a suitable refrigerator unit. Large freezers are much easier to come by.' He lifted a hand, index finger extended to make a point. 'But I'm not talking a much shorter period in this case. Maybe six days. Had it been shorter, there would have been a more obvious difference in levels of deterioration.'

'Two to three days to freeze, maybe six to defrost. We're looking at eight days minimum then?'

'It's hard to pinpoint–'

'Your professional opinion,' West said, pressing him.

Kennedy, no more than anyone, didn't like being pushed into a corner. He hesitated and then huffed in annoyance. 'Fine, if you insist, in my professional opinion the process of freezing and defrosting would have taken a minimum of eight days.'

West met Andrews' eyes. Then she can't have been seen on the previous Sunday or Friday. Muriel Hennessy's family had lied.

11

For the first few miles of the drive back to Foxrock, both West and Andrews were lost in thought.

It was Andrews who spoke first. 'He was right, though, wasn't he?'

West glanced at him. 'About us getting the oddest cases, you mean?'

'Yes.'

'I suppose he was. We've certainly had more than our fair share of doozies.'

'Doozies.' Andrews laughed. 'Lamprey eels, little kids in suitcases, a man crucified in the church–'

'He wasn't precisely crucified.'

'As good as. And now this. Why would Muriel Hennessy's family have frozen her? It doesn't make sense.'

'Maybe they had a row,' West said. 'Muriel had a heart attack and died. They were afraid they'd be blamed so they put her into the freezer while they planned what to do?' He indicated for the turn into Foxrock Garda Station and pulled into his parking space.

'Or maybe they put her into the freezer while she was alive

to kill her off, and she had a heart attack before she froze to death?'

'Motive?' West said as they walked into the station.

'She was troublesome and demanding or she had money and they wanted it?'

'Or both.'

'Or both,' Andrews agreed.

Sam Jarvis was on the phone when they went into the detective unit. West waved at him to get his attention and pointed towards his office.

'You were right,' West said a minute later as Jarvis hovered in the doorway.

The younger officer's face lit up. 'You spoke to Kennedy?'

'Yes, sit, I'll fill you in.'

Jarvis listened, his eyes growing wider. 'Frozen!' Shock made his voice sharp. 'Cara Donaldson and Liam Hennessy froze their mother, then defrosted her and dumped the poor old dear's body in that lane. Left her there for the rats to nibble!'

'Yes, but the cause of death is definitely a heart attack,' West said. 'We need to bring them in for questioning. The daughter lied to us about seeing her on the Sunday, and if Kennedy's time frame is correct, the son also lied about seeing her on Friday.'

'Mrs Hennessy may have had a heart attack and the daughter panicked when she found her dead. Putting her in a freezer is an odd thing to do but...' He shrugged.

'We've seen odder,' West agreed. 'Yes, that's a possibility as is the other idea, that the son or the daughter, or both of them, put her into the freezer in order to kill her and she had a heart attack from the shock of it.'

'Hmm.' Jarvis gave that idea some consideration. 'I suppose it would be a bloodless crime. All you'd need is a decent size chest freezer. Mrs Hennessy wasn't a big woman, even one person could have managed it. All they would have had to do is ask her to fetch something from the freezer, then when she was leaning in, grab her feet and toss her in.'

'I'm glad you're on our side,' West said with a raise of an eyebrow.

Andrews, meanwhile, was staring at Jarvis as if he'd never seen him before. 'I always thought butter wouldn't melt,' he said with a shake of his head.

Jarvis grinned. 'It's keeping company with you lot.'

West tapped a finger rhythmically on the desk. 'You are right, of course. It wouldn't have been hard to do. We need to find that freezer.'

'It might have been in her own home,' Andrews pointed out.

'Yes, indeed it might. There must have been keys found on her, or have they been handed back to the family?'

'I'll check,' Jarvis said, getting to his feet. 'Will I bring her son and daughter in for questioning?'

West frowned, his finger still drumming the desk. 'We need to go carefully; they have just lost their mother. Tell them something has come up and ask if they'll come in. We might need to get a search warrant to look for a chest freezer in their homes but we'll take a softly-softly approach for now, okay?'

The following morning both siblings arrived within minutes of each other wearing fixed expressions of confusion.

Liam Hennessy was a florid-faced, dumpy man with a receding hairline. Unfortunately, he'd decided to dye the remnant of his hair black, the result making him look remarkably like one of the Lego figures Jarvis's nephew liked to play with. Jarvis tried not to stare as he introduced himself. 'I'm Detective Garda Jarvis and this is my colleague Detective Garda

Allen. 'We appreciate your coming in and hope we can get this sorted as quickly as possible.'

'What exactly is *this*?' Hennessy said, crooking his forefingers in the air around the word. 'Apart from being most inconvenient, that is.'

'Honestly, you're always Mr So-Important.' Cara Donaldson, a petite, elegant woman with sun-streaked brown hair shot a scathing look at her brother before turning to Jarvis. 'We will, of course, do anything we can to help. I understand you wanted to discuss the results of the post-mortem with us.'

'That's correct,' Jarvis said. He raised a hand in the direction of the interview rooms. 'It's best to talk somewhere more private.' He stopped at the door to the Big One and pushed it open. 'Unfortunately,' he said, looking from one to the other of the siblings, 'rules prohibit us from speaking to more than one person at a time in the interview rooms.' He waved a dismissive hand and hoped they'd swallow the lie. Groups of people were frequently seen in the interview rooms – but not when they were under investigation. 'Rules and regulations, they'll be the bane of us, won't they?'

'If you would come with me,' Allen said to Liam Hennessy, standing back to allow him to pass.

Hennessy hesitated. 'If it's upsetting news, shouldn't I be with my sister?'

Cara laughed. 'What, so that I can console you? Don't be such a wuss, Liam. Go with the officer so we can hear what they have to say and get out of here.' She looked at Jarvis. 'No offence, but I've better places to spend my morning.'

'No offence taken,' he said, 'now if you'd take a seat, we can get started.'

West was already seated at the table. He stood and held out his hand. 'Detective Garda Sergeant West,' he said. 'My condolences on your loss, Mrs Donaldson, and thanks for obliging us by coming in so quickly.'

Cara gave him an appraising glance as she extended her hand. 'Thank you, and I'm happy to help but do call me Cara.'

'Thank you, now please, take a seat.'

Jarvis pointed to the camera mounted in the corner of the room. 'It's standard operating procedure to record all interviews and to read the interviewee their rights at the commencement of each,' he said, smiling as if to say the rules were crazy but had to be kept.

'Odd,' she said but showed no discomfort as she was read her rights and answered a bored 'yes' when asked if she understood. 'Honestly,' she said, 'if you have to go through this palaver every time you need to speak to someone, I'm surprised you get any work done.'

West sat back and kept his eyes on the woman as Jarvis opened the file in front of him. She seemed completely at ease but she looked like the kind of woman who quickly adapted to her circumstances. He'd read the little information they had on her before coming in. A financial adviser. Perhaps a poker face was an essential part of her role.

'The post-mortem showed that your mother died from a massive coronary,' Jarvis said, looking at the notes. 'There was an indication that she had long-standing coronary artery disease.' He looked up. 'Were you aware of any issues?'

Cara slowly shook her head. 'No, but that's not surprising. My mother was a very private woman, she didn't like to discuss her health.'

'But you didn't see any signs? Breathlessness, maybe a bluish tinge to her lips?'

'No, nothing like that. As far as I'm aware she was in good health for a woman of her years.'

Jarvis looked back to his notes. 'Were you aware her mobility was poor... that she found it difficult to walk more than a short distance?'

'Did she?' A note of boredom had crept into Cara's voice again and she shuffled restlessly in her seat. 'As I said, my mother didn't discuss her health with me. I called around to see her for an hour or so every Sunday unless I was away and that was the sum total of our relationship. I would classify myself as a dutiful rather than a loving daughter if that makes sense.'

Cold and self-obsessed was West's opinion of her. The flash of a diamond on her ring finger caught his eye and reminded him briefly of Edel and the mystery of the missing engagement ring. The thought almost made him smile. If he were going to start looking at every episode in his life as though it were straight from an Agatha Christie novel he would be in serious trouble.

'A dutiful daughter,' Jarvis murmured before closing the file and looking at Cara Donaldson. 'Tell me, did your mother have a will?'

The question was blunt and made her frown. 'Yes,' she said, making a two-syllable word from the one.

'Do you know the content?'

This time her frown deepened and she didn't answer, her eyes flicking from Jarvis's face to West's and back. 'I understood I was asked to come in to discuss the results of the post-mortem,' she said finally. 'Suddenly, I'm wondering if it *is* standard operational procedure to be read my rights... perhaps I should simply leave.' But she made no move to stand, the frown remaining as she looked from one to the other of the detectives again before finally fixing her blue eyes on West. 'Right, why don't you tell me what is going on?'

West looked to Jarvis and nodded.

'The initial assumption was that your mother became unwell,' Jarvis said. 'It was thought that, as a result, she was confused and took herself into that lane where she collapsed and died.'

'From a heart attack, isn't that what you said?'

'Yes.' Jarvis looked at her for a moment before speaking. 'You said you visited your mother on Sunday. Is that correct?'

Cara Donaldson weighed up the question as if looking for a catch. 'Yes.'

Jarvis tapped the file. 'You see that's where the problem lies... the state pathologist was quite emphatic... Muriel Hennessy died at least eight days before she was discovered in that laneway.'

Cara jerked back as if the words had jabbed her with a clenched fist. It took a few seconds for her to recover enough to bark out, 'Ridiculous!'

'No. Fact. The heart attack was only one of the things the post-mortem revealed. The other was that your mother's body was frozen and thawed before it was dumped in the laneway.'

West found himself staring in fascination at the range of emotions that flickered across Cara Donaldson's features. No longer poker-faced, shock was followed by horror and quickly by puzzlement that deepened her frown and furrowed her forehead.

'I have no idea what is going on, but I definitely saw my mother on the Sunday before she was found. And Liam said he'd called to see her Friday evening. But now, to answer your original question, which suddenly seems the correct thing to do since I assume you're searching for a motive for getting rid of her – my mother's estate, such as it is, is left in equal shares to me and my brother.' She held a hand up. 'Don't get too excited though, it's not much. With my encouragement, she released the equity in her house several years ago – one of those wonderful schemes which paid under the odds for the house but allowed her to stay for her lifetime. My mother,' she added, 'liked to go away for expensive hotel breaks. She also, believe it or not, liked expensive wine. I don't know how much is left but I doubt we'll get more than twenty K each.' She shrugged. 'If, as I assume you will do, you look into my finances, you'll see that I'm not in the need of any inheritance. I am not privy to my brother's affairs and I know he's had some trouble recently but he always struck me as being sensible about his finances.'

So perhaps money wasn't the motive. West pulled the file towards him, drawing Cara's eyes back to him. 'You said your relationship with your mother was dutiful rather than loving,' he said. 'Was she a difficult woman?'

But Cara Donaldson wasn't a fool. She got to her feet. 'It looks to me as if you're casting your nets trying to find a motive for my mother's death so I think I'll take myself off – unless you're going to arrest me?' She waited, staring at each of them in turn. 'Before I go, let me make something very, very clear. I saw my mother on Sunday.

'She was as irritating and downright feisty as ever but she was alive when I arrived and alive when I left. And that is all I'm going to say.'

12

'Well, that didn't go too well,' Jarvis said as the click-click of Cara Donaldson's high heels on the tiled floor of the corridor faded into the distance.

'What did you expect? That she'd fess up to killing her mother and stuffing her into a chest freezer?'

Jarvis picked up the file and got to his feet. 'I was hoping she'd look a little guilty or shifty but she didn't.'

West followed him from the room. 'She's a smart woman but this is early stages. You need to have patience. Let's see how the interview with Liam Hennessy is going.'

But when they opened the door into the observation room, they could see that the other interview room was empty. They found Andrews and Allen in the detective office, Andrews sitting at his desk, the younger man perched on the edge of it waving a hand around as he spoke.

'How did it go?' West asked, pulling a chair from behind another desk and sitting.

'It didn't.' Allen shook his head sending a lock of red hair falling over his brow. He pushed it back roughly. 'As soon as we mentioned reading him his rights, he reared back like a frightened mare and insisted on leaving with the stink of guilt following him like he'd trodden in a cowpat.'

Mick Allen had left his family's farm in Tipperary to join the gardaí but he spent most of his free time going back and his comparisons still tended to be farm-related. West had asked him once why he didn't transfer nearer home and Allen had looked at him with a grin. 'Not enough excitement there for me; plus I'd spend my time arresting my friends and neighbours. Me da wouldn't like that.'

'We fared a little better,' Jarvis said, bracing a shoulder against the wall. He gave them a summary of their conversation with Cara Donaldson.

'Did you believe her?' Andrews asked.

Jarvis looked at West and shrugged slightly. 'She works in finance; she's probably well used to parking her expression in neutral when she needs to but she looked shocked and puzzled when we told her. Bottom line is, she says her mother was alive on Sunday and we know that isn't possible.' He looked again to West, this time for confirmation.

'Dr Kennedy said eight days at least to freeze and defrost Muriel Hennessy's body. If Cara Donaldson saw her on Sunday, that only leaves five days before the mother was found on the Friday. It simply doesn't add up.' West looked around the room. 'Right, let's look for a motive. Check out Mrs Donaldson's claim that the house had been sold under equity release and her assertion that she wasn't in need of any inheritance. Same for Liam Hennessy. I want to know everything there is to know about them.'

'The keys to Muriel Hennessy's house were sent to the mortuary,' Jarvis said. 'Someone's dropping them in this evening. As soon as I have them, I'll call and see if there's a chest freezer in her house.'

'Okay.' West frowned. 'I'll speak to a judge, see if we have enough to get a warrant to search both Cara Donaldson's and Liam Hennessy's houses.'

'Maybe they're both lying about having seen their mother,' Andrews said. 'You know, they were both supposed to, neither did and they felt too guilty to admit that they hadn't. That would mean the woman hadn't been seen for almost two weeks.'

'There didn't seem to be much love lost between brother and sister,' Jarvis said. 'Maybe you're right, that it was a case of one-upmanship. Both wanted to appear to be the dutiful child, but in fact neither was.'

People lied for such a wide variety of reasons, nothing surprised them anymore. 'You could be right,' Baxter said, 'but we're still down to why anyone would want to freeze the old dear.'

'Let's concentrate on the son and daughter before we start looking at random people,' West said, getting to his feet. 'Jarvis, check out the house tomorrow. If you find a chest freezer, get the garda technical team out from Shankill to take samples. Meanwhile, I'll see if we have enough probable cause to get that warrant.' He looked around the eager faces. 'Tomorrow. But for now, let's get out of here.'

13

W est was relieved to see that Edel was wearing her engagement ring when he arrived home that evening. He'd been fussing about nothing.

'How's the writing going?' he asked as they sat over dinner.

'Good,' she said. 'Some days it almost seems to write itself and this was one of them.'

'I wish my cases were like that.'

'You've gone and got yourself another complicated one, have you?'

He looked at her with a smile. 'Kind of.' He filled her in on the siblings and their assertion that they'd seen their mother alive when she couldn't have been. 'She'd have been, as Niall Kennedy so elegantly put it, "frozen-turkey frozen".'

Edel spluttered on the water she was drinking. 'Honestly, he does come out with some dreadful things. So, what are you going to do?'

'The usual,' he said. He waited, wondering if she'd repeat her comment about digging for dirt. It was exactly what he was going to do. The thought made him sigh.

'Find out who is lying and why?'

It was a nicer way of putting it, even if it meant the same thing. 'We can't argue with the science. Only a complete freeze of the body would have resulted in the cellular damage, according to Niall, and that would take two to three days. There was some tissue damage that showed the body was defrosted a bit faster than it should have been. He estimated eight days in total. Which would have meant her dying on the previous Thursday.'

'So, the son and daughter could both have been lying.'

'Yes. Peter could be right, of course.'

'Peter often is,' she said, 'but what is he right about this time?'

West put his knife and fork down and sat back with his arms folded. 'They were supposed to visit her every week to keep an eye on her, check if she needed anything. Cara visited on Sunday, her brother on a weekday after work. Pete suggested that they were lying about having visited her.'

'Yes,' she nodded, understanding the thinking, 'and then were too embarrassed to say they hadn't bothered. I could see that, okay. So that would mean she hadn't been seen for about almost two weeks before she died.'

West said nothing for a moment, mulling over the idea that both son and daughter lied about visiting their mother. 'Muriel Hennessy had coronary heart disease and her death would have been put down to that if Jarvis hadn't read her medical file and queried how she managed to get to where she was found.'

'It's down to a chicken and egg scenario,' Edel said. She smiled at his raised eyebrow. 'You know – which came first? Did the woman die from a heart attack and was then, for some unknown reason, frozen, or did her darling son and daughter try to bump her off by throwing her into a freezer where she had a heart attack and died.'

They discussed the case as they cleared away.

'It's a puzzle,' Edel said, curling up on the sofa while West switched on the TV. 'I really can't see any reason for the siblings to lie.'

'But lie they did,' he said, putting an arm around her shoulder and pulling her close. 'Hopefully, tomorrow, we'll find out why.'

~

It was always good to be optimistic but by mid-morning the following day, they were no closer to finding a reason for anyone to have frozen the body of Muriel Hennessy.

Jarvis returned from her house and stood in the doorway of West's office. 'No joy, I'm afraid. All she had was a small fridge-freezer, nothing else. I checked the garage, just in case but nothing.'

'Right,' West said, running a hand over his head. 'We'll have the warrants to search for a freezer in Cara Donaldson's and Liam Hennessy's houses by late afternoon. Both work nine-to-five jobs. We'll call about 6.30: that should catch them home. You and I will stick with the lovely Cara and I'll get Andrews and Allen to call to her brother.'

'I'll give the garda technical team in Shankill a heads-up,' Jarvis said. 'They can come if we need them.' He took a step into the room and waved a tatty, worn book. 'I brought back the old lady's phone book. I thought I'd contact a few of her friends, see if I can get a feel for the relationship between Mrs Hennessy and her kids from that.'

'Good idea. Family friction is often enough of a motive for murder.'

As Jarvis took himself back to his desk, Baxter walked in with an expression on his face that told West he should be pleased to see him. Baxter sat, balanced his ankle on his knee and stared across the desk. Had Andrews been there he would have made a sarcastic remark about Baxter behaving like a diva and told him to get on with it. West had a smidgeon more patience. 'Well?'

'Our friend Darragh Checkley likes to play the big I am, but more importantly, he likes to play the stock market.'

'He's broke?'

'Hasn't, according to my very reliable source, got two brass farthings to rub together.'

West knew where Checkley lived. A large, detached house on Brennanstown Road in Carrickmines. 'What about his house?'

'Mortgaged to the hilt and they're behind in repayments.'

'Doris Whitaker's death works in their favour then, doesn't it?'

'It sure does. I spoke to a friend who works for an estate agent. He said her house would be worth at least five million because of the long road frontage. There's room, according to him, to build at least three large houses on the site.'

Five million would go a long way to paying off debts. 'Probably why Checkley was treating himself to an expensive Rolex at the weekend. Spending his inheritance. I think we need to pay our friend a visit, Seamus.'

'He works nine-to-five, but she should be at home.'

'Maybe that would work in our favour,' West said. 'We need to look at her car.' He chewed his lip for a second. 'It might be too late but ask one of the garda technical team to meet us there. We might get lucky.'

An hour later, they were pulling into the driveway of a large, detached house. It was modern, boxy, and not to West's taste even if he could afford the couple of million it would take to buy it.

'I prefer our house in Gorey,' Seamus said, getting out of the car and looking around.

West had been to his three-bedded semi at a house-warming/engagement party a couple of weeks before. His fiancée, Tanya, had made the house into a warm, comfortable home. 'So do I,' he said, walking up to the front door. A standard bay tree stood each side. *Nice,* West thought, reaching automatically to touch the nearest one, surprised to find it was fake. A bit like Darragh Checkley's bravado. He pushed the doorbell and stepped back.

A minute later, Lynda Checkley opened the door. Recognition was instant, surprise in her widened eyes before her expression turned carefully neutral. 'Detective Garda Sergeant West, isn't it?'

'That's right, and this is my colleague, Detective Garda Baxter. We have a few questions for you, would you mind if we came in?'

She lifted her wrist and stared at her watch with a frown. 'I have a meeting soon that I can't miss. You really should have called. Perhaps, tomorrow.'

'It will only take a moment,' West said, his voice firm. 'I'd hate to have to make it official and ask you to come to the station instead.'

This brought a flush of angry colour to her face. 'This sounds like police intimidation to me,' she said. 'I will remind you, since it appears to have slipped your mind, that we're in mourning for Darragh's cousin.'

Lynda had been tearful and distressed during her visit to the station. Now she was spiky and brittle. Had her distress been a calculated act? 'Actually, it's the reason we're here. We have a few questions to ask about her death.'

The angry flush faded, leaving Lynda paler than before. She was obviously weighing up her choices, then with a huff, she waved them inside.

14

Inside the house, it was obvious no expense had been spared. Lynda Checkley led them into a spacious and very elegant sitting room where accessories in varying shades of jade brightened a pale-grey colour scheme. Two charcoal-grey sofas faced each other across an overly large coffee table.

It was all very elegant but cold. Just like the woman who dropped casually onto one of the sofas. She rested an elbow on the back and linked her diamond-bedecked fingers together, a study in posed relaxation.

West and Baxter sat on the sofa that faced her.

'Were you close to your husband's cousin?' West asked her.

Lynda tilted her head to one side. 'Define "close"?' She pointedly looked at her watch.

West leaned back on the sofa and crossed his legs. 'We will finish with more speed if you answer the questions we ask without playing games, Mrs Checkley.'

'Fine,' she snapped. 'No, I wasn't particularly close to her. We got on okay, and I quite liked her but that's about it.'

'But you did visit her every week?'

Lynda dropped her studied pose and sat up straight. 'Only

because I had to. Darragh wanted to keep her sweet and he didn't have time to call around. Not that she'd have welcomed a visit from him, anyway. She wasn't overly keen on men.' She raised her hands and dropped them into her lap. 'So, I called around to keep the peace. Did any bit of shopping she needed, had a cup of tea or coffee with her and then escaped. Thirty minutes max, once a week.'

'Tell me about the day you found her.'

Her sigh was loudly exaggerated as was the lift of her hand as she checked her watch once again. 'I gave my statement to the garda who was at the scene and later I wrote it down.'

'You were no doubt distraught at the scene and the statement, I gather, was written the same day while you were still distressed. Sometimes, time and reflection allow a different take on what happened.'

She eyed him with dislike. 'Fine, I'll go over what happened again.'

And she did, giving an almost word-for-word account of what happened the day she found Doris Whitaker lying on the side of the road. West met Baxter's sharp eyes and knew he was thinking the same.

'And you recognised her immediately?'

'Not immediately,' Lynda said. 'At first I thought it was rubbish on the side of the road. It was only when I drew near that the colour caught my eye. The coat she was wearing, one she was fond of and wore frequently, was a particularly vivid shade of blue. Recognition hit me then so I stopped the car in the middle of the road and rushed over.' She shut her eyes and held her hand over her mouth for a dramatic few seconds. 'You hope that it's not true, that it can't possibly be... but, of course, it was.'

'The gardaí who responded, stated that you had moved the body.'

'It was an automatic reaction to gather her into my arms and offer what comfort I could. Honestly, I was in shock and wasn't really aware of what I was doing.'

Or she knew exactly what she was doing. Looking at her cold, calculating eyes, West didn't feel the need to couch his questions in more sensitive terms. 'Did you know she was dead?'

'No,' she said. Just as she'd written in her statement. West could see the lie on her face. She'd known damn well that the woman was dead. What they had to find out was, had she helped kill her?

He guessed that if there'd been any evidence on her car of a collision, it would be long gone. But still, they might get lucky. 'The gardaí at the scene missed a crucial step in the investigation.' West sacrificed the integrity of the two attending gardaí without compunction. 'They should have taken samples from your car to rule out any involvement... purely routine as I'm sure you understand... if it would be okay with you, we could do that now. A technical team is standing by.'

If he'd hoped to see a flicker of anxiety, he was doomed to disappointment. 'Seems like a terrible waste of time and resources,' she said in a bored tone of voice. 'But if it will get this all sorted faster, then be my guest, you're in luck, I won't be needing it.' She waved to the right. 'It's on the drive at the side of the house.'

'Thank you,' West said, getting to his feet. 'And for your time.'

Outside, they sat in his car to await the technical team.

'She's an ice-lady isn't she,' Baxter said, staring across the drive to the house. 'And her account, it was almost word for word what she wrote down. Not normal that, is it?'

'It did sound as if she'd memorised it,' West agreed. 'But that's not a crime.'

'She lied though, about not knowing her cousin-in-law was dead.'

'Yes, and it was an unnecessary lie which made it all the more foolish.'

Baxter stretched and tapped the flat of his hands against the roof of the car. 'Yes, she slipped up there I think, odd for a cold, calculating woman. Maybe our visit rattled her.'

'Maybe,' West said. 'Or maybe saying she thought Doris was still alive gave her a valid reason for moving the body.'

'True, but why would she need to?'

Why indeed. West had no idea but there was something off about this whole thing.

Baxter shuffled restlessly in his seat and checked the time. 'They should be here soon but I'd bet a fiver that we're not going to find anything on her car.'

West shook his head. 'No takers on that bet. She looked too smug when she told us to go ahead.'

A comfortable silence settled over them. It was broken by Baxter, who turned in his seat to look at West. 'I was going to say how odd it was that we were investigating two cases where both victims were octogenarians. But Doris Whitaker was ninety so what does that make her?'

'A nonagenarian.'

'I must use that on Andrews when we get back. Bet you a fiver, he'll be using it before the end of the day.' He looked towards the car pulling into the driveway. 'Here they are, I'll go and fill them in.'

West tuned the radio to a classical music station, put his head back and shut his eyes. An octogenarian and a nonagenarian – it didn't matter how old their victims were, they'd try their best to get justice for them.

15

The garda technical team couldn't find anything overtly suspicious but they took a series of swabs from Lynda Checkley's car and left.

'It was worth a try,' Baxter said, climbing back into the passenger seat. He raised an eyebrow at the music but wisely made no remark. 'We still going to talk to the husband?'

'There's not much point. His wife will no doubt have rung him as soon as we'd left so we've lost the element of surprise.' West started the engine and edged the car onto the road. 'They're an unlikeable duo, I'd like to find them guilty of something.'

～

'Nothing?' Andrews asked as he put a mug of coffee on the desk.

'Mrs Checkley is sticking to her statement,' West said, picking up the mug and taking a sip. 'Word for word which is suspicious in itself. We had the technical team take some swabs from her car but I'm not holding out any hope there.'

'She's had plenty of time to clean it,' Andrews said philosophically. He sat back and slurped his coffee. 'You think she's capable of cold-bloodedly running someone over?'

'They have one of those big houses on Brennanstown Road. Wide, curving entrance drive, manicured gardens. Inside, everything is high-end including Lynda Checkley. Contrary to her tearful performance when she was here, she came across as a cold, hard woman. She's used to living well, too, being broke wouldn't suit her.'

'Killing to protect her lifestyle... it's not the worst motive for murder I've ever heard.'

'We've no proof of any wrongdoing,' West said, putting his mug down and linking his hands behind his head.

'Yet,' Andrews said, getting to his feet. 'If they had a hand in the old dear's death, we'll find the proof.' He stopped in the doorway and looked back. 'We're still set for six to pay a visit on Liam Hennessy and Cara Donaldson?'

'Yes. Maybe we'll have better luck and find a freezer big enough to have kept Muriel Hennessy's body.'

'It would be nice to have either the octogenarian or the nonagenarian case solved,' Andrews said before heading back to his desk.

Baxter would have won his fiver, but West never bet on certainties. He switched on his computer and spent the remaining time on the never-ending paperwork.

At six, Allen, Jarvis and Andrews crowded into his office for a final meeting before leaving for the Donaldson and Hennessy homes.

'We know Muriel Hennessy was kept in a freezer for two to three days,' West said. 'She wasn't a big woman but it would still need to be either a chest freezer or maybe one of those full-size American-style freezers.'

'Do we impound it if they have one?' Jarvis asked. 'I'm thinking of the freezer in my parents' house. It's generally crammed with stuff.'

'Unless they have two,' Allen suggested. 'People do, you know, a small one in the kitchen for ice cream and stuff and a bigger one in the garage for–'

'Frozen turkeys and bodies,' Jarvis interrupted.

West held his hand up. 'If we find a suitable freezer anywhere, house or garage, we ring the garda technical team. I've already spoken to them. They'll oblige us again and come and take samples if we need them to.' He looked from one to the other. 'Of course, if it is an obvious crime scene–'

'Like if we find her dentures in the bottom of the chest freezer–'

'Or long nail scratches on the inside of an American freezer door,' Jarvis added.

West met Andrews' eyes and sighed. 'As far as I'm aware, her dentures weren't missing, and let's not drift into Edgar Allan Poe territory.'

'*The Fall of the House of Usher*,' Jarvis said with a grin. 'A grave not a freezer, I was using artistic licence.'

This time it was Andrews and Allen who exchanged glances. 'Let's head,' Andrews said to him. 'If they've started on Poe, they'll soon drift to Agatha Christie.'

'Not from Poe,' Jarvis said with an expression of mock horror. 'It would be to Wilkie Collins, of course, the writer of the first modern detective novel.'

But Andrews had long gone.

It was left to Jarvis and West to discuss *The Moonstone* as they made their way to the car park where Andrews and Allen were already pulling out.

Cara Donaldson lived in a moderate-sized semi-detached

house in Cabinteely. That the Donaldsons were comfortable, rather than Brennanstown Road rich, was West's estimation as they climbed out. Despite the impression Cara had given them, the car in the driveway was six years old, and the house itself looked as if it could do with a bit of TLC.

Or maybe, unlike the Checkleys, they were a family who lived within their means.

West parked on the road outside. 'Let's see what we find here then,' he said, getting out.

Light shone through a pane to one side of the uPVC door. West pressed the doorbell and heard the chimes echoing within. He stepped back, Jarvis at his side and waited. Only seconds passed before they saw a figure appearing down the hallway. It disappeared behind the solid door, then there was the rattle of a chain being put in place. Security conscious, or determined not to let visitors inside?

It was an unknown man's face that peered through the gap the chain allowed. 'Yes?' a deep voice asked.

West held his identification forward. 'I'm Detective Garda Sergeant West and this is my colleague Detective Garda Jarvis. We have a few questions to ask Cara Donaldson.'

There was a snap as the door was shut, then the rattle of the chain as it was removed before the door was opened wide. 'Cara's only just home,' the man said, standing to one side and waving them in. 'I'm Ross, her husband.' He shut the door behind them and indicated a room. 'Take a seat, I'll give her a shout. I assume this has to do with the death of her mother. A shocking business, she's really cut up about it.'

'It's always a difficult time,' West said neutrally. He'd not got the impression that Cara was in any way upset about the death of her mother but maybe she was simply good at concealing her grief. He needed to keep an open mind.

West and Jarvis sat as Ross left the room shutting the door

after him. They heard his quick step on the stair, then his deep voice reverberating through the floorboards followed by her voice, louder, higher-pitched. Definitely annoyed.

'We have that effect on people,' Jarvis said. He got to his feet and crossed to a tall shelving unit on one side of the mantelpiece. Framed photographs filled up spaces between rows of books; he examined each intently as if the answer to all their questions lay in them.

Amused, West sat back and strained to hear what was going on upstairs. The voices died away, followed moments later by heavy footsteps coming down the stairs. Ross didn't reappear. West heard the opening and shutting of another door, then the sound of a TV.

It was ten minutes before the door opened and Cara came in. If she'd been annoyed when she heard they were there, there was no evidence of it, her expression bland and almost bored. 'Sorry to have kept you waiting,' she said, sinking onto the small sofa in the corner. 'Now to what do I owe this interesting visit?'

West reached into his inside pocket. 'We have a warrant to search your house for a freezer, Mrs Donaldson.'

Instead of appearing shocked, Cara blinked, shook her head slowly and started to laugh. She had a deep earthy laugh that instantly made a listener smile, a contagious, genuine laugh that told West and Jarvis, who had sat again, that whatever they were looking for, wasn't going to be found there.

'You're serious,' she said, her laughter dying away. 'You think I might have killed and frozen my mother?'

'Someone did.'

Cara, for a change, seemed stuck for words. 'Right,' she eventually managed to say. 'I suppose you'd better come and see our freezer then. Luckily for me, you're going to be disappointed.'

She led them into a room that stretched across the back of

the house. It had obviously been extended at one stage, but it had been badly designed and the shape was awkward. A small sitting area was stuck in one corner with a too-large TV overpowering the space. Cara's husband sat, with his feet up on the sofa, engrossed in a football game. He spared a brief glance before returning his attention to the screen.

'Here you go,' Cara said, opening the door of an integrated fridge-freezer. The top freezer section was small. It would have been barely adequate to store food for a small family; it was definitely not suitable to freeze a body.

'Do you have a second one?' Jarvis asked. 'In the garage or an outhouse?'

'We don't have an outhouse,' she said. She pulled open a drawer of the kind found in every home, packed with all kinds of paraphernalia. Cara rummaged for a moment and pulled out a set of keys. 'Here you go. Have a look yourselves. We don't use the garage very much. Someday we're going to get it converted into another room.' She waved a hand around the higgledy-piggledy room. 'And get this sorted too. The previous owners made a right hash of extending.'

Jarvis took the keys and headed out the front door to investigate the attached garage.

Cara crossed the kitchen, picked up a glass and filled it with water from the tap and stayed with her back to West drinking it. When she turned her eyes were shining. 'My mother and I didn't have the closest of relationships but she was my mother. I wouldn't have wished her harm. You are convinced I am lying about visiting her that weekend. Believe me, Sergeant West, I did see her. There is no reason for me to lie.'

'Science doesn't lie either, Mrs Donaldson. And science tells us, that your mother had to have died at least eight days before she was found.'

Cara put the glass down carefully and folded her arms. 'I'm telling the truth. You think your science is telling the truth. It seems to me that there is something seriously wrong with that because we can't both be telling the truth. But I have an advantage, Sergeant West... I know I'm not lying.'

16

Not many miles away, Andrews and Allen were having an equally unsuccessful time.

When they arrived outside Liam Hennessy's small townhouse there was no lights at any of the windows and no response when they pressed the doorbell several times.

Allen stepped back and peered at the upstairs window. 'Looks like nobody's home.'

'We'll sit and wait,' Andrews said, heading back to where they'd parked their car on the roadside. 'He has two teenage kids, doesn't he? I wonder where they are.'

Since there was no way Allen could have known, he assumed Andrews wasn't expecting an answer. He rested his head back and shut his eyes.

'Tired, are we?'

'I don't know about you, but I'm knackered.'

'No stamina, you young lads.' Andrews turned on the radio and pressed buttons till he found a music station he liked.

The strains of country music filled the air. Allen opened one eye and groaned. 'My flatmate decided to buy a cat. It kept me awake most of the bloody night mewling; now I have to listen to that!'

Andrews shot him a look but reached down and turned the radio off. For a few minutes, there was silence in the car.

'Do you think they're in it together?' Allen asked. 'That they killed the old dear?'

Both this case and the death of Doris Whitaker had been spinning around Andrews' brain. Until they were solved, they'd be there, niggling him. 'Somebody froze Muriel Hennessy's body several days before she was found and her two nearest and dearest are swearing they saw her within that period. There is something wrong with the maths there; we need to find out what that is.'

'But it could have been an accident.'

Andrews looked at him. 'What? She accidentally fell into a freezer?'

'Happens.'

'In a bad TV series maybe. Not in real life.'

Allen opened his eyes, sat up and rubbed a hand over his face. 'There's some quote about stranger things happening in real life than on TV, but I can't remember what it is.'

'Good,' Andrews said bluntly. 'Next thing you'll be quoting Poe or Wilkie whatever his name.'

Allen opened his mouth to reply but stopped as a car pulled into the driveway. They watched silently as Liam Hennessy climbed out. He stood for a moment holding onto the car door, the bright interior light reflecting on his lined and weary face. Only when the light went out, did he push the door shut and trudge to the front door.

'He doesn't look too hot,' Allen said.

'Guilt can make a poor companion.'

'Is that a quotation?' Allen grinned and got out of the car.

By the time they got to the front door, only seconds later,

both had fixed suitably official expressions on their faces. Andrews pressed the doorbell, then pressed again a minute later but it wasn't until the third, longer ring, that the door was pulled open.

Liam Hennessy's face fell when he saw who was on the doorstep. 'I thought... I was hoping–' He shook his head and irritation flitted across his face. 'What do you want?'

'May we come in?'

Hennessy's glare told the story: he was going to shut the door in their faces.

'We do have a warrant,' Andrews said quickly.

Hennessy's eyes grew wide, his mouth opening and closing as his brain tried to understand. 'A warrant?'

'It would be better to discuss this inside.'

It was another few seconds before reality got through. Then Hennessy stood back and flung the door open with such force it banged off the wall behind, the sound startlingly loud.

The house was small. A kitchen to the front, and to the back a combined sitting-dining room that gave little space for either. Dirty plates and cutlery cluttered the small dining table and old newspapers formed a pile on one end of a two-seater sofa. A fine layer of dust covered the TV and a shelving unit that was empty apart from a few books and one frame holding a photograph of two children.

The room stank of stale food, neglect, and despair.

The two detectives followed Hennessy's stiff back into the room and took the seats he waved them to while he stood, one hand gripping the other.

'What's this all about?'

Andrews frowned. The man seemed on edge. He looked paler, more anxious than when they'd seen him last. 'Where are your wife and children? Are you expecting them home soon?'

A laugh rang out, startling both detectives. 'No, I'm not

expecting them home soon,' Hennessy's lips twisted and there was a sneer in his voice as he spat out, 'I'm not expecting them home... *ever.*'

Andrews and Jarvis exchanged glances. Trained to expect the unexpected, they were still often caught unawares by a change in circumstances and this was one of those times.

'Why is that, then?' Andrews asked, keeping his voice calm, treading carefully.

'None of your damn business.' Hennessy wrung his hands together and glared at the two men. 'This warrant... what's it all about?'

Andrews decided to leave the question about the wife and children for the moment and proceed with the reason they had come. He took the warrant out. 'This gives us the right to search the house, garage or outhouses for a freezer.'

Hennessy's laugh was almost amused. 'Well, that won't take long. The kitchen is through there. I don't have a garage or an outhouse.'

It took Allen only minutes to confirm what he said, and to rule out the tiny freezer in the kitchen as being in any way suitable to house the body of even such a little woman as Muriel Hennessy.

When Allen returned and gave an almost imperceptible head shake, Andrews stood, turned to Hennessy and jerked a thumb upwards. 'Do you mind if I use your bathroom?'

'I do.' A second passed before he lifted his hands in defeat. 'I suppose I'm obliged to say yes. Up the stairs, second door on the left.'

'Thank you.' Although he'd never spoken about it, Andrews knew all about West's traumatic experience prior to his transfer to Foxrock. The domestic incident that West and his partner had been called to... the murder of the partner... the dead body of the woman and her children in an upstairs bedroom.

Andrews gripped the handle of the first door and slowly opened it. There was nobody in the room. An unmade bed, a tangle of clothes on every surface, that stuffy, unpleasant smell that shouted neglect. No dead bodies.

He skipped the bathroom door and headed to the second bedroom. Two single beds neatly made. A small wardrobe. Andrews slid the door open and set the empty hangers rattling. It was a sad, desolate sound. He looked around the room. No personal belongings, no messy, childish clutter.

Frowning, he opened the final door to the small bathroom. He probably should have flushed the toilet to support his story about wanting to use it but he didn't want to continue with the deception.

Back downstairs, he joined Allen who was standing in the living room, his hands in his trouser pockets. 'He hasn't moved or said a word since you went upstairs.'

Andrews crossed the room and sat opposite the man whose face was half hidden by the hand resting over his mouth. 'Where are your wife and children?' There was no movement and he didn't think he was going to get an answer but slowly the hand was dropped and the pale face lifted.

'What? You think I might have killed them?' Hennessy sniffed. 'Is that why you wanted to go upstairs? To see if they were lying there, dead?' He took a handkerchief from his pocket and wiped it over his eyes. 'They might as well be. My wife is Russian.' He said it as if that explained everything.

'Russian?' Andrews suddenly wished that West were there because his own knowledge of Russia was limited to bad guys in Bond movies.

'You didn't know that, but then why would you?' Hennessy shoved the handkerchief back into his pocket and sat back. 'The company I worked for folded last year. I'd worked for them for several years and should have had a big redundancy package but it transpired that the company had been diddling the books for years. There was no money left so I got a statutory payout. A paltry sum but it would have been okay if I'd been able to find another job straight away.' He slumped down in the chair. 'I was out of work for several months and was afraid I'd never get another position so I did what I thought was best... sold our Rathgar house and bought somewhere smaller.'

Hennessy waved a hand around the room. 'This was the best I could do, but Annika, my wife, hated it. She complained it was so small she couldn't breathe.' Hennessy pulled out his handkerchief again, wiped it over his eyes. 'She hated the house and resented me... no, make that hated me... for my failure. Last month, she left, took the two kids and went to live in Moscow with her family.'

'You have rights,' Andrews said.

'Yes, and my solicitor is arguing them for me.' Hennessy sighed loudly. 'Unfortunately for me, Annika's family are rich. I'm talking Russian oligarch rich, you get me?'

And Andrews did. He might know little about Russia but he knew a bit about inequality. There was the law, and there was the law for the very rich. Only a fool thought it didn't make any difference. He saw the defeated face of the man opposite; he wasn't a fool. 'I'm sorry,' he said simply and got to his feet. 'We'll be on our way.'

Outside, Andrews looked back at the small townhouse. 'Poor man,' he muttered.

'I thought for a while there we were going to have a familicide on our hands,' Allen said as he buckled his seat belt. 'I was thinking of those mummified bodies we found and wondering if they could have been his wife and kids.'

Andrews looked at him with a puzzled frown. 'Those remains are nearly fifty years old.'

'Science can be wrong. Maybe there's a way of ageing dead bodies to make it look as though they're older.'

'That's why you and Jarvis get on so well,' Andrews said, doing a U-turn on the narrow road. 'You both talk a load of rubbish.' Stopped at the lights on the way back to the station, he turned to Allen. 'Best to check out his story though. Not that I think your daft story has any credence, but just in case we're having the wool pulled over our eyes.'

He pulled into a parking space outside the station. 'Go home,' he said to Allen. 'The morning will be time enough for the rest.'

Andrews wasn't surprised to find West sitting in his office. 'I hope you had more luck than we had.'

'Afraid not and, into the bargain, Cara Donaldson is adamant she saw her mother at the weekend. I told her about the impossibility of it, that to freeze and thaw a human body would take at least eight days and do you know what she said?'

'That the science was wrong?'

'Exactly,' West said.

'Allen said much the same thing on the way home although he was referring to a different matter.' He gave West a quick breakdown of their conversation with Hennessy. 'Allen's going to check his story in the morning but I think he's telling us the truth.'

West looked at him. 'Something troubling you?'

'I was thinking... maybe they're right. Cara Donaldson and Allen... maybe the science is wrong. You're going to laugh but I've actually thought of a perfect quote to explain what I mean. Arthur Conan Doyle said it, Mike. "When you have excluded the impossible, whatever remains, however improbable, must be the truth".'

17

'Andrews quoted Arthur Conan Doyle?'

West twirled spaghetti around his fork before replying. 'I thought he was going to admit to being a closet Sherlock Holmes fan, but he heard it quoted at a conference years ago and it stuck in his head.'

Edel laughed. 'Sounds more like it.'

'Cara Donaldson is sticking to her story. She swears that she saw her mother at the weekend. We said that was impossible, that Muriel Hennessy had to have been dead before that. So if we eliminate that...'

'Then she's right. Her mother was alive and the science is wrong.'

'Makes it sound so easy but I've a feeling Niall Kennedy is going to dispute that.'

'If I was writing this story, I'd make him the bad guy. He's altering test results for his own nefarious reasons.' Edel reached for the wine bottle and topped up both their glasses. 'Of course, I'd have to change his appearance. He's too boyishly handsome to be the bad guy; I'd make him moody and have his face heavily lined instead.'

West smiled. 'I wish it were that easy for me.'

Edel pushed her plate away and picked up her glass. 'But it's true, isn't it? If she's right, the science... and Niall... must be wrong. Okay, he's not altering results for nefarious reasons – this is Niall after all – but couldn't he simply be mistaken?'

'It is, unfortunately, something I'm going to have to look into.' West shook his head. 'It won't be the easiest conversation.'

'Bring him one of those big meringues that he likes, and you'll be fine.'

Next morning, it seemed the best idea to go straight to Drumcondra. West rang on the way and asked the administrator for five minutes of Dr Kennedy's time.

'Since it's you, he'll probably squeeze you in,' she said. 'I'll tell him you're on your way.'

It didn't bode well for the success of West's visit that when he called into Thunders, he was told the meringues weren't ready.

'Not for another hour,' the assistant said. 'If it's fresh cream you want, we have éclairs and cream donuts.'

Settling for two of each, he paid and carried the box to the car. He hoped the contents would sweeten what was going to be a trying conversation.

As it turned out, it wasn't as difficult as he'd expected. When West asked if the science could possibly be wrong, Kennedy, with his mouth full of cream donut, merely sputtered sugary crumbs over the table. 'Science, my friend, is never wrong!'

'I know, and I'd be the first to say exactly that, Niall. But I'm stuck with this one. The daughter swears she saw the mother when you said she couldn't possibly have done.'

Kennedy dusted sugar from his fingers and reached for an éclair. 'I prefer the meringues, but these are a good substitute.'

With the éclair demolished in a few bites, Kennedy stood and rinsed his hands in the small wash-hand basin. 'I only know what the results tell me, Mike,' he said, turning as he dried his hands. 'The level of cellular damage I saw would have required the body to be completely frozen. Based on mathematical and scientific calculations for a body of her weight, that would take two to three days depending on the freezer.' He sat behind his desk again. 'Since the body was not frozen when it was found, it had to have been defrosted prior to being dumped. That's roughly another six days.'

'Maybe it was frozen, and defrosted while it was lying there?'

Kennedy shook his head slowly. 'Rodents won't eat frozen meat.'

West remembered seeing the photographs of the damage done to Muriel Hennessy's body and shuddered. 'Horrible thought.'

'As I already explained to you, the level of degradation in peripheral tissues was inconsistent with the tissue deterioration of internal organs.'

'Yes, you did. Tissue on the outside was decomposing while her insides were still frozen.'

'Exactly.' Kennedy wagged a hand side to side. 'But there wasn't a huge difference – they didn't thaw the body somewhere warm, for instance, which would have made the disparity more significant. My guess would be in an unheated room or garage. It would take six days to defrost.' He thought a moment. 'Maybe five, but no less.'

'Not four.'

'Definitely not four.' Kennedy waited for that to sink in before adding, 'I do have some news for you though. And please notice I didn't say good news.'

'I would have preferred if you had,' West said. 'I suppose I should be grateful you didn't say bad. Go on, what is it?'

'We got the DNA results back. The skulls match the bodies we found. And even better, we now know that the younger adults were full siblings. One of the older bodies was the father of the two. The other is no relation to any of them.'

'A father, two children and a woman.' West shrugged. 'Baxter is trawling through the lists of missing persons but it's not an easy task. Have you been able to narrow down an age for us?'

'Oh, that's the good news,' Kennedy said. He reached for a file and flicked it open. 'It is pretty amazing what you can learn from a dead body. Okay, first: the man was between forty and forty-five. He broke his right arm when he was younger. The woman was a little younger, between thirty and thirty-five. She'd never given birth. The younger female was approximately twenty, she'd never given birth either. The boy was approximately twenty-one.' He waved the report. 'I've emailed the information to you.'

'Thank you.' West thought about what he'd just heard. Maybe it would help narrow down their search. 'Interesting. You're more certain of the younger ages than the older?'

'Ah, but there is a good reason, my friend.' Kennedy rubbed his head. 'Skull sutures. There is a scientifically accepted scale for estimating age based on how much they've closed since birth. Generally, they are completely closed by twenty-three. Both younger skulls had sutures that were significantly closed but not closed or fused. The scale indicated their ages as I've said to be approximately twenty and twenty-one. For the older two, I had to use different calculations which were less precise.'

'It'll all help paint a picture,' West said. 'There was no indication of violence?'

'You're looking for a cause of death and here, I'm afraid, I'm going to have to disappoint you. The toxicology screen isn't all back yet but initial results show that all four were in rudimentary good health.'

'The person or persons who killed them, mummified the bodies and decapitated them may be dead themselves. But someone cut the bodies up and dumped them. I'd like to find who that person is.'

'Yes, find that person, you might find who our four friends are. I'd like to see them get a decent burial.' Kennedy stood and laid a hand on West's shoulder. 'You found a name for little Abasiama. You can do the same for these.'

18

Back at the station, West saw Baxter hunched over his computer and called him into his office.

'I don't suppose you've any good news for me?'

Baxter shook his head. 'There are numerous reports of missing people but not entire families, Mike. I've put feelers out to our friends in the UK and a contact I have in Interpol.'

'Good. I've been to see Dr Kennedy this morning. He has some information that might help.' West switched on his computer and waited, frowning while it booted up. 'Someday,' he complained, 'they're going to have to give me a new one.'

'Cutbacks.' Baxter grinned and perched on the edge of the desk.

'Right, here you go. Their ages, a couple of other pieces of information that'll help to paint a picture of them.' He frowned as he read something Kennedy hadn't thought to mention. 'They're European so it might be worthwhile adding that and their ages to the information for Interpol.'

'Will do.' Baxter got to his feet, stretched his arms over his head and cracked his knuckles. 'I got a printout of all the vehicles that entered the recycling centre in the two-day period since the container had been emptied. Edwards is working through them to see if anything suspicious turns up.'

It was a long shot but sometimes their breaks came because of one. 'It would be good to give those four people a name,' West said. 'Let's keep at it.'

He forwarded Kennedy's report to Baxter and got to his feet. It was time to tell Inspector Morrison what they were up to. West had been putting it off: he knew exactly what would be said.

~

'How do you do it?' Morrison said, his thick, hairy eyebrows joining in mutual disbelief. 'Seriously, in all my years as a police officer I've never met anyone who can attract the weird and wonderful cases the way you do.'

'I don't do it deliberately,' West said, his shoulder propped against the wall.

'A frozen nonagenarian, the suspicious death of an octogenarian–'

'The other way around–'

'What?' Morrison's eyebrows rose almost to his hairline.

'It's a frozen octogenarian and the suspicious death of a nonagenarian.'

Eyebrows came down and to West's surprise, the inspector laughed. 'Sounds like something from between the pages of a bad novel.' He resumed his normal severe expression. 'Anyway, you've a frozen body, a suspicious body and the mummified remains of four bodies. Sounds like quite a mess to anyone's ears.'

West crossed his fingers behind his back. 'We'll get them sorted.'

'At least there are no priests involved this time,' Morrison said and waved him away.

West saw Andrews at the coffee machine as he passed through the main office. 'I need one too.' He sat behind his desk and rubbed a hand over his head. 'Mother Morrison is glad there are no priests involved in any of our messy cases.'

Andrews put a mug of coffee on the desk. 'It's about the only positive thing to be said for any of the three. We're not getting anywhere.'

'That's not quite true.' West filled him in on his conversation with the state pathologist. 'So we're building a picture of the four.'

'A pretty bare picture.' Andrews held a hand up in apology. 'I know, it's slow but sure.'

'Slow anyway.' West lifted his mug and took a sip. 'What about Checkley? Have we anything?' He saw Andrews shake his head. 'We need to speak to Doris Whitaker's solicitor. Checkley is a cousin. How did he end up being her next of kin anyway?'

'It's Pritchard and Lane Solicitors in Dun Laoghaire,' Andrews said. 'You want me to make an appointment?'

'I can't think of anything else to do. Yes, go ahead. It might get us somewhere.'

'We might be able to paint another picture.' Andrews grinned, took the two empty mugs with him and left.

He was back before West's computer had powered up. 'That was quick.'

'I'm super-efficient,' Andrews said. 'A solicitor by the name of Ashley Pritchard will see us at 2pm. You don't know him, I suppose.'

'It's five years since I worked as a solicitor. Lots of new faces in five years.' West looked at the computer screen, then tapped a few keys to shut it down. 'Let's go, we can get some lunch on the way.'

For convenience, as the solicitor's practice was on George's Street Upper, they parked in Dun Laoghaire shopping centre and had lunch in one of the many cafés. It was noisy, packed, and the sandwich West had chosen wasn't very good, but the coffee was excellent. He pushed the second half of the sandwich away.

Andrews, far less fussy, raised an eyebrow and when his sandwich was finished, he reached for it. 'Shame to let it go to waste.'

'I asked Kennedy about the science being wrong.' West raised his voice to be heard over the cries of a baby sat at the next table.

'Ha,' Andrews said around a mouthful of avocado and brie. 'I bet he loved that.'

'Actually, he wasn't in the least offended. Probably, in fairness, because his mouth was full of cream donut.'

'Thunders?'

West nodded absently. 'He insists it would have taken two days to freeze Muriel Hennessy's body to cause the level of cellular damage he saw. And another five to six days to defrost it.'

'Maybe the body was dumped in that laneway when it was still frozen.'

'Exactly what I said, to which Niall replied that rodents didn't eat frozen meat.'

Andrews picked up a piece of tomato that had escaped from his sandwich and popped it into his mouth. 'Yes, I see his point there. There was quite a lot of damage done to her face, ears and fingers.'

'Thankfully, she was dead before that.' West glanced at his watch. 'We'd better head.'

The office of Pritchard and Lane Solicitors was across the street from the shopping centre. Above a shop, it was accessed through a narrow door which led to an even narrower steep stairway.

To make up for the less than salubrious entrance, the reception area was decorated in aubergine and gold with dramatic paintings in ornate gold frames on every wall. *Trying too hard,* West thought, as they gave their names to the elegantly dressed woman behind the desk.

They weren't kept waiting. A door behind opened almost immediately and a short, slight man bustled through with a hand extended. 'Come into my office,' he said, shaking each of their hands in turn.

The office, with tall windows looking out over the street, was large and bright. Ashley Pritchard took his seat behind the desk and waved to two chairs the other side. 'Sit,' he said, then resting his elbows on the desk he steepled long thin fingers together and looked over at the two detectives expectantly. 'Now, what is it I can do for the gardaí?'

'You are Doris Whitaker's solicitor.'

A wary expression came over the solicitor's face. 'That's correct.'

West chose his words carefully. 'We believe her will was read recently. We know, obviously, that until probate is cleared, it's not in the public domain but would you be able to answer some questions for us?'

Pritchard's long middle fingers tapped soundlessly against one another as he considered the question. 'Ask them,' he said finally. 'If I can answer, I will.'

'Fair enough. None are too complex. Some are things we already know and we simply need confirmation. For instance,' West said, 'we are aware that Darragh Checkley is Mrs Whitaker's next of kin. Can we assume he inherits her estate?'

'You are, of course, entitled to assume whatever you wish. But I'm not obliged to tell you the contents of the will.'

Not an unexpected reply. West tried again. 'How long has Darragh Checkley been her next of kin?'

This made the solicitor drop his hands and sit back. 'Perhaps if you would share why you're investigating Mr Checkley I might be of more assistance.'

'Even a conservative estimate would value Mrs Whitaker's house and garden at around five million. It was Darragh's wife, Lynda, who found her on the road, the victim of a hit-and-run. So, Mr Pritchard, we have a wealthy ninety-year-old who leaves her estate to her next of kin, found dead by that next of kin's wife following a hit-and-run that nobody witnessed. You can see why we'd be a little bit suspicious, especially as Darragh Checkley comes across as a...'

Pritchard jumped into his hesitation. 'As a prize prick?'

'I couldn't have said it better, myself. So, what can you tell us?'

'I only met Checkley once when he brought Mrs Whitaker in to change her will.' The solicitor joined his hands together again.

'And this was recently?'

'Yes, about three weeks ago. I'd inherited Mrs Whitaker as a client from a partner who retired several years ago so I'd had no dealings with her. It was several years since she'd written the previous will and it isn't unheard of for people to change their will after a long period. I did suggest that I call around in view of her age but she insisted on coming in.'

'Those stairs up can't have been easy,' Andrews said.

'I gather that's why Checkley came with her: he virtually hauled her up the stairs.'

'Not surprising if she was changing her will in his favour. He wanted to make sure she didn't pop her clogs beforehand.'

The solicitor gave West's remark the courtesy of a slight smile. 'Mrs Whitaker sat and introduced Checkley as her cousin.

She told me that he and his wife were supporting her, and she wanted to repay their kindness by changing her will in his favour.'

West frowned. 'There was no indication that Checkley was putting undue pressure on her?'

Pritchard shook his head emphatically. 'I didn't take to the man but had there been the slightest intimation that he was putting pressure on her I'd have refused to proceed.'

'Maybe the pressure had been exerted before they arrived. Something along the lines of... leave everything to me or I won't support you any longer.'

'I had no sense of that being the case. Mrs Whitaker came across as sharp as a tack. I put some deliberately pointed and complex questions to her about her various bequests and there was no indication of any lack of comprehension. Her voice was low and quite frail, and when she picked up the pen to sign there was a noticeable tremor in her hand, but I'd have to swear that she was of sound mind and was making the change completely of her own volition.'

'You don't think it suspicious that less than three weeks later, she was the victim of a hit-and-run, and Checkley's wife was the one to find her?'

If he did think so, Pritchard wasn't admitting it. 'My hands were tied. I couldn't refuse her request.'

West said nothing, he knew the restraints the solicitor was under.

Andrews, however, wasn't so willing to be silent. 'Looks like you might have helped sign her death warrant, though, doesn't it?'

19

'A bit harsh,' West said as they walked through the shopping centre to the car park.

Andrews wasn't backing down. 'Didn't he have a responsibility to his client?'

West stopped and turned to him. 'The same as we have a responsibility to the people we're supposed to protect. It isn't always easy. Remember Ken Blundell?' The man was always in West's thoughts. He frequently tortured himself by going back to the decision he'd taken that had cost the man his life.

Andrews held a hand up in defeat. 'Yes, of course, you're right. It just galls me to think that poor old dear was conned by that nasty piece of work Checkley.'

'We'll get him, Pete,' West said, wishing as he spoke the words that he believed them. Simple truth was, they didn't always get their man.

There was nothing more said as they made their way through the hordes of shoppers to the car. West opened the car door, then stood leaning on the bonnet looking across at Andrews. 'Let's have a meeting before end of shift, see where we are with all three cases. Morrison would be happy if we could at least solve one of them.'

'We aren't able to solve every case,' Andrews said, 'but if we have a choice, can we get that Checkley guy?'

'He certainly hasn't made any friends, has he?' West exited the car park onto Marine Road and joined the slow queue of traffic, taking the side roads automatically until they were back in Foxrock. 'That conundrum with Muriel Hennessy's body is going to drive me insane unless we solve it,' he said as he and Andrews walked back into the station.

'We're stuck with that unless we can change Cara Donaldson's story and I don't think that's going to happen.'

'Or change the science.'

Andrews laughed. 'You arguing against the science? That has to be a first.'

'It shows how frustrated I'm finding it. Maybe the lads have turned up something interesting.'

In the main detective office, Baxter and Edwards had their heads together but the bark of laughter that greeted West and Andrews told them that whatever they were looking at it wasn't to do with the case.

Unembarrassed, Baxter launched into an update. 'No news on the misper search. I'm still waiting for my contacts to get back to me.'

'Nothing here either.' Edwards stretched his hands out and flexed his fingers. 'I've managed to contact the owners of almost half the vehicles that visited the recycling centre over the two-day period. Nobody remembers seeing anything suspicious. A couple of them laughed and said everyone was carrying black bags so how could they tell.'

'Keep at it,' West said. 'We'll have a meeting at 6pm, see if we can find somewhere to go in any of these cases.' He filled a mug with coffee, headed to his office and sat sipping it, hoping the caffeine would enlighten him.

It didn't seem to do much good and he switched on his computer. Waiting for it to power up, he sent a message to Edel. *I'll be home around 7pm, why don't we go to the Italian?*

When she didn't reply, he guessed she was deep in the world of her characters working out who had done what. He wished it was as easy in real life.

A few emails needed his attention keeping him too busy to watch the minute hand ticking around the face of the clock sitting over the office door.

'We're waiting,' Andrews said from the doorway.

West glanced at the time on the corner of the screen in surprise. 'Right, just let me finish this.' A minute later he was done and joined the rest of the team, noticing a lack of enthusiasm on every face.

'Okay,' he said, heading to the Wall where the sparse details of their three cases were laid out. 'It's not looking too great, is it?' He turned, perched on the edge of a desk and looked around. 'Anyone got anything?'

'I've been doing some digging on Liam Hennessy's finances,' Baxter said. 'Up to a year ago, they were living in a big, detached house in Rathgar. The company he worked for pulled a fast one with their accounts and when it folded, he got a far smaller redundancy package than he should have. The bare minimum. It didn't pay the mortgage and bills so he took the sensible step and downsized. He's doing okay and has a new job. The paltry sum he'll receive from his dead mother's estate isn't going to make any difference to him.'

Allen held up a hand. 'I checked out his story about his wife and children. They flew to Moscow four weeks ago. Annika's father is–' he lifted a notebook and read the name, stumbling over the pronunciation, '–Misalov Isaak Yakovich.' He tossed the notebook down. 'The family are in banking. Seriously wealthy. I'm talking about private jets and large yachts kind of wealthy. Annika and the two children are living in a mansion outside Moscow and the two kids have been enrolled in private schools. It looks like they're staying.'

It explained Liam Hennessy's miserable defeated expression.

'Doesn't Muriel Hennessy have a house to sell?' Allen asked, puzzled. 'It must be worth a bob or two.'

'It was sold on an equity release thing,' Jarvis said. 'You know the way – they sell it well below the market value but then they are allowed stay in it for as long as they live.'

'Anything on Cara Donaldson?' West hoped his words didn't have a lick of desperation. Three cases and they'd nothing.

Allen raised his hand again. 'She works for Stanton's, an investment bank. Well regarded. Not as much as a parking fine recorded. One daughter living in New York. Husband is a teacher, again well regarded.' He shook his head. 'Average, middle-class family.'

'Even average middle-class families have secrets,' West said. 'Dig a little more.' He glanced at Edwards who was leaning back in his chair looking bored. 'Have you finished working through that list yet?'

'Not yet.' Edwards' slightly prominent brown eyes flicked to the printout he'd dropped on the desk. It was scored with thick, black parallel lines. 'About twenty-five to go. I'm not sure it isn't a waste of time.'

There was a sudden silence and the rest of the team looked awkwardly at their feet.

West stood up. 'Get it done before you go off shift,' he said sharply then looked to where Baxter was slouched against the wall. 'Any progress on the missing persons' search?'

'One of my Interpol contacts got back to me.' He shook his head. 'A surprisingly large number of families go missing every year but many are from African countries. When I put the European ancestry into the mix it narrowed it down to only a few and none that matched the age group of our bodies.'

'Right, chase up your other contacts.' West looked at the photograph of the body parts and skulls someone had stuck in the centre of the Wall and frowned. 'It might be one we have to let go,' he said, turning back to the team. 'But not until we've checked every avenue. Okay?'

Nods all around.

West filled them in on their meeting with the solicitor. 'Three weeks before Doris Whittaker died, she changed her will to leave everything to the charming Mr Checkley. Then his delightful wife Lynda just happens to be driving by after Doris is knocked down and killed in a hit-and-run. We all know coincidences happen but this one stinks.' He glanced to where Edwards sat keeping his head down. 'On Monday, Edwards, I want you and Baxter to go over everything again. Talk to the uniforms who were first on scene, the ambulance driver and anyone involved. Shake their stories till something falls out, understood?' He waited until Edwards muttered 'Yes' before looking away.

'Anything else?' When all West got were blank stares in reply, he turned and headed back to his office.

20

West wasn't surprised when Andrews appeared in the doorway a few minutes later. 'You should go home,' he said without looking up from his keyboard.

'It's Friday. I thought you might fancy going for a pint.'

West looked up at that, surprised. 'You're not rushing home to Joyce?'

'I can rush home after a pint just as easily.'

'Okay, you're on.' West looked at the email he'd started. It could wait until Monday. He switched the computer off and stood. 'Right, let's go.' He took his jacket from the hook on the back of the door and pulled it on. 'I could do with a drink.'

In the main office, Edwards was the only member of the team remaining. He had a marker in his hand and scored through another line of the printout with rather more force than was necessary.

West was slow to anger and quick to forgive. 'Go home, Mark. It'll do on Monday.'

Edwards looked up, colour flashing across his sallow cheeks. 'I don't mind staying to finish.' He fiddled with the marker in his hand. 'I'm sorry if I sounded like an arse earlier. It wasn't meant to be a criticism.'

West stopped by his desk. 'These cases are frustrating for us all. It's probably going to prove impossible to find out who those mummified bodies are. We might never be able to prove that Darragh and Lynda Checkley were involved in Doris Whitaker's death and we may never know why Muriel Hennessy's body was frozen or who was responsible.' He picked up the printout and looked at it. 'Detective work is ninety-five per cent a boring trudge through things like this, Mark. It may seem a colossal waste of time and I've no doubt it's boring but maybe, just maybe, you'll find something interesting.' He put the sheet down. 'Go home when you're done. See you on Monday.'

He met Andrews in the car park of The Lep Inn and they walked into the pub together. It was busy, bustling with staff from nearby offices still in their formal suits. Some of the men had undone their ties to mark the end of the working week and for the same reason, perhaps, some of the women had undone one more button of their shirts.

'Over there,' Andrews said and without waiting, negotiated the crowd to an empty table he'd seen at the back.

'I don't know how you do it.' West sank onto a chair. 'No matter how busy it is you always manage to get a seat.'

'It's a knack. You having a Guinness?'

When West nodded, Andrews looked around, caught the eye of one of the lounge staff and waved her over. 'A pint of Guinness and a pint of Heineken.'

'These cases are frustrating,' Andrews said. 'Plus, we didn't get a break after that murder in the church.'

'Or the child in the suitcase. One brilliant crime novel title after the other.'

Andrews opened his mouth to say something just as their drinks appeared. 'Slainte,' he said, lifting his pint.

'Cheers.' West swallowed deeply. 'I needed that.'

'Yes.'

'That's all you're going to say?' West was surprised at his reticence. Normally Andrews was the first to jump in with his opinion.

'Edwards was being his usual smart-arse self. He needed telling.' Andrews drank more of his pint before putting it down. 'Won't do him any harm to be put in his place now and then.'

West gazed into his pint. 'Morrison will push us to drop both the dismembered bodies and the hit-and-run case next week if we can't get anywhere with either. And the Hennessy case won't be far behind.'

'Let's hope that nothing comes in over the weekend to require our input. Morrison will only moan if they start queuing up.'

West's mobile buzzed. He checked the caller and stared at Andrews. 'You jinxed us, Pete. It's the station. Probably a double homicide.'

Andrews barked a laugh. 'Foxrock isn't the murder capital of Ireland, you know.'

West pressed to accept the call, gave his name and listened. 'Really?' His eyes widened and he thumped Andrews' shoulder with his fist. 'Okay. No, Monday will do fine. They're not going anywhere.' He laughed at whatever the other person was saying before cutting the connection and sitting back. 'You're never going to believe this.'

'I might if you tell me.'

'That was Edwards. He's working through that list of cars that visited the recycling centre during the two days before the body parts were found. The next car on his list... you'll never guess who it belongs to?' West lifted his pint and sank the remaining Guinness. 'I'll tell you because you'd never guess. Darragh Checkley.'

'Checkley!' Andrews' eyes narrowed. 'Now that's a surprise.'

West's brain was spinning. He'd known there was something off about Checkley. Coincidences happened but they were building up around the man. 'We know four things about Checkley: three weeks before Doris Whitaker died, she left him an estate worth around five million; he's broke; his wife was first on the scene after Doris was killed in a hit-and-run; and he was seen driving into the recycling centre where we found the remains of dead bodies.'

Andrews decided to play devil's advocate. 'It is possible it's a huge coincidence.'

'No. There's something.' West slammed the flat of his hand on the beer-sticky table hard enough for the sound to draw attention in the noisy pub. He waited for everyone to resume their own lives before leaning forward and saying quietly, 'Maybe... and you're going to think this is seriously weird... but maybe Doris Whitaker left him her five-million-pound estate with conditions.'

21

Trying to persuade Andrews that Doris Whitaker had left all her money to the Checkleys on the condition that they get rid of dead bodies she had hidden away took time. As a result, it was after 7pm when West pushed open the front door of his house. Normally, he liked to change out of his suit but it was half an hour's walk to the Italian restaurant so he'd go as he was.

The hall light was on but there was no sign of Edel and only the sound of Tyler's paws clip-clipping on the kitchen floor broke the silence.

'Edel,' West called as he climbed the stairs. He was sorry he'd suggested going out after all. It would have been nicer to have eaten in, had a few glasses of wine, maybe a whiskey or two and chilled out. He wasn't physically tired, but he was mentally exhausted.

Soft music drifting from the spare bedroom told him Edel was still working. He was surprised, she didn't normally work so late. He tapped on the door and opened it slowly. Sometimes she was so engrossed in what she was doing that she didn't notice what was going on around her.

He stood looking at her as she sat in the glow of a lamp. She was crouched over the keyboard, fingers flying over the keys, a rapt expression on her face. Totally engrossed. And still, he noticed with a smile, wearing her writing clothes. He took a step backwards and shut the door gently.

There was still no sign of Edel stirring when he came out of their bedroom ten minutes later, his suit replaced by well-worn jeans and an old flannel shirt. Downstairs, he took a beer from the fridge, opened it, and drank from the bottle as he rang the restaurant to cancel the table, apologising profusely for the late notice. He searched for the Indian takeaway menu, dialled their number and ordered a variety of food to be delivered. Then he went into the sitting room to finish the beer.

He sat in silence for a while before reaching for the remote to turn on the TV. As usual it was switched to a news channel where that evening the topic under discussion was a salacious political scandal. With that to keep them occupied they'd have little airtime to spare for the octogenarian, nonagenarian and the collection of dismembered corpses. It was a small mercy.

West nursed his beer and thought about the cases. That they'd found a connection between two of them was unexpected... and downright bizarre. A tentative connection, true, but it was there. Edwards had learned a valuable lesson too. The boring jobs sometimes paid off.

But they'd a long way to go yet. West's idea that Doris Whitaker had changed her will on the condition that Checkley would dispose of the bodies was bordering on far-fetched. Andrews had scoffed at the idea and probably only agreed that it warranted looking into to shut him up. Morrison would think he'd lost the plot. Maybe he had.

He lifted the bottle to his mouth, discovered it was empty and was about to get to his feet when he heard movement overhead and seconds later a clamber on the stairs as Edel took the steps in twos.

'Mike,' she said, bursting through the door. 'I'm sorry. I hit a sweet spot and the words were falling from my fingertips so I forgot completely about everything.' She looked at her watch in horror. 'I can't believe it's so late. Give me five... no, maybe you better make that ten minutes and I'll be ready.'

West stood and slid an arm around her waist to pull her close. 'Relax. I've cancelled the restaurant and ordered a takeaway. Sit, I'll get a bottle of wine and we can have a glass while we're waiting for it.' He checked his watch. 'It should be arriving any minute. We'll have it in here, shall we?'

'Sounds perfect,' Edel said, flopping onto the sofa and dragging her feet under her.

Ten minutes later, containers with aromatic food were spread out on the coffee table. West had brought cutlery and glasses and opened a bottle of wine. For a few minutes they ate and drank in silence.

'I hadn't realised how hungry I was,' Edel said, spooning more chicken korma onto her plate. 'This was a good idea, Mike, thank you.'

He topped up her glass. 'I'm glad your writing is going well.'

Her mouth full, she murmured 'Mm-hm' enthusiastically. 'How about your day,' she asked when able.

'You know the three cases we're working on. The octogenarian–'

'The nonagenarian and the dismembered bodies,' she said with a gurgling laugh. 'Honestly, I would love to use it as a title for a book. I could see it on the bookshelves in Eason's.'

'I'm starting to think of all our cases as book titles. That's your influence.'

She raised her glass to him. 'I'll take the credit for that. Go on, what were you going to tell me about the cases? Don't tell me you've solved them.'

'I wish. And Morrison very much wishes. No.' He sipped his wine and went over the idea in his head again. 'Andrews said it was a crazy idea.'

'Peter often thinks your ideas are crazy, then he has to back-pedal when he finds out they weren't.'

Dishing up the last of the lamb rogan josh, West sat back with the plate in his hand. In between mouthfuls, he told her of Edwards' discovery and his theory about the link with the Checkleys.

Edel's eyes widened.

'You think it's ridiculous?' West hoped she'd see his theory as having some validation. He respected her brain... if she thought it was possible it would make it easier to face down disbelief from the rest of the team.

'No,' Edel said. Then she tilted her head and looked at him strangely. 'I'm not sure you've thought it through far enough though.'

West frowned. 'I don't understand.'

'The nonagenarian... Doris Whitaker, isn't it?' When West nodded, she picked up her glass and took a mouthful of wine. 'Fifty years ago, she'd have been forty. Did she have a husband? Children? If so, where are they? Or any other relatives? Maybe those bodies are her *family*.'

It was West's turn to widen his eyes. She was right: he'd not thought it through far enough. Because, of course, she was right: that could be who their dismembered, mummified bodies were.

22

The weekend, as it often did, passed in a blink with West spending most of the time working in the back garden.

Edel was still, as she phrased it, *in a sweet spot* with her writing and wanted to continue. 'You don't mind, do you?'

'Of course I don't,' he'd assured her. 'How many times have I had to abandon you for work. Only fair that it works both ways. Anyway, it'll give me the perfect opportunity to tackle the garden.'

The borders, where roses and fuchsia were supposed to be growing, were choked with weeds. It was hard but satisfying work to pull them up. He dug over the borders, whistling between his teeth as he did, getting mud caked into his nails and his boots.

On Sunday, he dragged Edel away from her keyboard to a garden centre and bought several plants and spent the afternoon digging and planting while she wrote. It was all very civilised and for the first time in a long time, he didn't think about the job.

~

Monday, as if a switch clicked, he was back in work mode. He sat at his desk in the station, relieved to see there was nothing new to add to their workload from the weekend. A few robberies which his robbery division counterpart Sergeant Clark might be able to handle – or at least delegate to Garda Foley to sort out. Nothing to make Morrison worried.

The clock never ticked fast enough for West when he wanted to get on with things. The Office of the State Pathologist didn't open until 9am. He'd be on the phone on the dot to ask Niall Kennedy to compare DNA from Doris Whitaker to that of the dismembered bodies. If there was a match... if they could formally link the two then they might be able to put pressure on the Checkleys to admit their part in the disposal of the bodies. He still couldn't prove they had a hand in Doris's death but he'd take what he could for the moment.

When he saw Andrews walk into the main office at five to the hour, he went out to join him. 'Did you give what I said on Friday any thought?'

Andrews took off his jacket and hung it on the back of his chair. 'And a good morning to you too.' Without another word, he headed to the coffee machine and poured two mugs of coffee. He picked up the carton of milk, opened the spout and held it to his nose for a second before adding some to both mugs, then stirred three packets of sugar into his. 'Here,' he said, handing the second mug to West before sitting. 'Something tells me I'm going to need caffeine before I hear whatever it is you're going to tell me. Because there's something... I can tell by your face.'

West grinned, hooked a foot around the leg of a nearby chair and pulled it closer. He sat, took a mouthful of coffee and told Andrews about Edel's brainwave. In his head, the whole idea sounded feasible but when he put it into words it sounded, even to his ears, like a crazed script for a bad movie. 'What do you think?'

Andrews drained his mug and put it down. 'You so often get wild ideas that turn out not to be so daft that I did give your idea some thought over the weekend.' He reached out and thumped West on the shoulder hard enough to make him wince. 'It seems Edel and I think alike because that was exactly what I'd come up with.'

'Morrison will never believe it.'

'He'll be so pleased to have two cases solved that he won't care. Although,' Andrews admitted, 'he will say, again, that we get involved in the weirdest cases.'

'First, we have to prove our theory. Get the team to do a search on Doris Whitaker as a priority. There must be a record somewhere of a family. Meanwhile, I'm going to ring Niall Kennedy and get him to do a DNA comparison.'

West was in luck. Kennedy was in reception when he rang. 'Another second and you'd have missed me,' the pathologist said, sounding as if he were sorry that second hadn't happened. 'What do you want this early on a Monday morning?'

'It'll take too long to go into details if you're heading out. But I'd like a DNA comparison between Doris Whitaker and the dismembered bodies.'

Kennedy's soft groan drifted down the line. 'Something tells me you've come up with some weird and wonderful theory that will have us all scratching our heads in wonder.'

'If we're right, that comparison will prove it.'

'Okay, I'll get one of the technicians to do it as soon as, but it will be tomorrow afternoon, at the earliest, before we'll have results, okay?'

Better than West had expected. 'Great, thanks, Niall.'

'I'll have the usual payment next time you're around this way.'

West hung up and sat back, tapping the handset against his chin. It would have been nice to have dragged the Checkleys in and grilled them till they popped. He smiled at the thought, one he'd picked up from a dated US crime movie he'd watched recently. He couldn't grill the Checkleys; he couldn't even bring them in with what they had. They needed that DNA comparison and more information on Doris Whitaker.

The handset rang, startling him. 'West.'

'Would you come up to my office, at your convenience?'

Morrison. First thing on a Monday morning. 'I'll come straight away, Inspector.' In fact, it was a few minutes before he moved. He sat with his forehead creased in puzzlement as he tried to figure out why Morrison wanted to see him.

'You in a daze?' Andrews said from the doorway.

'Mother wants to see me.'

'First thing on a Monday morning?'

'My thoughts exactly.' West got to his feet. 'I suppose I'd better go and find out.'

'Are you going to tell him your theory?'

West held his hand out horizontally and tilted it side to side. 'Depends on why he wants to see me.'

23

Morrison's office on the next floor was dominated by a large untidy desk. It wasn't a place that encouraged anyone to linger, especially since the only chair in the office was the one he was sitting in. West resented having to stand like a naughty schoolboy and usually rested his shoulder against the wall when he had the need to be there.

Today, however, puzzled by the summons, he stood in front of the desk.

To his surprise, Morrison got to his feet and reached for the coffee pot that was gurgling on a trolley behind him. He poured two mugs, added milk to both and handed one to West.

'Thank you.' West took it and sipped, keeping his eyes on the inspector, tempted to bark out *what's going on*. Because something was. This was not normal.

Morrison stayed standing. He picked up his mug, then put it down without drinking. 'My wife plays golf, did you know that?'

West shook his head. The only thing he knew about Jennifer Morrison was that she was considerably younger than the inspector.

'She does. Very good at it too, has a handicap of eleven. She plays for The Grange Golf Club. Has done for years. Made some good friends there.' He picked up his mug and this time took a sip of coffee. 'She's friends with Yvonne Cunningham whose husband owns Cunningham's Jewellers in the Meridian Shopping Centre.'

West knew this had to be going somewhere, he simply couldn't figure out where.

'She was out with her on Saturday – a girls' night out, you know the kind of thing.'

'Yes.' It was the only thing West could think to say.

'They got talking about this and that.' Morrison put the mug down and sat in his chair, steepling his hands together on the desk in front of him. 'Yvonne was in the shop last Monday waiting for her husband when a customer came in to sell some jewellery. The customer happened to comment that the diamond ring she was bringing in – an old engagement ring – seemed to sparkle better than her new one. Out of curiosity, the assistant had a look at the new one and broke the bad news.'

'It was a fake?'

'Yes, some man-made stone I'd never heard of. The customer was shocked. It seems the ring was bought in a reputable jewellers and cost around eight grand.'

West, who was beginning to wonder if this was going anywhere, stared at the inspector with narrowed eyes. 'Edel.'

'Yvonne was in the office when the assistant brought the paperwork in and the name caught her eye.' Morrison held up his hand as West opened his mouth to interrupt. 'No, she doesn't know you, but there was all that hoo-ha last year when you and Edel were trapped down in that cave and I told Jennifer about the two of you. She doesn't normally gossip but she thought the whole rescue thing was so exciting and romantic.' Morrison raised his thick eyebrows and shook his head. 'So romantic, that she mentioned it to Yvonne. If you remember, photographs of both you and Edel were in the papers following the rescue. So, when Yvonne saw Edel in the jewellery shop she recognised her from somewhere, then saw her name and...' He lifted his hands. 'You know the rest.'

West did. Only too well. He'd been conned. 'I can't imagine Debeerds are involved in anything dodgy.'

'I took the liberty of ringing Jim Cunningham. He agrees with you. It seems Edel told them that the assistant in Debeerds took the ring away for cleaning after you'd made the decision to buy it and he was gone for a couple of minutes.'

'Yes, he was. Time enough to pull a switch.' West pushed a hand through his hair. He'd been distracted by Checkley sitting on the other side of the shop instead of paying attention to what was going on.

Morrison leaned forward. 'The assistant said Edel didn't want her fiancé to know that the ring was worthless.'

'No, she wouldn't.' West remembered how excited she was about the ring. 'The rings she was bringing in must have been her engagement and wedding ring from her first disastrous marriage. A real diamond for a bigamous marriage. She would have been horrified to find that her new engagement ring was fake.' More than horrified. He knew the way her brain worked. No wonder she'd been leaving it off.

'What are you going to do?'

'Get the real ring back.' He wasn't sure how he was going to do that but he'd do it.

'I had a feeling you'd say that. Let me know the outcome.'

It was a dismissal but West waited. 'Since I'm here I may as well give you an update on the three cases... or on two of them at least.' He summarised where they were, watching as Morrison's expression drifted from sympathetic to flabbergasted.

'You think the Checkleys dumped the body parts in return for being left everything in Doris Whitaker's will.'

'And that the bodies are related to Doris in some way. Yes, that what we're working on.'

Morrison shook his head slowly. 'Just the kind of ridiculous case that you and Andrews embroil yourselves in.'

There didn't seem any point in saying they didn't do it deliberately. 'But it does mean we'll get two out of the three cases solved, Inspector.' With that as a parting shot, he turned to leave but stopped with his hand on the door and looked back. 'I appreciate you telling me about the ring, Inspector. And please, pass on my thanks to Mrs Morrison.'

24

West was sitting in his office staring into space twenty minutes later when Andrews appeared in the doorway. 'That bad?'

West looked at him blankly before giving a quick shake of his head. 'It wasn't about our cases although he does think we've managed to embroil ourselves in yet more crazy ones. I swear he thinks we do it deliberately.'

Andrews laughed and sat on the spare chair. 'We're magnets for the odd ones.' His forehead creased as he realised what West had said. 'It wasn't about our cases though?'

'No.' The ring dilemma had been rolling around in West's head. He had no doubt Debeerds would take the allegation seriously and not dismiss it out of hand as an attempt at extortion. He was a garda, after all. But it would be a mess and it would cast a long shadow over his and Edel's engagement. It was probably the reason she'd not mentioned it. He guessed, too, that she was worrying it was a bad omen. No wonder she'd taken to leaving the ring off.

That blasted thieving assistant had a lot to answer for. It

wouldn't have been the first time he'd pulled a switch either; it had been too slickly done. West couldn't allow him to get away with it. 'I have a problem, Peter.'

Andrews reached over and pushed the office door shut. 'Go on.' He listened without interrupting as West filled him in, lines across his forehead deepening. 'Clever. And you were unlucky. He'd probably been waiting a while for the right person – someone who would choose that particular ring, who it would fit without needing alteration. Easy then to do a quick switch.'

'Unlucky!' West rubbed a hand roughly over his head making his hair stand on end. 'Edel is probably seeing it as a bad omen. The irony that she was there to get rid of her first engagement ring – which is real by the way – hasn't escaped me. A real ring for a fake relationship, and now a fake ring–'

'You're doing it again, taking yourself too seriously,' Andrews interrupted him. 'What are you going to do about it?'

West shook his head slowly. 'I don't know.'

'You're too close to it. How about you leave it to me to sort it out?'

'Leave it to you?' If there was one person West would trust with anything it was the man sitting opposite. 'Okay, why not.' He held a hand up quickly. 'Nothing illegal though.'

'As if.' Andrews grinned and got to his feet.

West watched him go feeling tension ease. If there was something that could be done, Andrews was the man to find out, and do it.

Putting the ring and the ramifications of it from his mind, West concentrated on the important matter of proving there was a link between the Checkley case and the dismembered bodies.

In the main office, he looked around. Jarvis and Allen were out dealing with a complaint. Drug dealing outside a local secondary school. They'd speak to the school head and organise a uniform presence for a period. They might be lucky and catch the dealers in the act. Chances were that they'd move on pretty quickly once they saw they'd been spotted. West made a mental note to warn his colleagues in Dun Laoghaire and Stillorgan. Drug dealers didn't go away, they simply moved on.

With Jarvis and Allen temporarily unavailable, he zoned in on the two detectives who were hammering away on keyboards, expressions fixed and intent.

'Good work, Mark,' he said, drawing Edwards' attention.

A final tap of the keyboard and the younger detective looked up. 'I'd have given up, though, and would have missed it if you hadn't pushed me to carry on.'

'The important thing is that you didn't give up and you found us what might be an important link between two odd cases. Any success with tracing Doris Whitaker's relatives?'

'I'm going through reports from the Central Statistics Office and Baxter is trawling through the births, marriages and deaths in the General Register Office. When we have everything, we'll collate it and make a report.' He tapped the edge of his keyboard. 'It's slow-going. Maybe in a couple of hours.'

'Good.' West checked his watch. 'We'll have a catch-up at 1pm.' He passed Andrews' desk as he slammed the phone down with unaccustomed irritation. 'Someone annoying you?'

Andrews sat back and stretched his arms out. 'I've been on the phone for the last hour trying to find anyone who would agree with Cara Donaldson's claim that the science had to be wrong and that her mother either hadn't been frozen at all or that it had occurred in a much tighter time frame.'

West sat on the edge of the desk. 'And?'

'And every one of them agreed with Dr Kennedy.' Andrews brought a clenched fist down hard on the table. 'Donaldson has to be lying to us.'

'It's a bit like one of those locked-room mysteries.'

'Poe again?'

'No, not this time. John Dickson Carr. He wrote *The Hollow Man*, one of the best examples of a seemingly impossible crime, one of which occurred in full view of witnesses who swore they saw nothing. It was solved by an amateur detective, Gideon Fell.'

'Maybe you can ask him to come and give us a hand,' Andrews said sarcastically. 'Because this room is well and truly locked.'

'As I said to Edwards on Friday... keep at it.' West thumped him on the shoulder. 'And look how that turned out.' He stood and headed for his office, turning back to remind him, 'We'll have a catch-up at 1pm. See where we stand.'

Jarvis and Allen appeared before he'd sat behind his desk. 'A quick word?'

'Of course, come in,' West said, hoping this wasn't going to be trouble.

Both men stayed standing. Jarvis, his hands jammed into the pockets of his trousers, was first to speak. 'We've been to the school and had a word with the head. She said she noticed two older boys hanging around the entrance on Friday morning. When she noticed the same boys there in the afternoon, she became suspicious but when she approached them, they fled. When they were outside the school again this morning, she decided to ring us.'

West frowned. 'Had they approached any of the students?'

'Yes,' Allen said. 'But according to the head, no money or drugs changed hands. They have a proactive anti-drugs policy, but she's no fool: she knows if these lads keep it up there'll be some idiots who'll be lured into it.'

West knew she was right. 'Fine, so what's the plan?'

Allen and Jarvis exchanged glances. 'If we simply post uniforms, the two guys will do a runner and turn up somewhere else within a day or two. We'd prefer to catch these two and get them off the street.'

'Okay. But take a couple of plain-clothes gardaí with you.' He saw a flash of excitement cross their faces and held up a hand. 'Remember your surroundings and don't take risks, please.'

Then they were gone, muttering together as they planned their course of action. The two drug dealers would likely spot them before Jarvis and Allen had got out of their car and be gone, drug-fuelled energy taking them flying through the laneways. They'd turn up again though. Maybe somewhere nearby, giving Allen and Jarvis a second opportunity. But if the dealers were running, they weren't selling.

West rang his contact in the drug squad. It was no harm to keep them apprised of dealers in their area and to find out if there was anything new they should be worried about.

Inspector Bob Phelan gave a gruff laugh when he was told there were two dealers. 'Only two. You'd be lucky, Mike. Tip of the iceberg, I'm telling you, tip of the iceberg.'

Not what West wanted to hear. 'Anything new on the street, Bob, or is it still our old friend, Zombie Z?'

'Still Zombie Z, although I did hear a whisper that there's something new.'

There was always something new, and always whispers. 'Nothing we should be too concerned about at the minute?'

'No, you'll get the usual update if any concrete intel comes in. Let me know if you need a hand with your two dealers.' Another gruff snicker before he hung up.

Phelan knew, as well as West did, that even one dealer was one too many. But he'd allow him his moment's amusement. He knew from stories Phelan had told him in the past that there weren't many of them.

It was almost 1pm but when West went into the main office,

he saw Edwards and Baxter, their eyes glued to their monitors, fingers flying over their keyboards with a speed he envied.

Andrews was tapping away more in his style. Not quite two fingers, but not many more. 'Anything?' he said, hovering above him.

'Nothing but a colossal headache. Coffee might help.'

'Your wish is my command,' West said and he crossed the room to the percolator. He'd finally remembered to buy some decent coffee for the station, the aroma making him sniff in satisfaction. He poured two mugs, added sugar to one and milk to both and brought them back to where Andrews was sitting back with fingers linked behind his head. 'Here you go.'

'Ta.' Andrews slurped loudly before putting the mug down. It instantly left a ring on the desk which he ignored. 'I'm not sure we should waste any more time on the Muriel Hennessy thing, Mike. It's going nowhere. And yes,' he said, lifting a hand to stave off what he guessed would be the answer, 'I'm aware that Edwards succeeded when he persevered but he was looking into something. There's nothing in the Hennessy case to look into. There is no motive. No reason at all to kill the old dear that I can find–'

'Yet she was killed.' West pulled a chair up and sat.

'Or died of natural causes.'

'And accidentally froze herself afterwards?' West drank some coffee, wishing there was a large whiskey in it. 'I hate giving up.'

'I do too, you know that.' Andrews waved a hand at the pile of pages he'd scribbled notes on. 'But I'm chasing my tail.'

'Give it to Jarvis or Allen when they get back. Maybe fresh eyes will see something.'

Andrews didn't take umbrage. It had happened before that fresh eyes had seen something one of the team had overlooked. It had, in fact, been Edel who'd given them the key for the last case. 'You should ask Edel, she has a good mind for these things.'

'I might just do that,' West said. 'Meanwhile, keep at it.' Unusually, he had the last word and took his coffee back to his office.

25

It was almost five. West was reading a report that seemed to make little sense when his desk phone went and he lifted it absently. 'West.'

'Mike, there's been a stabbing.' Sergeant Blunt, the big, bluff desk sergeant who West had never seen anything but stoic, had a distinct tremor in his voice. 'At the school. It's Jarvis. It doesn't sound good.'

West dropped the phone. For a second, he was unable to move or think. Then he picked up the handset again. 'We're on our way.'

Grabbing his jacket, he stood in the doorway of his office. 'Drop everything, we're needed.' His tone of voice along with his suddenly pale, drawn face left the rest in no doubt – something had gone wrong. 'Baxter, you drive.'

Baxter grabbed his jacket and keys and hurried after West who was striding from the room.

'It's Jarvis,' West said as all four climbed into Baxter's car. 'He's been stabbed. Blunt says it doesn't look good.' Best if they were forewarned. It might help them to face whatever they were going to find.

Siren blaring, they made it to the school in minutes. Baxter pulled up behind a squad car, West, Andrews and Edwards clambering out before the engine was off.

'There's Allen,' Edwards said, pointing towards the school gate.

Leaning heavily against the gate, Allen was so pale it looked as if his freckles were floating. His jacket hung open, the white shirt underneath streaked with blood. A paramedic was trying to persuade him to go with him but wasn't having much luck. He threw his hands up and backed away when the four detectives approached.

'You hurt?' West asked. Lots of blood but he couldn't see an injury.

'No. The blood is Sam's.' Allen shuddered. 'There was so much of it. I tried to stop it but my hands grew slippery.' He held out two bloodstained hands.

West glanced back at the ambulance. If Jarvis were alive, the paramedics would be working on him and he would only be in the way. In any case, it was soon enough to hear bad news. 'What happened, Mick?'

Allen dragged his attention from his bloody hands. 'It all happened so quickly. The two dealers were already here when we arrived, but we parked on a side street and they didn't see us until we were almost upon them.' He frowned as he tried to remember the sequence of events. 'Jarvis identified us as gardaí and asked them to come with us... then before we had a chance to do anything, one of them pulled a knife from his belt and lunged. It caught Sam right in the belly.'

'Okay. Now–' West crooked a finger at the hovering paramedic, '–I want you to go to the hospital and get checked out.'

'I don't need to, I'm fine.' Allen was leaning heavily against the fence. West guessed he'd be unable to walk.

The paramedic had obviously come to the same conclusion. With a wave to his colleague in the second ambulance, a gurney appeared and trundled towards them. The detectives backed away to leave the paramedics to their job.

'He'll be okay when the shock wears off,' Andrews said, watching as Allen was helped onto the gurney.

As it disappeared into the waiting ambulance, their attention was drawn to a paramedic who had stepped from the second vehicle and was proceeding to shut the doors. They quickly closed in on him. 'Sam's our colleague,' West said. 'How is he?'

The paramedic finished what he was doing as he answered. 'He's alive but he's lost a lot of blood. We're taking him to the Mater and he'll be going straight to theatre.' With a nod, he was gone and a minute later, sirens howling, the ambulance raced away.

A short, plump woman stepped through the gate and made her way across to them. 'I'm Trina Newcombe, the school head,' she said. 'I'm so sorry for what has happened.'

West couldn't bring himself to utter the usual platitude, that it was all part of their job. The sound of the ambulance faded into the distance. He listened to it as long as he could... a siren meant Sam was still alive.

'I'm sure you probably don't want to hear this right now,' Trina went on. 'But a couple of the students filmed the whole thing on their mobiles. I've looked at the footage. The two drug dealers... their faces are clear.'

All part of their job and now it was time to get back to it.

The school head had been right. When they watched the footage, not only were the faces clear, but one of the uniforms who'd answered the emergency call asked for a closer look.

'That's Mossy Hayden,' he said firmly. 'I'd recognise that face anywhere.'

'And the man with the knife?' West expanded the picture as much as possible. 'Recognise him?'

'No, but Mossy hangs out with a few rough types. Could be any one of them.'

'Right, pick him up,' West said. 'And all of his friends too.'

He didn't have to ask twice. Both squad cars present took off, their combined sirens drawing all eyes for a few minutes before they drifted back to the detectives. The two plain-clothes gardaí who had arrived with Jarvis and Allen made themselves useful, moving on the voyeurs, and the students who hovered in the background.

'Take the names of all the students who were around when it happened,' West told them. They already had the names of the two students who'd filmed the attack. They'd get statements from them later.

'They're badly shook,' the head said, approaching West a few minutes later. 'Their parents are coming to pick them up, and the school will arrange counselling. If you could leave off speaking to them until tomorrow, that would be for the best.'

'Tomorrow will be okay,' West said. Tomorrow they'd probably know if they were talking about an assault on a garda or the murder of one.

'We need to contact Jarvis's parents,' Andrews said as she moved away. 'Before they hear about it from that lot.' He indicated the news reporters who had arrived and were already standing with their microphones poised and their cameras filming the bloody stain on the pathway.

'Yes, I know.' West dragged his eyes away from the reporters. 'Best if we go around.' He turned to Edwards and Baxter. 'I'll take your car, Seamus. Get a lift back to the station, wait for the suspects to turn up. Everything by the book, okay.' He waited till they agreed before he took the keys Baxter offered and headed towards the car, Andrews a step behind.

Neither spoke as they drove to Stillorgan where Jarvis's father ran a general practice from an extension to the side of his home.

'We need to speak to Dr Jarvis,' West said to the receptionist, holding forward his identification. The reaction was automatic: a widening of eyes, quick pallor and indrawn breath.

'Sam?' The receptionist held a hand over her mouth before getting to her feet and hurrying away. She returned less than a minute later, her face pressed into lines of stress. 'He's with a patient and will be with you in just a minute.' She pointed to a door on the left. 'Dr Wilson isn't in this morning; you can wait in his office.'

The small room was windowless and low-ceilinged and the two detectives almost filled what space remained between the overlarge desk and door. They remained standing, neither finding words to fill the silence.

Bringing bad news never got easier but bringing it about a colleague wasn't something either had had to do before. Their very arrival was a forewarning, though, and Dr Jarvis, when he entered a couple of minutes later, didn't need to be told.

'Is he alive?' His question cut straight to it.

'He was stabbed in the stomach.' West remembered Allen's bloody hands. Could anyone survive that much blood loss? 'They took him to the Mater where he'll be going straight to theatre.' He hesitated before adding, 'There was a lot of blood.'

Dr Jarvis swallowed loudly. 'Okay. I'll go and tell my wife and we'll get in there.' He took a deep breath. 'Sam is young, fit... tough. He'll make it.' Words of reassurance for himself or the detectives, it didn't matter, they all hoped he was right.

Back in the car, West sat with the engine running. He would have liked to go to the hospital and wait while the surgeon battled to save Jarvis but if they managed to pick up Mossy Hayden, his place was in the station.

26

Sometimes things went their way. When the uniformed gardaí arrived at Mossy Hayden's house and rang the doorbell, it was opened almost immediately by a middle-aged, tired-looking woman who heaved a sigh when she saw them.

'Good, I'm glad you've come. Saves me the trip to the station. Mossy told me what happened. I warned him if he got involved with that idiot Anto it would end in trouble.' She blinked a tear away. 'My son is not very bright but he's not taking the rap for stabbing a guard.' Leaving the gardaí on the doorstep, she turned away and yelled up the stairs. 'Mossy, get down here. Now.'

The figure that came down almost immediately was a more subdued character than the one the gardaí had seen in the mobile phone footage. 'It wasn't me.' The age-old cry of the juvenile.

Both gardaí had heard it before. 'You need to come with us, Mossy.' They read him his rights while his mother, arms folded, stood looking on with a resigned expression on her tired face. When they were finished, she reached behind to where a pile of clothes hung over the newel post of the stairway and pulled a jacket from the top. 'You'd better take this.'

Garda Mackin watched as Mossy dragged it on over a distinctly scruffy sweatshirt. 'It will work in your favour, you know, if you tell us who your friend with the knife is.'

'I can tell you that,' Mrs Hayden piped up. 'It's that scumbag Anto Devlin, that's who.'

'That right, Mossy?'

Mossy, caught between the gardaí and his mother, obviously decided he'd had enough. 'I didn't know he had a knife.'

'Sounds like you were mixing with the wrong sort. Where does this Anto Devlin live then?'

Mossy glanced at his mother. Whether it was her tear-filled eyes or the realisation he was in bigger trouble than he'd expected when he'd headed out that morning, he told them what they wanted to know.

Mackin radioed his colleagues in the other squad car and gave them the details. 'Right,' he said to Mossy. 'Let's go.'

It was with a sense of satisfaction rather than celebration that less than three hours after Sam Jarvis was stabbed, the two responsible were sitting in the interview rooms in Foxrock Station waiting for their free legal aid solicitors.

West and Andrews arrived back to find Morrison sitting in the main office talking to Baxter and Edwards.

The inspector got to his feet when he saw them. 'You're probably not going to like this, but it's for the best so don't argue. I'm having Hayden and Devlin transferred to Blackrock and the detectives there will handle the investigation. Detective Sergeant Enright has agreed to take it over and deal with it personally.'

It wasn't unexpected. 'I understand.' West pulled out a chair and sat. 'Any news on Sam?'

'He's in surgery.'

In surgery. It was almost good news. He hadn't bled out on

the way to the hospital, dying alone in the ambulance. Each of the men had their own thoughts and silence settled over the group.

'No doubt you'll be heading over there,' Morrison said finally and got to his feet. 'Keep me informed.'

Baxter headed to the coffee percolator, poured four mugs of coffee and handed them around.

'Thanks,' West said, taking the mug. 'Any word on Allen?'

'He's okay, they've released him,' Edwards said. 'Sergeant Blunt has sent a car to pick him up and bring him home.'

Andrews grimaced when he tasted his coffee. He crossed to the sugar and ladled three teaspoons in. 'We going to the Mater?'

It was a relief for West not to have to think about dealing with the two men they had in custody. Morrison had been right. As usual. 'Yes, we might as well be worrying about Sam there as here.' He looked at Edwards and Baxter. 'You don't need to come; we'll ring if we hear anything.'

Both men shook their heads. 'May as well worry there as at home,' Baxter said. 'I'll give Tanya a ring and let her know I'll be late.'

'Under the thumb,' Edwards said with an attempt at humour that managed to raise a slight smile on all their faces.

West rang Edel and explained the situation. 'I might be very late.'

'Poor Sam,' Edel said. 'But he's young, healthy, he'll pull through, Mike.'

'Hopefully. I'll ring you when I'm on the way home.'

Andrews rang his wife and filled her in.

'Oh no,' Joyce said with quick sympathy. 'Are you all okay?'

'We're all a bit shocked,' Andrews admitted. 'I was going to fill you in on something else tonight but it might be late when I get home.'

'Something else? Sounds mysterious.'

'I'll explain but just in case you were making plans, could you meet me in town tomorrow, around 1pm?'

'In town? Even more mysterious – but I don't see why not.'

West, standing in his office door, saw a grin flash across Andrews' face and wondered for a second what he was up to.

He didn't have a chance to ask, with Edwards and Baxter bustling over, eager to leave.

There was little chat on the long cross-city journey to the Mater hospital. Parking around the old, hugely extended hospital was notoriously bad. Baxter, who was driving, didn't bother searching for a space. Instead, he parked in an emergency services parking space and put his Garda Síochána Official Business sign on the dashboard.

Andrews appeared to know where he was going, striding along the hospital corridors with the rest on his heels. He pushed open a door into a narrow, quiet stairway, took the stairs up to the next floor and exited to another corridor. 'This way,' Andrews said without stopping.

They rounded the next corner and came to a halt, a flurry of patient trolleys in and out of a doorway ahead indicating Andrews hadn't led them astray.

'There's Allen!' Edwards pointed to a figure standing on the other side of the operating theatre entrance. The hospital staff had obviously taken pity on him and removed his bloodstained clothes. He was wearing a scrub suit a size too small: the fabric of the top stretched across his chest, and the bottoms stopped at least six inches too short to show off colourfully striped socks.

West put a hand on his arm. 'You should be at home. Blunt was supposed to organise someone to pick you up.'

'They came. I sent them away. I guessed you'd all arrive here.'

'At least sit down before you fall down.'

'I'm fine, honestly. Dr and Mrs Jarvis were here, they've gone to make phone calls. We've been told it'll be another hour at least before we hear anything.'

There was no waiting room, just a few uncomfortable chairs positioned along the corridor where Mrs Jarvis sat when she returned, her eyes fixed on the entrance to the operating theatres.

Dr Jarvis alternated between sitting with her, and speaking to the detectives, and it was he who persuaded a reluctant Allen to take one of the other chairs. 'You'll be doing me a favour,' he said. 'Tell Maggie some stories of your adventures in the guards.'

It was two hours before a scrub-suited man exited the theatre and after a quick glance either direction, headed their way. 'Dr Jarvis?'

'That's me.' He waved a hand to include the detectives. 'We're all here for Sam. How is he?'

'Lucky,' the surgeon said bluntly. 'One millimetre deeper and we wouldn't be having this conversation. The knife nicked his aorta and he'd lost a considerable amount of blood by the time we opened him up but,' he said firmly, 'he's going to be okay.'

27

Relief had them smiling, shaking hands with the surgeon, thanking him, patting each other on the shoulders and creating so much noise that eventually a head popped out from the theatre and shushed them loudly.

'I'd better get back before they throw me out along with you,' the surgeon said, extricating his hand from Mrs Jarvis's grip with difficulty. 'Sam will be in recovery for another ten minutes or so before he's sent back to his room.'

'Not to intensive care?'

'It's not necessary.' The surgeon reassured the anxious mother once more before giving a wave and disappearing back into the theatre suite.

Despite the good news, nobody wanted to leave until they'd seen Sam coming out. But when he did, deathly pale, intravenous infusions in both arms, a monitor beep-beeping, their voices faded to a whisper.

There was no delay, the hospital staff negotiated the turn and manoeuvred the trolley into the lift with casual expertise. Then he was gone.

'We're staying until we see him wake up,' Dr Jarvis said.

West took out a business card and handed it to him. 'If you need me. Or need a lift anywhere, please ring. The station will happily organise something... anything.'

'Thank you.' The lift door opened and Dr Jarvis and his wife vanished inside.

'Right,' West said. 'Let's get out of here.'

'We won't all fit in my car, you know.' Baxter looked from one to the other as if mentally wondering who to make walk.

'Don't worry about me.' Allen looked past them to where a figure approached. 'I've organised my lift home. Here it comes.'

They all turned automatically to see an attractive woman in a white coat closing in on them, a look of concern on her face that faded when she saw Allen. 'You ready to go?'

'Yes.' Allen put a hand on her arm and turned her to face the other detectives. 'You've heard me speak about this lot often enough.' He did quick introductions. 'And this is Dr Izzy George, my flatmate.'

'Flatmate, my ass,' Baxter said a few seconds later as Allen and the doctor vanished around a turn in the corridor. He rubbed his face briskly. 'Anyone else need coffee?'

'Sounds good,' Edwards agreed.

Andrews pointed back the way they'd come. 'There's a drinks dispenser near the accident and emergency department. If we follow the stairs to the lower ground floor, it's along there somewhere.'

Much of the older building of the Mater hospital had, over the years, been converted into offices with the wards moved into the newer high-rise extension. All the lower ground floor was now offices and minor departments. This late, most were shut and the corridors were quiet, the detectives' footsteps echoing eerily on the tiled floor.

'It's a bit spooky down here.' Edwards glanced around. 'I bet it's haunted.'

They turned a corner and found themselves in a long, poorly lit corridor. 'You sure this is right?' Baxter said. 'I'm not sure I wanted coffee this desperately.'

West pointed to a directional map on the wall. 'Let's find out.'

They gathered around it, trying to follow the faint directions in the poor light. 'See,' Andrews said, pointing, the *I told you* left unsaid.

A loud squeak drew their attention. They turned in time to hear an even louder clunk as a door swung shut behind a man who hurried down the corridor to disappear through double doors at the far end.

'I'd recognise that walk anywhere,' West said. 'That was Darragh Checkley.'

'Definitely,' Baxter agreed. 'Why's he creeping around here this time of the night?'

'Let's have a look and see.'

They stopped outside the door Checkley had come through. 'Department of Clinical Anaplastology,' West read aloud and shook his head. 'I've no idea what that is, does anyone?'

After a collective head shake, they walked on and through the door at the end of the corridor. It opened into a bright open space. Double doors to one side led into the accident and emergency department and further double doors ahead were clearly marked *exit*.

Rows of chairs were fixed to the floor and behind them stood a line of dispensing machines. A few of the chairs were occupied. A couple of people, obviously drunk, were swaying back and forth and singing raucously. A woman was sitting with her head buried in her hands, the young man beside her patting her on the back looked like he was barely keeping it together. There was no sign of Darragh Checkley.

Armed with coffee and bars of chocolate, the detectives left the hospital and made their way around to where they'd parked the car. They were all tired so the only sounds heard on the journey back were the slurp of hot coffee, the crackle of paper and the loud snap as pieces of chocolate were broken off and eaten.

'Here we go,' Baxter said as he pulled into the station car park. They all muttered a 'Thanks, Seamus' as they got out and he drove off with a wave.

'G'night. That was some day,' Edwards said before crossing the almost empty car park to his car.

West turned to Andrews. 'Some day indeed! Right, I'm going in to let the night shift know Jarvis is okay. I'll see you in the morning.'

Inside the station, it was unnaturally quiet. The front desk was unattended but West heard the murmur of voices from the office behind. He went around and tapped lightly on the door. It wasn't a complete surprise to find Sergeant Blunt there, sitting behind the desk while the night sergeant, Chad Delaney, leaned a shoulder against the wall. Both straightened when he came through, their faces instantly relaxing when they saw West's expression. 'He's okay?' Blunt said.

'Yes, he was lucky. The surgeon said another millimetre and he wouldn't have made it.'

'Good. And you'll be glad to know those two toerags, Hayden and Devlin, are neatly locked away in Blackrock. Detective Sergeant Enright is delighted: they're desperate to get themselves off the hook and giving up everyone they know.'

It would be small fry, West knew, and Devlin might do less time for attacking Jarvis as a result. But he knew Enright well, he'd not let them off lightly.

28

West had sent Edel a text from the hospital to tell her Jarvis was going to be okay. When he got home, she was curled up on the sofa watching a movie. She jumped to her feet and put her arms around him. 'What a terrible day. You want something to eat? There's some chicken casserole.'

West shook his head and pulled her closer. 'No, I'm not hungry. Exhausted though, it has been a hell of a day.'

'And Sam will definitely be okay?'

West pulled back and kissed her on the forehead. 'He'll be fine according to the surgeon.' He didn't tell her that another millimetre and they'd be having a different conversation. She didn't need to know that. 'I fancy a whiskey though.'

'Coming up.' She returned a moment later with one for each of them, sat beside him and reached for the remote to switch off the TV. 'It was a daft movie.'

'Guess who we saw when we were leaving the hospital.'

'Lots of doctors and nurses?'

'Apart from them. Someone we wouldn't have expected to see.'

'Inspector Morrison?'

'Ha, no, not him either. Darragh Checkley. Coming out of one of the departments on the ground floor.'

'I wouldn't have thought any of the departments would be open that late.'

'I doubt if they are.' He sipped his whiskey. 'He came from the department of clinical anaplastology.'

'Anaplastology? I've never heard of it.' She put her drink down on the coffee table and reached for her iPad. 'I'll have a look on the internet, see what it is.' A few seconds later, she was peering at the screen. 'Listen... anaplastology,' she read, 'is a branch of medicine dealing with prosthetic rehabilitation of an absent, disfigured or malformed part of the face or body.'

'Like glass eyes and prosthetic ears?' West was puzzled.

Edel was still reading and scrolling through the information. 'Yes those, plus noses, chins, cheekbones. There are some photos.' She held the iPad forward for him to see. 'Maybe Checkley has a glass eye and that's why he was there.'

'That late at night? A bit odd, wouldn't you say?'

Edel was reading on. 'They train to be anaplastologists in Stanford University Medical Centre. Americans... maybe they keep odd hours, you know, so they can speak to their colleagues in the US.'

'Maybe.' It was a possibility. Anyway, whatever it was, Checkley's medical history was no business of the gardaí.

Edel was still scrolling through, reading out snippets now and then. West's eye was drawn to her ring. That damn ring. It looked perfect to him but it annoyed him to know it wasn't. That they'd been conned. He wondered what Andrews was planning. Remembering his devious expression from earlier, West hoped that whatever the detective had in mind was legal and wouldn't get both of them into trouble.

The iPad was shut with a snap. 'Fascinating,' Edel said. 'I might have to use it in a story sometime. Maybe get an evil anaplastologist to make a new face for himself to commit crimes with... you know, one he could slide on and off as a disguise.'

'As long as you don't give any of our criminals the idea.' West knocked back the last of the whiskey and got to his feet, pulling Edel up beside him. 'We already, as Inspector Morrison kindly pointed out, attract the weird and wonderful cases, we could do without any weirder.'

Getting to sleep after such a tough day was always going to be difficult. West tossed and turned for a long time before drifting off only for his dreams to be disturbed by yobs carrying larger-than-life cartoon-like knives that went through his body as if he were invisible. He woke and stared into the darkness for a while before drifting back to sleep. This time it was criminals wearing silicone masks that chased him down twisted alleyways.

At five, he gave up. He couldn't find the T-shirt he usually left on the chair so in desperation he grabbed Edel's robe from the back of the door. The pink colour probably did nothing for his image, it was a bit tight but it was warm and surprisingly comfortable.

Coffee perked him up a little. And a slice of toast smothered with butter and marmalade took away the niggling hunger pangs. He found the previous day's newspaper and read through it without any interest as he ate. When he was finished, he dusted the crumbs from his fingers and looked at the clock.

Five thirty. It was going to be a long day and there was no point sitting there waiting for it to pass when he had so much to do. First on his agenda, was a visit to the Mater to see how Jarvis was. Only then could he face the rest of the day. At least, this early, he'd beat the rush-hour traffic.

As quietly as he could, he showered and dressed in the spare bedroom. Edel usually slept through his morning ablutions so he wasn't surprised to find her curled up when he opened their bedroom door fifteen minutes later.

It was a shame to disturb her but he knew she'd hate it more if he went without saying goodbye. He bent and planted a kiss on her lips, smiling as she immediately stirred, her eyelids flickering open. 'I'm heading off early. Go back to sleep. I'll call you after I've seen Sam.'

She looked at him sleepily. 'Stay safe.'

'I promise.' He kissed her again and left.

The traffic was light, the journey across the city faster than he'd expected. What he hadn't taken into account, though, was to find the front door of the Mater hospital shut tight. Swearing softly, he made his way around to the accident and emergency entrance and tried to use the door they had exited the night before. But he was out of luck. It, too, was shut tight.

A nurse stared at West's Garda Síochána identification blankly and told him to return when it was visiting time before hurrying away to deal with a patient who was attempting to pull off ECG leads.

Unwilling to give up, West wandered over the sprawling grounds for several minutes before finally locating a security guard on his beat. He showed his identification and told him why he was there. 'Can you get me in?'

'Sure thing.' The guard pointed towards a dark laneway between two buildings. 'We can get in this way. It's a bit of a warren but I'm free for a bit so I'll take you.'

After five minutes' walk along narrow passageways and up and down two different stairways, the guard stopped at a keypad, tapped in a code and opened a doorway onto a brightly lit wide corridor. 'This is the McGivney wing. St Laurence's Ward is on level five.' He pointed to lifts opposite. 'When you get out of the lift turn right. You can't miss it.'

And he was right. A few minutes later, West was standing at the end of Jarvis's bed. Luckily, a nurse who came to shoo him away was impressed by his identification. 'Okay, but don't get in our way.'

'How's he doing?'

'Not a bother,' the nurse said, reaching forward to adjust the intravenous drip. There were still two in place. One blood, one a clear fluid. 'His observations have been stable all night. He was awake and talking a while ago but he had some pain so I gave him a shot that's knocked him out.' She smiled at someone behind him. 'His ma and da were able to chat to him so that was something.'

West turned to see Dr and Mrs Jarvis looking tired but less anxious than the previous night. 'Sam sounded just like his old self,' she said.

'Good. When he wakes again will you tell him I called in. I've no doubt the rest of the team will be in, too, over the course of the day.'

'We're going to head home soon,' Dr Jarvis said. 'Dr Wilson is covering my clinics for me so I'll get some sleep and come back later.'

'I'll send a car to bring you in,' West said. 'Save you having to find parking each time.'

Dr Jarvis looked as though he were going to refuse but his wife put a hand on his arm. 'That would be extremely kind, thank you.'

'Anything we can do to help, we'll do.' With that organised, West said his goodbyes, took a final look at the sleeping Jarvis and left.

The journey back to Foxrock wasn't as bad as he anticipated, and less than an hour later, he turned into the station's car park.

The night desk sergeant, Delaney, shook his head when West pushed through the door. 'You ever sleep?'

'I've been in to see Jarvis. He's doing okay.'

'Good to hear.'

The detective unit was empty. The coffee percolator was still switched on, the contents a sludgy grey colour. West threw it out and made a fresh pot. It would help him get through the day.

29

In the period of quiet before the rest of the team turned up, West worked through paperwork pertaining to the events of the day before. It was a cold way of looking at it, but paperwork wasn't emotional and he tried to distance himself from the memory as he described the blood on the path and on Allen's clothes and hands.

He had it almost done before Andrews came through the door. 'I'll have some more coffee. It's not long made.'

Andrews vanished and returned a minute later with two mugs. 'You haven't been here all night, have you?'

West laughed. 'No, I was home. But I didn't sleep well and woke early so decided to visit Jarvis before I came in. He's doing okay according to a nurse I spoke to and had been speaking to his parents not long before I arrived.'

'I'll get in to see him later.' Andrews took a mouthful of the coffee. 'You want to have a meeting this morning, see where we are with Doris Whitaker.'

'Wait till this afternoon, hopefully we'll have the DNA result to link her to those body parts and tie everything together.'

'Checkley isn't going to give it up easily.'

West picked up his coffee and tapped his free hand on the desk. 'It will be him against the DNA–'

'Don't say science doesn't lie,' Andrews said, holding up a hand. 'We're still stuck on that Muriel Hennessy conundrum.'

'Don't remind me.' West groaned. 'Right, let's have a catch-up at 1pm–'

'Can we make it later?'

Surprised, West raised an eyebrow.

'I need some personal time... just a couple of hours. If it's not convenient...'

'No, that's fine,' West hurried to say. He was instantly suspicious but a request for *personal* time didn't allow for questions. 'What time will you be back?'

'3pm. At the latest. I'll organise a meeting of the team for then.' Andrews stood, then obviously thought of something, and sat again. 'Did you find out about the department that Checkley was visiting?'

'Yes. It deals with prosthetics. Maybe our friend has a glass eye.' West shrugged. 'He might have simply been visiting a friend.'

'Probably.' Andrews, always suspicious, didn't look convinced. 'I might have a nosy later when I'm visiting Jarvis.'

If there was anything suspicious attached to Checkley's visit, Andrews was the perfect man to find out. He could squeeze information from the strangest of places.

But what Checkley was or wasn't up to in the Mater wasn't Andrews' key concern that day. Back at his desk, he took out his mobile and rang his wife. 'All set for 1pm,' he said. 'I'll meet you outside Brown Thomas, okay?'

'Grand,' Joyce said. 'I'm looking forward to it. Are we going to use fake names? It's all very exciting.'

'Don't get carried away,' Andrews said calmly. 'No fake names, and stick to what we said, okay?'

'Spoilsport.' Joyce laughed and hung up.

Andrews parked his car outside Pearse Street Garda Station and walked around Trinity College to Grafton Street. Joyce was early, waiting in the doorway of Brown Thomas as they'd arranged. She was a beautiful woman in her usual casual clothes but she'd made a special effort that day and was wearing a coat he hadn't seen in some time. Even at a distance he thought she looked stunning.

She saw him, lifted a hand in greeting and smiled. Not for the first time, he acknowledged what a lucky man he was. 'You look lovely,' he said, slipping a hand around her waist.

She kissed him lightly. 'It's my disguise.'

'We should do this more often. Maybe next time just for fun though.' He reached for her hand and held it tightly in his as they walked the short distance to Debeerds. 'You remember what I told you?'

'I'm to pretend to be such a silly woman that I'm dazzled by the engagement rings on display and ask him to choose what he thinks would suit my hand. Once we've chosen, if he takes it away to be cleaned, we have him. If he doesn't, we've to scarper before we have to fork out a ridiculous amount of money for a ring.' She turned to Andrews with a grin. 'Do I have it?'

He gave her hand a squeeze. 'Perfect.'

Debeerds was empty which was in their favour. But there were two assistants behind the counter, which wasn't. But Andrews had already done some work. He knew the assistant in question was the only male working in the shop so ignoring the woman, he addressed the man. 'We're looking for an engagement ring.' He put an arm around Joyce's shoulders. 'One good enough for this beautiful woman.'

'We're delighted you chose Debeerds,' the assistant said. 'Please, take a seat and we'll see what we can do.'

Diamond ring after diamond ring was taken out for their perusal. Andrews wasn't sure if Joyce was acting or not, but her eyes were growing rounder and rounder.

'I'm bedazzled,' she said, having tried on the tenth ring. 'They're all so beautiful.' Her fingers lingered on the most opulent of the rings, a diamond and sapphire cluster. 'This is lovely but I'm not sure.' She looked up at the assistant. 'Which do you think suits my hand better?'

'That one is lovely,' he said. 'But you have such dainty hands, I think something simple would be better.' He picked up a solitaire, a marquise diamond that glittered beautifully under the lights. 'This is a particularly fine stone. Half a carat in a simple four claw design with tapered shoulders to enhance the appearance of the stone.' He slipped it on her finger. 'And look, it fits you perfectly.'

Joyce lifted her hand. 'Wow, you're right, it's absolutely beautiful.' She turned to Andrews, waving her hand towards him. 'What do you think, darling?'

'I think it's perfect.' He looked to the assistant. 'Looks like your job is done.'

'I don't need to take it off,' Joyce said happily.

The assistant was taking the credit card machine from under the counter and Andrews felt a moment's panic. Even if he wanted to go through with it, his credit card would laugh hysterically. The ring, at the least computation, had to be way beyond their means.

The assistant slipped an invoice discreetly across the counter to Andrews who looked at it with his best poker face. Seven thousand euro. He had to brazen it out for a moment more.

'Fine,' he said. He reached for his mobile. 'I'll just need to transfer some funds. It'll take me a minute.'

'No problem, while you're settling that, I'll take the ring for a final polish.'

With great reluctance, Joyce slipped it off her finger and handed it across.

As soon as the assistant was out of sight, Andrews put his phone away and jumped to his feet. He turned the sign on the door to 'closed' and locked the catch. The woman behind the counter gasped and took a step back. 'Garda Síochána,' Andrews said quickly. He pulled out his identification and waved it at her. 'Is there a manager here?'

She pointed to a door behind.

'Get him out here, please.'

The assistant, who didn't need to be told twice, opened the door and disappeared inside and seconds later, a grey-haired man came out, eyes darting around the shop before stopping at Andrews. 'Guards?'

'Detective Garda Andrews.' He held his identification out again. 'This is my wife Joyce. We need your assistance with catching a thief.'

Puzzlement creased the manager's forehead but he nodded slowly.

'If you'd wait behind the counter,' Andrews said, and quickly took his seat when he heard footsteps approach. 'Here you are,' the assistant said cheerfully. 'All polished for you.' His attention was on the ring and the couple on the other side of the counter and he paid no attention to the manager staring from the other side of the shop.

'That's great,' Andrews said, taking the ring. He turned with it in his hand and held it out to the manager. 'Could you have a look at this for me?'

'What?' the assistant said, glancing up to see the manager making his way towards them. 'What's going on?'

'I'd like this half carat diamond to be double-checked by your manager. Have you a problem with that?' Andrews saw the quick dart of panic as the assistant glanced at the corridor behind, now blocked by the bulk of the manager, then to the front door.

'I wouldn't try it,' Andrews warned. 'It's locked.'

'I'm not sure what is going on here,' the manager said. He took the ring from Andrews and looked at it, then with a frown pulled a loupe from his pocket, screwed it into his eye and looked at the ring again.

With a sigh, he allowed the loupe to drop into his hand. 'I think we'd better go into my office.' He wrapped long fingers around the assistant's arm and pulled him along with him. 'Perhaps you could open the shop again, Miss Dickson.'

The manager's office was spacious and well appointed. The assistant was pushed into a chair as the manager took his seat behind the desk. He waved Andrews and Joyce into other chairs.

'My name is Noel Charlton,' the manager said. 'I've worked for Debeerds for the best part of twenty years and this–' he held up the ring between his thumb and first finger, '–has never happened before.'

'It's not a diamond,' Andrews said.

'No, it isn't. The green/blue light it gives off would lead me to favour it being moissanite – probably a man-made variety too. It looks good, and would fool most people, but it is not a diamond.' His face tightened. 'The fact that you're here leads me to believe that this isn't a one-off swap.'

Andrews shook his head and quickly filled him in on Edel's visit to Cunningham's Jewellers and her discovery that the ring they'd bought was a fake. 'Neither she, nor Sergeant West, wanted to make a fuss and spoil what had been a special day so I decided to step in with a sting of my own making.'

'You did a good job,' the manager said. 'And thank you. I know Jim Cunningham, I'll have a word, tell him it's been put to rights.' He met Andrews' eyes. 'This isn't something we want broadcast. It could damage our reputation beyond repair.' He turned to the assistant. 'How many?'

Sweat beaded the assistant's forehead. 'Four.'

'Four!' Charlton looked horrified for a moment, then gathered himself together and turned to Andrews. 'If Debeerds assures you that all four will be contacted and compensated, can we keep this from leaving this office?'

'This is strictly off the books,' Andrews admitted. 'I've done this for my colleague.' He turned to the assistant who was sitting with his head down. 'What did you do with the real rings?'

'I kept them for a couple of weeks in my locker in case the buyer returned them. Had they done so, I'd have swapped them back before anyone noticed.'

'A few weeks? Do you still have the original ring you sold to Mike West and Edel Johnson last week?'

There was a slight hesitation before the assistant nodded. 'Yes, it's still in my locker.'

Accompanied by the manager, the ring was retrieved and handed to Andrews who opened it. 'This will make their day.' He snapped the box shut, put it into his pocket and looked at the young man. 'You were lucky this time, you may not be in the future. Take this as a valuable lesson.'

Charlton walked to the shop door with them. 'I am most grateful,' he said again.

'What are you going to do about him?' Joyce asked.

'Keep him on. He's good at what he does, good with the customers.' He shrugged. 'But I won't be stupid. I'll have a CCTV camera set over where he works to ensure he never has a chance to be tempted again. And he'll repay any compensation that we need to pay out.' With final words of gratitude, he returned inside.

'That was exciting.'

Andrews took her hand. 'It worked out better than I expected. Mike and Edel will be happy.'

They walked along Grafton Street to the DART station on Stephen's Green where they were in luck, one was waiting to leave. Andrews pulled Joyce closer and kissed her lightly. 'Thank you for helping.'

'I had fun.' Joyce hopped on board and sat on a seat, looking out at him. She raised her hand in a wave.

Andrews waited until the DART pulled away before retracing his steps down Grafton Street, his fingers closing over the box in his pocket. It had been a job well done.

30

When West hadn't heard from Niall Kennedy by 2.30pm, he picked up the phone to ring him. Unfortunately, he was out of luck and the pathologist was in the middle of a meeting.

'I can get him to ring you when he's free,' the receptionist said.

'Good. Tell him it's regarding the DNA results.'

West hung up feeling frustrated with cases that seemed to be going nowhere. He rang the hospital for an update on Jarvis and put the phone down when he was reassured by the nurse that he was improving by the hour. Good news there at least.

It wasn't yet 3pm, but he was restless and went out to the main office to stare at the Wall in the hopes that the information there might inspire him. It didn't. Within a few minutes he was joined by the others.

'You doing okay?' he asked Allen. 'You didn't need to come in today.'

'No reason for me to stay home.' Allen looked embarrassed. 'I didn't get stabbed.'

'And you weren't to blame for Jarvis getting stabbed either.

He was unlucky, you were lucky. It's the way it goes sometimes.' West waved a hand at the Wall. 'But I'm glad you're here, we need all heads together to try and make sense of this.'

Baxter stepped up and stuck a sheet of A4 paper to the Wall with a wad of Blu Tack. 'We might be getting somewhere. Not all the info is back but Edwards and I have put what we have together.' He looked at his watch. 'It's not quite 3pm, d'you want to wait.'

Almost as if he were conjured by the words, Andrews came through the door on a wave of voices that vanished as it shut behind him. 'Not late, am I?'

'Baxter was about to solve the mystery of the Whitaker case for us,' West said.

'Not precisely solve.' Baxter grinned.

'A mug of coffee and I'm all ears,' Andrews said, crossing to the percolator.

'Right, so what do you have?' West folded his arms and sat on the desk behind while Baxter stepped up to the Wall and tapped the sheet of paper he'd fixed to it. 'It took a bit of digging but–' he tipped his head at Edwards, '–we think we've got it together.

'When she was eighteen, Doris Black married Benjamin Whitaker. They lived for several years in Sallynoggin where they had two children, Rebecca and Benjamin Junior. When the children were in their late teens, early twenties, Doris inherited money from her parents and they moved from Sallynoggin to the house in Foxrock.' Baxter looked around. 'So far, all very straightforward but then we get to the interesting bit. Benjamin Whitaker worked in a variety of poorly paid, unskilled jobs over the years and never stayed in any one job for long. Then forty-nine years ago, he stopped paying tax. And there's no further record of him. The two kids were enrolled in university but we couldn't find any record of them graduating. And neither ever paid tax in Ireland.'

'Maybe they went abroad,' West suggested.

'I checked tax records for all three in the UK and there's nothing,' Edwards said. 'We're waiting to hear back from the US regarding Benjamin Whitaker but according to the passport office neither Rebecca nor Benjamin Junior were ever issued with a passport so they couldn't have gone.'

West felt success at their fingertips. 'So, at the same time an older male adult and two younger adults were killed and their bodies somehow preserved, Doris Whitaker's family disappeared.'

Baxter stepped back from the Wall and perched on a desk. 'Doris Whitaker never reported her husband and children missing because she'd killed them.'

'We've no idea who the fourth body is,' Edwards said. 'We checked the previous census reports. The occupants of the house were listed as the parents and two children, nobody else.'

The ring of the phone distracted them. 'It might be Kennedy with our DNA result. Facts will lock our theory together.' West headed to his office and picked up the phone.

'Sorry for the delay in getting back to you, it's been manic here.' Niall Kennedy's voice sounded weary. 'I heard about Jarvis. He doing okay?'

'Yes, they say he should make a full recovery.'

'Good. Right, the DNA results.'

'We've just been discussing it. Doris Whitaker's husband and children haven't been heard of for forty-nine years so we're hoping you're going to confirm it's them.'

'Well, I'm afraid that's not going to be possible.'

West blinked in surprise. 'There isn't a match?'

'Nope. DNA from the dismembered bodies doesn't match DNA taken from the hit-and-run victim, Doris Whitaker.'

They'd been so sure they were on the right track. He knew the answer to the question before he asked but asked it anyway. 'No chance there's been a mistake?'

'I should take umbrage,' Kennedy said. 'But I'm too tired. No mistake. Not a match.'

West waited a moment before he headed back to join the rest of the team. This wasn't what they wanted to hear.

Andrews saw him coming across the room, shut his eyes, and muttered under his breath. 'You're kidding me,' he then said aloud.

'Afraid not. Dr Kennedy says there isn't a match.'

Baxter and Edwards spoke together, both vociferous about the DNA results having to be wrong. Even Allen, always the quieter of them, put his word in.

West held up a hand. 'The DNA doesn't match. I'm not going to say the science can't be wrong because I'm less certain of that than I was only a week ago... but we're stuck with what we have–'

'Which is now nothing,' Baxter interrupted, scowling.

'We know Doris Whitaker's husband and two children disappeared around the same time as our dismembered corpses were killed. That's too much of a coincidence. What we have to do, is to get the facts to fit the science. We weren't expecting a DNA match to the adult male – they were husband and wife after all – but we were expecting a match to the two children... so why isn't there one? We know the man and children are related... so maybe they used a surrogate. Find out. I know we're onto something.'

He left them to it and returned to his office, Andrews following closely behind.

'Damn DNA,' West said, flopping onto his chair. 'We need a break with this. If we can't get proof, we'll never tie Checkley in with the bodies.'

'Science is giving us a lot of headaches these days.'

'I'm less sure of the Hennessy case. It's down to estimation of time, after all. But you simply can't argue with DNA.'

The sound of voices drifted from the main office, followed by Baxter's very distinctive laugh.

Andrews pushed the door shut. 'We were lucky with Jarvis.'

'We use that word far too often, d'you know that?'

'Part of our life.' Andrews reached forward and placed a small box in the middle of the desk. 'What we have to remember is that it's often on our side.'

West stared at the box in disbelief. He knew Andrews would do something but he never thought he'd get the ring back. His hand slid across the desk, fingers closing over the box, eyes still on Andrews. 'It's really the ring?'

'The assistant hung onto the rings he swapped for a couple of weeks in case the customers changed their minds.'

West opened the box, took the ring out and held it up to the light. 'It looks exactly the same as the one she's wearing, you know.'

'But it isn't, and that's important to Edel.'

The ring was put back into the box, the lid shut with a loud snap. 'I don't know how to thank you.'

'It's in my interest,' Andrews said as he got to his feet. 'You're far less grumpy when you're happy.'

31

'Let me get this straight,' Edel said over dinner that night. 'This woman, Doris Whitaker, was married with two children and they and her husband seem to have vanished off the face of the earth. You have three bodies from the same time frame, and yet you can't say for sure they're the same?'

'That's about it.'

'How extraordinary! I bet Morrison loved that.'

West jabbed his fork into a piece of chicken with more vigour than the overcooked fowl needed. 'I haven't told him yet.' Edel's laugh rang out, making him smile. 'If only Morrison would laugh. Instead, he puts on his hard-done-by expression and frowns so much that his eyebrows come together in one huge, hairy caterpillar.'

'He's right though, you do get some odd ones. It will be a long time before I forget those lamprey eels.'

The memory of Eoin Breathnach's body floating in the pond with the lamprey eels sucking the life out of him was the kind of image that was destined to last. 'I should never have brought you there.'

'Far as I remember, I didn't give you any choice. Anyway, if I remember correctly, it was me who found the murder weapon.'

'Shouldn't that be, it was *I* who found the murder weapon?'

'Ha, nobody loves a smart-arse,' Edel said, getting to her feet.

A few minutes later, order restored to the kitchen and dining room, they were relaxing in the sitting room listening to the news on TV.

'What about the other case?' Edel asked as some politician whose name she didn't know was spouting forth about the economy. 'You know, the frozen body one.'

'We've hit a dead-end with that, I'm afraid: Kennedy swears the time frame had to be several days, but Cara Donaldson insists she saw her mother on the Sunday.'

'Maybe there was a mix-up in the mortuary and the bodies were mislabelled or something. It happens, you know.'

'In crime novels and movies, maybe, not in real life.'

Edel twisted around to look at him. 'Rubbish! I bet it happens all the time. Did the family identify her there or in the hospital before she was transferred?'

West smiled at the excitement in Edel's eyes. It was good to be able to talk about his cases, even if she did put a fictional spin on them at times. 'They identified her in the mortuary.'

'Oh, pity. It would have worked better my way.'

He put an arm around her and pulled her close. 'Sorry not to be able to oblige you.'

'It would have been better, because if they'd been lying, if the woman wasn't their mother, that would solve the problem.'

West's hand tightened on her shoulder. 'What did you say?'

Edel moved away from his embrace and turned to look at him, startled by the sharpness in his voice. 'Sorry, I was joking.'

'No,' he said, 'say it again.'

'What? That if the woman wasn't their mother it would solve the problem?'

West pulled her to him again and kissed her firmly on the lips. 'Yes.' He reached into his shirt pocket for his mobile. 'Peter, it's Mike. Sorry for disturbing you but I wanted to check something. Cara Donaldson and her brother... did they actually see their mother or did they identify her from her belongings?' He listened for a moment. 'No, I'll explain tomorrow. G'night.'

He tapped the phone on his thigh, trying to get his thoughts in order.

'If you don't tell me what's going on soon, I'm going to explode,' Edel said.

'Muriel Hennessy's body had been in that alleyway for possibly a couple of days. There was rodent damage to her face, parts of her body. When it was explained to her son and daughter that they might prefer not to witness the damage, that they could formally identify her by the distinctive ring she always wore, that's what they did.'

'What!'

'There was never any doubt. Their mother had been missing for up to five days. There was no other elderly female reported missing so the logical conclusion was that the woman was Muriel Hennessy.' He laughed at the look of astonishment on Edel's face. She looked... what was that word... flabbergasted, yes, that was it. 'You look flabbergasted.'

'I am,' Edel said with a shake of her head. 'Completely. But if it's not her, who is it? And where's Muriel Hennessy?'

32

There was only one way to prove he was right, West decided as he dressed the following morning. Their old friend DNA would have to ride to the rescue again.

They had testing kits in the station. The sooner he could get a sample from one of the Hennessy offspring to bring to Kennedy for comparison, the sooner they'd know. Cara Donaldson he guessed would be the better option.

He stopped in the station to grab a kit and headed to her house. At 7.30am he rang her doorbell hoping she'd not yet left for work.

It was a puzzled, and sleepy-looking husband who answered the door, eyebrows shooting into his hairline when he saw West standing there. 'Very eager or a little desperate,' he said in lieu of good morning. He didn't appear to expect an answer, standing back and waving West in. 'There's coffee just made. Help yourself. I'll go get Cara.'

The coffee smelled good so West accepted the casual invitation and helped himself, adding milk from the Tetra Pak nearby. He stayed standing, sipping it as he stared out over a well-planned, neat back garden.

A bored voice made him turn. 'What is it this time?'

West had debated how much he should tell her. It was all speculation after all. But if he wanted a DNA sample, he'd have to be honest. 'It's been difficult trying to marry the facts as you told them, and the science as our expert is telling us. We've come to an odd conclusion that is, as yet, purely speculative.'

Cara's eyes narrowed. 'You should have been a politician; you have a great knack of speaking and saying nothing.' She opened a cupboard, took down a mug and poured coffee from the pot. 'How about you tell me what you want?'

'A DNA sample.'

She stared into the coffee before lifting it to her lips and taking a miniscule sip. It gave her enough time to weigh up his request and to come to the right conclusion. 'Of course.' She shook her head in amused disbelief. 'If *I'm* right, and the *science* is right, then it's the body that has to be wrong.'

West had to admire her. He couldn't have put it better. 'You identified your mother from a ring she wore, isn't that correct?'

'Yes. Neither Liam nor I wanted to look at her after we were told the damage that had been done by rodents.' She shivered. 'Anyway, the ring was very distinctive. It was one she'd worn forever – a hideous garnet and peridot concoction my father had made for her as an engagement ring. Garnets were her favourite stone and green was her favourite colour so he had the bright idea to combine the two.' She shook her head at the thought.

'It sounds unique.' It also made the situation more troubling. If the body in the laneway wasn't Muriel Hennessy, how and why was she wearing her ring?

'It is... very... so it seemed logical to assume it was Mum when we saw it. Now you're indicating it might not be.' The same thought crossed her mind. 'So why was she wearing Mum's ring?'

'I wish I could come up with a plausible reason but I haven't got one.' West took the sample kit from his pocket and handed it to her. 'Best if we get the proof one way or another. If you'd put some saliva in the pot, please.'

Cara took the kit and looked at it with dislike. 'Suddenly, my mouth seems obstinately dry.' She removed the sample pot. 'You don't mind if I turn my back, do you? Spitting, even for such a good reason as this, goes against my nature.'

When West nodded his agreement, she took a few steps away and turned her back to him.

'Disgusting,' she said a moment later, handing over the packet with the specimen pot plainly visible through a clear plastic window. 'When do you get the results?'

'I'll take it over now. Dr Kennedy is very efficient, if I beg nicely, he'll have the results by tomorrow.' He rolled the packet up and slipped it into his pocket. 'Thank you for your help, I'll let you know the results as soon as we hear anything.'

Back in his car, West sat and considered his next step. It was too early to go to the State Pathologist's Office, too early to call to Thunders for the necessary bribery. Instead, he drove to the Mater to visit Jarvis.

He tried the same entrance the security guard had taken him through the last time. Relieved to find it open, he headed down long, dimly lit corridors hoping he wouldn't get lost and have to ring someone to be rescued. But a few minutes later, he keyed in the code he'd seen the security guard use and pushed open the door into the main hospital.

Jarvis was asleep. West was relieved to see that the intravenous lines were gone, as were the monitoring leads. Only a simple device attached to one of his fingers remained. The numbers on the screen made no sense to West but it wasn't flashing warning lights or alarming so he took comfort from that. Deciding to stay a while, he grabbed a chair from a stack near the door, placed it beside the bed and sat.

Immediately, Jarvis opened his eyes. 'Hi.'

'Hi yourself. How're you feeling or is that a silly question.'

Jarvis slid his hand across the bed and felt for the control. Pressing a button, the head of the bed lifted. 'That's better.' He shuffled a little and sighed. 'I feel okay. The wound is a bit sore but they say it will be easier when the staples come out.'

'Staples?'

'High-tech stuff stopping my insides from falling out.' He pointed to a glass on the bedside table and West picked it up and held it for him while Jarvis slurped through the straw. 'Thank you.'

Because he knew Jarvis would be fascinated, West told him about the idea that the body found in the laneway wasn't, after all, Muriel Hennessy. 'I'm going to ask Kennedy to do a DNA comparison between her and Cara Donaldson. We should know tomorrow.'

'Makes sense, doesn't it. If the science was right, and the daughter was right. It had to be the body that was wrong.'

'Yes, we're all seeing it now. Inspector Morrison is going to be apoplectic.'

'I can imagine what he'll say.' Jarvis imitated Morrison's rather pedantic way of speaking. 'Instead of solving cases, Detective Sergeant West, you seem obsessed with making them more complicated... or should I say, more ridiculous!'

West laughed. 'Pretty close. You'd better not let Morrison hear that.'

Jarvis shuffled in the bed again, the movement causing him to wince. 'These beds are so damn hard.' He pressed the control again, the bed's angle changing slightly. 'Better.' He lifted the control. 'The only exercise I'm getting.' He dropped it on the bed. 'If that body isn't Muriel Hennessy, will you have to start the search for her again?'

'We'll certainly be opening the missing person's file on her again but at this stage I can't see us finding her alive.'

The door opened and a nurse came through. She stopped when she saw West sitting there and shook her head. 'I suppose there's no point in my saying it's not visiting hours; you'll simply say it's garda business and wave your identification the way those other lads did last night.'

West looked at Jarvis, an eyebrow raised in question.

'Baxter, Edwards and Allen. They came en masse to see me.'

'Ah, yes,' he turned to the nurse, 'it's important that we get detailed statements about what happened.'

'Yes, and if it causes great hilarity, all the better,' she said with a wink in Jarvis's direction. She checked the monitor, jotted down the recording on the chart she was holding and with a warning to West not to overstay his welcome, she vanished as quietly as she'd arrived.

West left a short while later and since it was after 9am, parked outside Thunders and went inside to see what form bribery would take that day.

A short while later he rapped on Kennedy's office door. When he heard the shout to come in, he opened the door and held the box inside like a white flag.

'That better be meringues and not more body parts.'

West pushed the door fully open. 'Neither, will you settle for cream donuts and éclairs? I'll have to plan my visits for later to get meringues.'

'Planning your visits by telling me you were coming might be a good idea too,' Kennedy said, but there was no criticism in the words. 'What's it this time?'

'Another DNA check, please.' West handed over the kit. 'Can you check this against Muriel Hennessy's. It might solve our conundrum.'

'The science versus witness one?'

'Yes.'

Kennedy paused in the act of sliding an éclair into his mouth. 'Ah, I see where you're going. If science and the witness are both right... the body has to be wrong.'

'You're the third person to say that this morning. If we're all so clever, why did it take us so long to see it?'

His mouth full, Kennedy waved a hand. 'We're theorising... wait until we do the DNA comparison before we decide it's a fact.'

'Sherlock Holmes never had this problem,' West said irritably. He picked up an éclair and demolished it in two bites.

33

Back in the station, West filled the team in on the latest development. 'For now, it's only a theory that the body found in the laneway is not Muriel Hennessy. Tomorrow, when we get the DNA result, we'll know for sure. Meanwhile, it wouldn't do any harm to check to see if an elderly female has turned up in any of the hospitals, because if the body isn't Muriel Hennessy, she has to be out there somewhere.'

'I'll start on that,' Allen said. 'Plus, if the body isn't her, who is it? I'll check for any missing persons citywide.'

'Morrison is going to love this,' Baxter said with a grin.

West shot him a quelling look. 'Inspector Morrison likes cases being solved, so how about we do our job and get one of these blasted cases closed.'

'You mean rather than making them more complicated,' Edwards replied with a shake of his head.

There was a moment when none of them knew which way it was going to go, but then West started to laugh and soon they were all at it. 'Yes, indeed, if we're right, it means we've turned our three cases into four. I might keep that from the inspector for the minute. Right,' West said, 'let's see if we can turn this around. Anything more on Doris Checkley's family.'

Baxter raised a hand. 'I found six Benjamin Whitakers living in the UK; only two were of the appropriate age but I managed, finally, to rule both out. There's no record of a man of that name legally emigrating to the US in that period... of course, he could have done so illegally and is working there using an assumed name.' He shrugged. 'No way of finding that out.'

'The two kids couldn't have gone to the US anyway, they didn't have passports,' Edwards reminded him. He shoved his hands into the baggy pockets of his tweed jacket. 'According to the birth certificates of both Rebecca and Benjamin Junior, they were born at home. So maybe it was a surrogate thing... Doris couldn't have children so they hired someone. It would explain why the DNA of the father matches the children but doesn't match Doris.'

'We were looking for a family group when we searched for missing persons,' Baxter said. 'Since we've proved the older female isn't related, I'll do a search for missing single females in the same time frame. Maybe we'll get lucky.'

There it was, that damn word again. 'Okay. Keep at it,' West said and returned to his office.

By the end of the day, they'd nothing more to add to the miserly information on the Wall.

'Nothing.' West shoved a hand through his hair in frustration.

'Nothing yet,' Andrews qualified. 'Lots of theories and tantalising snippets, just nothing concrete. Getting the DNA results tomorrow might help solve the Hennessy mystery though.'

'And leave us with another headache. Where's Muriel Hennessy, and who is the frozen woman?' West rocked back, his chair squeaking in protest as the front wheels were lifted off the ground. 'DNA didn't help us much with the Checkley case. It's so frustrating... we know those bodies must be Doris Whitaker's family but we can't prove it, and without that proof there's no way we can tie Darragh Checkley into the disposal of the bodies.'

'We may fail here, Mike. It's been two weeks. The only reason Morrison isn't yelling blue murder is that nothing more important has come along to need our attention plus, of course, he's playing softly-softly because of Jarvis.'

'Yes, I know.'

'Tomorrow, we'll catch a break.'

'Optimist.'

'That's me.' Andrews leaned forward and dropped his voice. 'Changing the subject, what did Edel say about the ring?'

'I haven't told her yet.' West laughed at his surprise. 'I have a plan, don't worry.'

'A plan?' Andrews, sounding puzzled, got to his feet. 'I'd better get on.' He turned back at the door with a final comment. 'As long as you know what you're doing.'

Did he? Since Edel had come into his life West wasn't always sure. He dropped the chair down on its four wheels with a crash. But this would work, he was sure of it.

34

West had a dart of guilt when he saw Edel wasn't wearing her ring again that evening. He didn't question it and later it was back in place. Maybe she left it off all day so that it wouldn't remind her that some relationships were fake... or was he overthinking things? He almost gave in and told her that he knew about the switch and that he had the real ring. But he'd asked her to marry him on the spur of the moment. She'd been dishing up lasagne at the time. It was hard to think of anything more unromantic than that. He had a second chance to do it properly. She deserved it.

His deception was only for one more day. He had a plan. The next night, he was going to put it into action and it would all work out perfectly.

Until then, he'd concentrate on his job and try to get even one of these blasted cases sorted.

~

'Inspector Morrison wants to see you,' Sergeant Blunt said when West arrived in the station on Thursday morning.

West was startled. This was becoming a habit... and not a good one. 'What's he doing in so early?'

'No idea.'

There was no point in putting it off so West went straight up and rapped on the edge of the open door. 'You wanted to see me, Inspector?'

'Come in.' Morrison was standing by his percolator. 'Coffee?'

'Please.' Not a bollocking then. Something more civilised. 'You're in early this morning.'

'I went to see Jarvis. Seemed a sensible time to be negotiating cross-city traffic.'

'I saw him yesterday,' West said, accepting the coffee that was handed to him.

'Doing well, he tells me.' Morrison sat behind his desk. 'That or he's putting a brave face on it.'

'I spoke to the nurse before I left yesterday; she said they were pleased with how he was doing.' West rested a shoulder against the wall. 'It'll be a while before he's fit to return to work though, plus he'll need to see a counsellor.'

'Indeed.' Morrison put his coffee down and folded his arms. 'It was why I wanted to see you this morning. I'm not planning on leaving you short. Some of the uniformed gardaí have shown an interest in joining the detective division, you've worked with a couple of them already.'

'Garda Mackin shows promise.'

'He does, but I've been worried about the lack of diversity so I was thinking about Gemma Ryan.'

West frowned as he tried to put a face to the name. 'Ah, yes.' His face cleared. 'She helped us out with those Cornelscourt muggers last year.' He remembered her as being eager, and more importantly she seemed to have common sense. If they couldn't have Mackin, she'd do. 'Young Mackin will be disappointed.'

'He'll live.'

West wondered whether he should bring up the progress... or lack of it in their current caseload but decided against. Later that day he might have something positive to report.

'Bring the mug back when you're finished with it.'

It was a clear dismissal. 'Will do,' West said and took himself off.

The detective unit was empty. He stood in front of the Wall while he finished the coffee, going over the little they knew and the tangle the cases had become. Two cases – despite lack of proof, he was still convinced the Checkleys and the dismembered bodies were linked.

'Hi.'

West turned, surprised to see Gemma Ryan standing hesitantly in the doorway with a nervous smile. Her hands tugged at the edges of a jacket. West guessed she'd probably bought it for an interview years before, hadn't worn it since, and discovered only that morning that it was a shade too small.

'Hello. Come in.' West waved her over. 'I hear you're going to be with us for a while.'

'While Detective Garda Jarvis is out of action. Which I hope won't be long, of course, but I am grateful for the opportunity.'

'You did well last year. The Cornelscourt muggers. We're glad to have you as part of the team. Now,' he turned to the Wall, 'let me fill you in on our current confusing and frustrating cases.'

Ryan stood silently listening as he went through the details, sparse as they were. 'We're waiting for DNA results to confirm our theory about the body in the laneway.' He tapped both the photograph of Muriel Hennessy taken before her death and the blown-up photo of her face taken in the mortuary, the damage done by the rodents graphically detailed. 'And that's her son Liam, and her daughter Cara Donaldson,' he said, indicating the photographs that sat alongside.

'And in the other case we're working on–' he pointed to another series of photographs, '–Doris Whitaker, victim of a hit-and-run last week, her cousin Darragh and his wife, Lynda. The team are trying to find a link between the dismembered bodies that were found in the recycling centre and Mrs Whitaker and hopefully we'll be able to charge Checkley with the disposal of the bodies. Unfortunately, it's not proving to be too easy.'

'Inspector Morrison was right,' Ryan said.

West turned to her, an eyebrow raised in question. 'Inspector Morrison frequently is, but about what in particular this time?'

'He said I'd be surprised at the bizarre cases you get here.'

'Bizarre.' West laughed. 'That's an improvement on the "ridiculous" he was using last week.' He looked back to the Wall. 'Probably because I haven't actually filled him in on our latest theory.'

The door opened and Andrews and Baxter came through deep in conversation. They stopped when they saw Ryan.

'Garda Ryan is joining us while Jarvis is off,' West said. He pointed to a desk in the corner. 'You can use his desk, Gemma. Settle yourself in. Get yourself a coffee and don't be put off by anything Baxter says, he's pretty harmless.'

He left Baxter chatting to her and took Andrews into his office. 'She'll be a good addition.'

'I agree. She's smart and quick-witted. Nice to have a woman on the team too.'

'That's what Morrison said when I suggested Mackin.' West sat behind his desk. 'The inspector didn't ask about the cases and I didn't volunteer anything. Let's hope we get something concrete today.'

'I'd settle for anything that wasn't smoke.' Andrews tipped his head towards the main office. 'What d'you want me to put Ryan on?'

'I gave her a quick rundown on the cases we're working on;

get Allen to take her through them in detail. We'll go from there.'

If they were hoping for a quiet morning to concentrate on their search for information regarding Doris Whitaker, their luck had run out and mid-morning, apart from Andrews and West, the detective unit was empty.

'Nothing complicated, so at least that's something.' Andrews stood in West's doorway. 'An alleged assault in Stillorgan shopping centre and a burglary at a premises on Sandyford Industrial Estate.' He held his hand up when he saw that West was going to interrupt. 'Yes, I know that one should be dealt with by the robbery division, but Clark and Foley are tied up dealing with a home burglary in Leopardstown.'

West grimaced. 'We've been lucky this long. How far had they got with their search?'

'They were still trawling through reports. I've taken over but it's slow-going. Hopefully, these new cases will be uncomplicated and they'll get back before too long.'

'Contrary to what Morrison thinks, we do get straightforward ones. Send me whatever Edwards was working on and I'll work through it.'

It was a boring, eye-watering task and West had to remind himself of what he'd told Edwards not many days before. Focusing on lines of data required frequent mugs of coffee and he was getting his third when the door opened and Baxter came through holding a tray of takeaway coffees. Edwards, behind him, waved a bag of donuts.

'We stopped on the way back,' Baxter said, putting the tray down. 'Thought you might need sustenance.'

Edwards plonked the donuts beside the coffee and tore open the bag. 'Sugar-rush heaven.'

A sugar rush might help. West reached for a jam donut and bit into it, sucking up the jam that immediately escaped. 'These are good, thanks.' It was gone in three bites leaving him with sugared fingers. It was tempting to do what Baxter was doing and brush his fingers against the leg of his trousers but he couldn't bring himself to do it and crossed to the sink. 'What about the alleged assault?'

'A sanctimonious idiot, too well-versed in his rights.' Edwards crooked his index fingers around the last word. 'He was in O'Brien's when another customer rushed in, brushed against him and knocked his coffee cup from his hand. It was a black coffee so he was a little scalded and started shouting the odds, accusing the other customer of assault. Unfortunately, instead of apologising, the other customer accused the first of being overweight and taking up too much room in the café thereby forcing people to detour around him.'

'I thought that was quite witty.' Baxter spoke through a mouthful of his second donut, granules of sugar falling from his lips. 'But it made the other customer more irate and he insisted that the staff call security.'

'The security man was Bill Grainger. You know him, Peter,' Edwards said as Andrews joined them.

'Unfortunately,' Andrews said, and reached for a donut. 'I thought they'd got rid of him.'

'They've tried but he's like chewing gum, hard to get rid of. Anyway, when he arrived, Mr Sanctimonious started spouting about his rights, and holding forward his slightly reddened hand so Grainger, never one to put himself out, decided to offload him onto us.'

Baxter dusted sugar from his hands and picked up a coffee. 'By the time we arrived the two customers were sitting at opposite ends of the café shooting daggers at each other. They both started speaking at once, each of them blaming the other so I told them they'd have to come to the station to make a statement. Since Mr Sanctimonious was talking about damages, I told them they'd need to get themselves solicitors first.'

'You should have heard him,' Edwards said. 'I swear he's been listening to you too much, Mike, he was spouting stuff about slander and reputational damages.'

'Reputational damages?' West looked from one to the other. 'I'm impressed, it sounds good but there's no such thing.'

'It sounded good,' Baxter said with a grin. 'That's all that mattered, and it worked. Mr Sanctimonious backed down and said he'd accept an apology which was offered almost before he'd finished speaking. The owner came over and offered them both lunch on the house and that was that.'

'Well done.' West had to smile. It was certainly one way to solve a case. 'Right, finish your sugar and caffeine fixes and get back to work. I want to be able to tell the inspector we're getting somewhere. We'll have a catch-up at four. Hopefully, I'll have the DNA results by then.'

Allen and Ryan arrived back not long afterwards. 'Sergeant Clark arrived and told us to take ourselves off.'

'Good. You were doing the missing person search, weren't you? Explain to Ryan the lengths we go to in our effort to trace a body. Impress her, but find out who that woman was.'

Allen grinned. 'Will do my best.'

When he hadn't heard from Kennedy by 3.45pm, West rang to be told the pathologist was in a meeting and couldn't be disturbed. West left a message and hung up. 'No results yet,' he told the team at 4pm. He looked around, seeing no excitement on any of their faces. 'Nothing?'

'We searched a five-year period and a twenty-mile radius and found three women who were reported missing,' Allen said. 'We're working through them looking for more details.'

'Okay, keep at it.' West looked around. 'Nothing else?'

Into the silence, the sound of the phone ringing was loud

and jarring. West picked up the nearest handset. 'Dr Kennedy,' he said. 'I'm hoping you can make my day.' He listened, murmuring uh-huh and mm-hm as he did. 'Seriously?' he said finally, his fingers tightening on the handset. West caught Andrews' eye and gave him a thumbs up. 'For this, Niall, I'll leave a standing order in Thunders for a weekly delivery of meringues, chocolate éclairs and cream donuts.'

West hung up and wiped a hand over his mouth. 'Never in a month of Sundays are you going to guess what Dr Kennedy has told me.'

35

W est paced the room. 'Bloody hell, Morrison is going to have a seizure when he hears this.'

'We're going to have a seizure if you don't tell us what's going on,' Andrews said.

'It's crazy. But give me a minute to work it out because...' West looked at the photographs on the Wall, then paced some more, his brow furrowed. 'Okay, bloody hell, I think I've got it!' He held a hand up to silence the questions that were being fired at him. 'We asked for Cara Donaldson's DNA to be compared to that of the frozen body to see if it was her mother, Muriel Hennessy. Dr Kennedy passed the instruction on to one of his technicians, but Kennedy was in a hurry and simply asked for it to be compared to the elderly female victim from Foxrock. The efficient technician checked to see who Cara Donaldson was and when he did, he compared her DNA to that of the frozen woman. As we'd speculated, it didn't match.

'What happened next was an unexpected bonus. The technician, deciding to leave no room for error, compared Donaldson's DNA to the *other* elderly female victim who had come from Foxrock following a hit-and-run.' West looked around, then moved to the Wall and tapped Doris Whitaker's photo, excitement lighting his eyes. 'He got a match.'

'What?' Baxter squeezed his eyes shut. 'You're telling us that Cara Donaldson is Doris Whitaker's daughter.'

'No, that's not what I'm saying.' West peeled off the photograph of the woman they'd found in the laneway with her rodent-ravaged face and stuck it under the photograph of Doris Whitaker. 'I'm saying that the hit-and-run victim is Muriel Hennessy and I'm betting that this poor woman we found in the laneway is Doris Whitaker.'

The team were stunned into silence, then everyone spoke together, a hullaballoo that made West smile. Never in a million years would he have put this together. He still couldn't quite believe it. But the science, after all, didn't lie.

'I'm stunned,' Andrews said.

'This is unbelievable,' Baxter and Edwards said almost at the same time.

'The Checkleys almost got away with it,' West said.

'Nobody ever questioned the identification of the hit-and-run victim.' Andrews rubbed a hand over his head, his expression bemused. 'Lynda said it was Doris Whitaker so there was no reason to.'

'But why?' Baxter's tone of voice suggested he was struggling to accept this bizarre turn of events.

'That's what we have to find out.' West looked around, his eyes settling on Andrews. 'You've the most meticulous brain, Peter, take us through it.'

Andrews folded his arms across his chest. 'On Tuesday 5th, there's a hit-and-run. Lynda Checkley happens to be passing and identifies the woman on the road as her husband's cousin, Doris Whitaker.

'The following day, Liam Hennessy calls to visit his mother, Muriel, and finds her house empty and cold. She hadn't been seen since the previous Sunday. A decomposing, rodent-chewed body is found on Friday. Due to the injuries, the family identify their mother from an unusual ring she always wore.'

Baxter held up a hand. 'Okay, so somehow, Muriel Hennessy's ring found its way onto Doris's body, yes?'

'Lynda Checkley had time to remove it after the hit-and-run,' Allen said.

'But why did she do that?' Gemma moved closer to the Wall and took down the photograph of the frozen woman, her face screwing up at the damage. 'Why did they want to convince us the body in the laneway was Doris.'

'Ashley Pritchard.' Andrews slapped the desk he was sitting on, the sound falling into the silence as everyone was lost in thought.

'Who?' Edwards asked for everyone.

'Doris's solicitor.' West reached for the phone, holding up a hand to stop further questions. 'Dr Kennedy, please.' The call was put on hold and West took the opportunity to voice yet another theory. 'What if Doris was frozen longer than a few days?'

'Like maybe three weeks,' Andrews said. 'Well now, that would be perfect. A five-million-euro motive for whatever the Checkleys did.'

'Niall, hi, it's Mike, sorry to be ringing you again. A quick question. Is it possible that the frozen body was kept frozen for a number of weeks?' He listened intently. 'Excellent, thank you. I'll let you know when we have it all figured out.' He hung up and took a deep breath. 'I think we have it.'

'He says it's possible?'

'Yes.'

Andrews frowned. 'Okay, so who visited the solicitor? Lynda Checkley would never pass for a ninety-year-old.'

'They might have roped someone else in to help,' Edwards suggested.

'The more people involved, the more likely they are to be discovered. Anyway, does Darragh Checkley strike you as the sharing type?' West paced, then stopped. 'Of course! The department we saw Checkley coming from – they do facial prosthetics. Maybe that's why he was there, to pay a debt.'

'Oh yes,' Gemma Ryan said. 'I have a friend who works in RTE as a make-up artist. He uses silicone prosthetics to age characters for parts when it's needed. He's shown me photographs and honestly, you'd never know.'

'Pritchard had never met Doris before,' West explained. 'It made it easier to fool him.'

'No wonder he thought the ninety-year-old was so sharp,' Andrews said with a laugh. 'It was Lynda Checkley.'

'They had the will changed to benefit them... and then what?' Allen frowned. 'They killed the poor old lady?'

West tapped the post-mortem report. 'The post-mortem indicated she died of heart disease. It may be that she died of natural causes but at an inconvenient time... she hadn't yet changed her will in their favour.'

'So instead of reporting it, they freeze the old dear and concoct this elaborate plan.' Andrews ran a hand over his face. 'Checkley... we knew he was a wrong 'un from the start.'

'Yes,' West said. 'And I haven't told you all of it yet.'

36

West pointed to the ghoulish photographs of the dismembered bodies and skulls. 'Our technician friend was the same one who had previously looked for a DNA match between the bodies and the hit-and-run victim. When he discovered a match between Cara Donaldson and the victim, he used his initiative and compared the DNA from the frozen body with the dismembered bodies.' West picked up the photograph taken at the recycling centre, the various body parts lined up in a macabre display, and fixed it beneath the rodent-damaged face of the woman they'd found in the laneway.

'He found a match between the frozen woman, who we now think to be Doris Whitaker, and the younger two bodies.'

'We were right.' Baxter thumped a fist into his palm in satisfaction.

'It looks like we were.'

Allen waved a hand, his face screwed up in lines of puzzlement. 'Have I got this right? The hit-and-run victim we thought was Doris Whitaker is really Muriel Hennessey, and the woman from the laneway, the frozen woman who we thought was Muriel, is really Doris?'

'Bizarre as it sounds, that's the way the DNA is pointing. Now we just need to prove it all. Right, first thing tomorrow I want Darragh and Lynda Checkley brought in.' He looked at his watch and tutted. 'Too late to get a warrant now but I'll organise one in the morning. If Doris died from natural causes, it was probably at home since by all accounts she was a recluse, so there might be a great big body-sized freezer in her house.'

Gemma held up a hand, colour rising in her cheeks when all eyes turned to look at her. 'The hit-and-run. Could it have been deliberate?'

West rubbed his eyes wearily. 'One of the reasons Jarvis's suspicions were raised about the frozen body initially was because Muriel Hennessy was a distance away from her house and she physically wasn't able to walk that far. Torquay Road is further away again, two miles, maybe two and a half from her home... how did she get there? So, to answer your question, Gemma, it is certainly suspicious.' He looked around. 'We've a lot of work to do to prove any of this. Go home, rest, come back for a long and probably tough day tomorrow.'

It was after nine before West pulled up outside his house. He'd rang earlier to warn Edel he'd be late. Usually, she'd have dinner and keep him something to heat up when he got in but that night, the table was set and there was no sign of her.

The sound of music drifted down from the room where she worked. He took the stairs slowly, the tangled cases weighing heavily on his mind and pressing him down.

Edel turned as he opened the door.

'Hi.' She held up her left hand... no sign of the ring, he noticed... to stop him. 'One sec, I need to get this down.' Then she stood and stepped forward, putting an arm around his neck. 'You look exhausted. Rough day?'

'I'll tell you about it over dinner since it looks as though you've not eaten.'

'I was on a roll and didn't want to stop. This book is really starting to take shape.' She pulled away. 'I put a lamb casserole in the slow cooker. It's going to be very, very well done.'

It was, but it was delicious. 'Perfect,' West said.

'Luckily.' She laughed. 'Right, now tell me, have you sorted out your crazy cases?'

Crazy cases... now reduced to one unbelievably crazy one. 'It's become a little more complicated.' Maybe explaining would get it clear in his head. It would also be a good practice run for telling Inspector Morrison in the morning. 'Okay, here's what we know...'

When he finished, Edel's round-eyed look of disbelief made him laugh. 'Yes, I know, unbelievable, isn't it?'

'Put it this way, if I wrote a story anywhere near as convoluted and incredible as that, readers would leave me a slew of one-star reviews.'

'You can't beat real life for throwing an interesting spin on things.' Tilting his plate, he spooned up the remainder of the gravy. 'That was delicious, thank you. Don't forget, tomorrow night we're going to the Italian.'

'Are you sure? It sounds like you're going to have a tough day. That Checkley guy doesn't seem like he's going to make it easy.'

'Whatever happens, I'll be home in time for us to go to the Italian at 7.30pm.' For once, he was going to put his personal life above his job. He stared at Edel's naked ring finger. Tomorrow... everything was set.

37

West had arranged to meet Andrews, Baxter and Edwards in Foxrock Station car park at 7.30am. As usual he was early but when he pulled in at 7.20am they were already there. Andrews sitting in his car, probably listening to country music; Edwards and Baxter deep in conversation that stopped when West pulled up. 'My bad habits are rubbing off on you, I see.'

Andrews got out of his car and stretched, yawning widely. 'I don't know about the rest of you, but I barely slept with this deranged case running through my head.'

'I stayed with Edwards last night.' Baxter explained his early arrival. 'Tanya doesn't mind and I wanted to make sure I didn't miss this.'

'Good. Right, you and Edwards take Lynda Checkley in. Andrews and I will bring in Darragh. The provisional charge is the concealment of a death and the false identification of a corpse with intent to defraud. I don't have to tell you not to forget to read Lynda her rights. Everything by the book, okay?' West waited for their agreement before continuing. 'We'll meet up outside their house and decide then how to proceed.'

It was a little after 7.45am when they pulled into the driveway of the Checkley house. A security light set high on the corner of the house lit up the drive. It went off a minute later when nobody got out.

West switched the engine off and surveyed the house. Dark windows stared blindly back. 'They're not early risers, are they? Let's wait until they're ready to leave.'

Edwards and Baxter were parked next to them awaiting instructions. Andrews sent a text, *Wait*. He put his mobile away and glanced at West. 'You don't think we should move now and catch them totally off guard?'

West undid his seat belt and stretched. 'No. We'd have to let them dress; they'd have an opportunity then to talk. I'd prefer to catch them by surprise and immediately separate them before either could reassure the other.'

'Good point.' Andrews pushed the seat back to get more leg room. 'You going to talk to Morrison when we get back?'

'Yes, I'm hoping he'll organise a search warrant for Doris Whitaker's home while we're interviewing them.'

'I'd like to be a fly on the wall when you tell him.'

'I have it planned.' West laughed. 'What does Mother love more than anything? Cases closed, yes?'

'As you've always said, it's his *raison d'être*.'

Andrews pronounced the phrase so perfectly, West guessed he'd been practising and waiting for an opportunity to use it. 'Yes, that's exactly right. He lives to have the cases closed so he can add them to his precious statistics. When I call around later this morning and tell him that not only do I have one case solved for him, but three, he'll be ecstatic.'

'Then you'll tell him what the cases are, and his ecstasy will turn to disbelief!'

'I can see his face already.'

Andrews held his forefingers out in front of him, brought them together and wriggled the combined duo. 'His eyebrows will come together like some fierce giant caterpillar and he'll glare at you from under them.'

'Then use words like ridiculous–'

'Preposterous,' Andrews suggested.

'Maybe ludicrous.' A light from the house caught his eye. 'They're waking.' He checked his watch. '8.05. Shouldn't be long now.'

It wasn't. Twenty minutes later, the front door opened, and Lynda Checkley stepped out. Her car was parked directly outside. She didn't look past it, aiming her car key to unlock, the sound loud in the quiet of the morning.

It was the signal for the detectives to move.

Lynda stopped with her hand on the car door and looked up in alarm as all four men approached. 'Goodness. To what do we owe this honour?' Alarm made her words sharp, but nervousness made her eyes shift from one to the other and back to the house. 'Do you want to speak to me or to Darragh?' She raised a slim wrist and looked at her watch. 'It really isn't convenient for me, I'm afraid.'

'That's unfortunate,' West said. 'We need you to come down to the station to help us with our enquiries. Detective Garda Baxter and Edwards will escort you.'

Lynda paled and leaned against the car. Caught off guard, she struggled and failed to find anything to say.

West waited until she was seated in the back of Baxter's car before he and Andrews stepped up to the front door. 'I doubt Darragh will remain so quiet,' West said. He peered through the glass panel of the door. There was nothing to be seen and he pressed the doorbell.

Baxter and Edwards had driven away before their repeated

ring succeeded. A visibly irate Darragh Checkley pulled the door open with more energy than was required, the door banging against the wall behind. His ire didn't lessen when he recognised the two detectives, his mouth twisting in an angry sneer. 'There better be a damn good reason for you hammering on my door at this unearthly hour!'

'There is,' West replied calmly. 'We need you to come to the station to assist us with our enquiries.'

Checkley looked over the detective's shoulder to where his wife's car sat. 'Lynda?'

'She's gone with our colleagues.'

'There is a good reason for this, I assume.' Checkley's manner was devil-may-care as he reached to tighten the knot on his grey silk tie, but a vein pulsed in his temple and his fingers trembled as they straightened the collar of his jacket.

'The preliminary charges are that you concealed a death and falsely identified a corpse with intent to defraud. Other charges may be laid pending the outcome of our investigations.'

Checkley said nothing and his expression didn't change as Andrews read him his rights. He grunted a 'yes' when he was asked if he understood. 'Before I go anywhere with you, I'm ringing my solicitor.' He glared at them as if expecting an argument and when none came, he huffed and took out his phone. His conversation with whomever he rang was short, succinct and a couple of minutes later, he was sat in the back seat of West's car.

In Foxrock Station, with Lynda Checkley in the Other One, Darragh was escorted to the Big One. 'Take a seat,' West said. 'Can I get you some coffee?'

Checkley sat rigidly upright, folded his arms across his chest and glared at him. 'Earl Grey tea.'

'No problem.'

Outside, Andrews rolled his eyes. 'Earl Grey tea!'

'They have some in the canteen. I think it's been there for decades but he won't know that.'

Baxter came from the Other One, Edwards trailing behind. 'She wants a solicitor.'

West jerked his thumb at the door. 'Checkley has phoned, they're sending one for each of them so we'll have to wait till they arrive. I'm going to update the inspector and I'll ask him to organise a warrant for Doris Whitaker's house.' He checked his watch. 'Allen and Ryan are heading into the Mater to speak to the person in charge of the department of anaplastology. Hopefully, they'll get confirmation that some facial prosthetics were made for the Checkleys.' He looked around at the intent faces. 'We're getting there but we need to play this bit carefully.'

With a wave he was gone, taking the back stairs two at a time. Inspector Morrison's office door was open. The inspector had obviously only arrived, still wearing a coat and a wool hat pulled down over his ears. He pulled it off when he saw West at the door and smoothed a hand over his flyaway hair.

'I hope you're not a harbinger of doom,' Morrison said as he took off his coat and hung it from a hook on the back of the door. 'Of course, it could be that you're coming to see me this early to let me end my week with some good news.' The chair rocked and squeaked as he sat heavily.

West dredged up a smile. 'That's more or less what I came to tell you. We're hoping to close all three of those odd cases we've been battling with recently.'

Unfortunately for West's plan, Morrison focused on the words *more or less* rather than *close* and his eyebrows joined in one giant hairy line. 'I have a bad feeling about this. Tell me.'

West did, trying to keep the report from becoming more tangled as he spoke. He watched the inspector drop his face into his hand and rub his eyes. 'We're hoping when we get a warrant to search Doris Whitaker's house we'll find the freezer that was used. It should all fall into place then.'

'Should it?' Morrison lifted his face and glared at him.

West took some consolation from the fact that the eyebrows had separated into individual parts. 'We have the Checkleys for falsely identifying Muriel Hennessy. If we find the freezer, we'll be able to make a case for their part in freezing Doris Whitaker–'

'But not killing her?'

'Probably not. I'm guessing she died of natural causes and they were using the death for their own ends. They used the prosthetics to pass Lynda off as Doris to change the will in Darragh's favour.'

Morrison squeezed his eyes shut for a second. 'Okay, I can see why they'd want a few weeks to pass between the will being changed and Doris's body being found but what I can't understand... why didn't they simply dispose of the body somehow?'

'Because they couldn't. If they'd simply reported her missing, it would have taken years to inherit. They were in a quandary, because if they'd left her frozen body to thaw, then rang to report that she'd passed away, there'd have been a post-mortem and the freezing may have been discovered. Their game would have been up.' West rested a shoulder against the wall. 'They needed a dead Doris Whitaker to inherit and a fresh body to identify as her. Somehow, they came across Muriel Hennessy.'

'And killed her?'

'Mrs Hennessy would never have been able to walk to Torquay Road where her body was found. Somehow, one or the other of the Checkleys... and my money is on Darragh... enticed her into their car and killed her, then made it look like a hit-and-run.'

'And I suppose you have a logical reason for the dismembered bodies too?'

There was nothing logical about any of these cases. West rubbed a hand over his head. 'We know from the DNA that Doris Whitaker was related to the two younger bodies. We also know that Doris's two children and husband disappeared almost fifty years ago... and Dr Kennedy had previously estimated that the bodies had been mummified around that time.'

'Mummified!' Morrison's face screwed up in disgust. 'There's no way to prove Doris killed them at this stage although I agree, it does seem the only conclusion.'

'It was possibly some kind of domestic incident... maybe the husband threatened to leave her and she got her revenge by killing him and the two children. The unidentified woman may have simply been in the wrong place.' West shrugged. 'We may never know unless there is something in her house that enlightens us.'

'You need a warrant. Okay, leave that with me and I'll get it done.' He looked at West suspiciously. 'There's nothing else, is there?'

'No, I think that's about it. We're waiting for the solicitors to arrive.' He checked his watch. 'I'm hoping we'll have confirmation of our theory from the department of anaplastology by then to strengthen our case against the Checkleys.'

'Anaplastology.' Morrison shook his head. 'Only you and your team, Mike. Right, I'll get on with organising the warrant. Keep me informed.'

The team were waiting in the detective office, all eyes focusing on West as he came through the door.

'The inspector will organise the warrant for us,' he said. 'Any word from Allen?'

Andrews shook his head. 'Not yet. Nor any sign of the solicitors. They're not rushing to the rescue.'

'Don't blame them. Darragh Checkley's an arrogant git and the wife's a piece of work,' Baxter said.

Edwards turned to West and rolled his eyes. 'Lynda told him he drove like he was a bit-part actor in a third-rate US cop show.'

'What does that even mean?' Baxter said, decidedly unimpressed at this slight on his driving.

West left them to it and went into his office, unsurprised when Andrews followed a minute later, a mug of coffee in each hand. 'Did you get Checkley his Earl Grey?'

'As you said. In the canteen, ten years past its use-by date. I had to shake a moth out of the packet but it probably won't affect the taste.' Andrews sipped his coffee. 'Morrison was really okay about it?'

'I think he was a bit stunned, Pete. It is one for the books, this case, isn't it?'

'Every time we get a weird case, I think we can't get weirder but this... we couldn't possibly beat this one.'

West's desk phone rang. 'Hopefully, good news.' He answered and listened in silence. 'Okay, good job. See you back here.' He hung up, met Andrews' eyes, and grinned. 'Closer and closer.'

'The department of whatever coughed up?'

'The department of anaplastology did indeed cough up. It appears that to fund a growing number of cases where people can't afford to have prosthetics made, the department has a lucrative, and official, sideline making masks for people. Checkley told the department manager that his wife wanted an old woman mask for a fancy-dress party, he paid a deposit and was supposed to pay the remainder when the mask was delivered. In what seems typical of Checkley, he waited until the department threatened to take legal action before paying the rest. That, it appears, is what he was doing the night we saw him in the hospital.'

'All done to fool Ashley Pritchard.'

'And to get their greedy paws on an estimated five million euro.' West looked up when Baxter appeared in the doorway.

'Two solicitors have turned up to represent the Checkleys.'

'Right,' West said, getting to his feet. 'Let the games begin.'

38

West told Baxter and Edwards to watch from the observation room. 'But as soon as that warrant comes through, I want you over to Doris Whitaker's house looking for a freezer. Give Shankill the heads-up that we may need someone from the technical team to take samples.'

He turned to Andrews. 'You ready?'

'Who are we going to start with?'

'The weakest link,' West said, heading for the Other One.

Lynda Checkley sat with her elbow casually resting on the chairback. Studied elegance. Too studied, and it couldn't conceal the shiftiness in her eyes or the way her clasped fingers tightened on one another.

The sharp-suited man beside her stood as they entered. 'I'm Xavier Bradshaw, acting for Ms Checkley.'

'Detective Garda Sergeant Mike West and Detective Garda Andrews.' West pulled out a chair and sat. 'Now that we've all identified ourselves for the recording, I'd like to ask Mrs Checkley some questions.'

Bradshaw held up a hand. 'My client tells me that she is being accused of falsely identifying a hit-and-run victim and of concealing the death of her husband's cousin. She denies categorically that she was involved in any wrongdoing. She was traumatised by seeing a woman lying injured... nay, dead,' he added with dramatic flair. 'And further traumatised by the realisation that it was someone she knew – a realisation which was triggered by the dead woman wearing clothes similar to ones her cousin-in-law regularly wore and by the woman being of the same age and colouring. If there was an error, she insists that shock was the reason.'

West opened the file he'd brought with him, took out a photograph and slid it across the table. 'Do you recognise this ring?'

Lynda glanced at it and shook her head.

West nudged the photograph further towards her. 'Muriel Hennessy's husband had it made for her as an engagement ring. According to her family, she never removed it.' He tapped the photograph. 'Yet, she wasn't wearing it when her body was brought to the mortuary and the ring subsequently turned up days later, on the finger of the dead woman we now know to be Doris Whitaker.'

'How odd.' Lynda injected a note of boredom into the two words. West was expecting her to yawn at any moment, maybe to flap her hand over her mouth for added effect. But she couldn't hide the tightening of her lips or the flickering of her eyelids.

'I gather you like fancy-dress parties.'

The question caught Lynda off guard. She laughed nervously and shot the solicitor a look that said he should answer.

Bradshaw responded immediately. 'If there's a reason that my client's personal life is of interest, I'd like to know.'

'Happy to oblige,' West said. 'The department of anaplastology in the Mater confirm that your husband bought a silicone mask... one that would effectively and convincingly age you. He said it was for a fancy-dress party.'

Lynda took her elbow from the back of the chair and folded her arms across her chest, her hands curling around her upper arms, fingers splayed, red-painted nails digging in. 'Oh yes, I remember now. Friends were going to have a fancy-dress party.' She shrugged. 'They changed their mind so I threw the horrible thing out.'

'All that trouble for a party that never took place.' West tut-tutted loudly. 'But perhaps you found another use for it?'

Bradshaw pushed back the double cuff of his shirt to check his watch, straightening the cuff again before looking across the desk. 'Is this going somewhere, sergeant?'

'Are you aware that Doris Whitaker changed her will a few weeks ago, Mr Bradshaw?'

The solicitor gave the question some consideration, weighing up the advantages and disadvantages of replying. Finally, he inclined his head. 'I am aware. I have been liaising with Mr Pritchard on behalf of the Checkleys.'

'What would you say if I told you, that at the time Doris Whitaker was supposedly changing her will, she was lying dead in a freezer?'

Solicitors were used to hearing all manner of things and most had perfected a carefully neutral poker face but even Bradshaw couldn't help widening his eyes at this. He recovered quickly. 'I would say "show me the proof", sergeant.'

West opened the file again and flicked his fingers over the reports before pulling out one. 'Here you go.' He laid it flat on the table and pushed it over. 'It might make more sense to you; the jargon tends to go over my head.'

Bradshaw scowled. 'Fake humility doesn't suit you.' He picked up the report and scanned it.

'If you turn to the next page, Dr Kennedy has written a

summary which states that the body had been frozen for a period of time.'

Bradshaw turned the page. He read silently, then dropped the report. 'It says that the freezing and defrosting process would have taken a minimum of eight days... it says nothing about her being frozen for weeks.'

'The cellular change in the body is due to the freezing process, there is no reliable way to estimate exactly how long Doris Whitaker had been kept frozen.'

'Therefore, she may have been frozen for only a couple of days.'

Ignoring the solicitor, West fixed his eyes on Lynda. 'The post-mortem indicates that Doris Whitaker died of natural causes so I'm guessing you found her dead. Was it your idea or your husband's to mount an elaborate charade to have the will changed?'

Lynda licked her lips. 'No comment.'

'That's okay. You don't need to say anything.' West reached for the photograph and the report and slipped them back into the file. 'We have the fact that you falsely identified a woman's body. We have Muriel Hennessy's ring miraculously appearing on Doris Whitaker's finger with the sole purpose of deception. We also have a statement from the department of anaplastology that your husband purchased a prosthetic that enabled you to disguise yourself as an old woman.' He lifted the file and tapped it on the desk. 'I think we have enough to go to the director of public prosecutions, don't you?'

A knock on the door disrupted the moment. West glanced around in irritation to find Baxter peering around the edge of the door. 'Yes?'

'Just wanted to let you know we got it, and me and Edwards are heading over there now.'

Bradshaw lifted both hands up in annoyance. 'Is this interruption necessary?'

'Detective Garda Baxter is informing me that we have a warrant to search Doris Whitaker's house. We hope to find the freezer she was kept in. I think we have enough to make a good case without it. But it's always good to have more.'

'No, you can't!'

All eyes turned in surprise to Lynda who sat with a shaky hand over her mouth. Whereas before, her eyes were restless with duplicity, now they were wide in fear. 'You can't,' she said again, her voice little more than a whisper. She turned to the solicitor. 'Tell them they have no right to go into her house. That it's under probate... or something.'

'Unfortunately,' Bradshaw said with a glance in West's direction, 'if it's a properly executed warrant, I have no right to prevent it being enacted.'

West looked to where Baxter still stood in the doorway. 'You have it?' He took the folded sheet of paper from his hand and passed it across to the solicitor.

Bradshaw's lips narrowed as he read. Folding it, he handed it back and turned to Lynda. 'I'm afraid there's nothing I can do.' He place a hand on her arm. 'If there's something you need to tell us about the house, now is a good time.'

39

Lynda Checkley took her hand away from her mouth and rested it on the table in front of her. It was trembling slightly. She kept her eyes on it rather than look up to meet any of the eyes that were staring at her.

West looked at the bowed head of the woman. She was a chameleon, changing rapidly to suit the circumstances... but what was it about the house that worried her? 'What is it you need to tell us, Mrs Checkley?'

It was a few seconds before Lynda lifted her head but she kept her eyes down. 'Doris Whitaker was a second cousin of Darragh's. They're not a close family so he didn't know she existed until two years ago when his mother died and he was clearing out her house. He found her address book and was flicking through it when he came across Doris's name and address.' She looked up then and met West's gaze. 'Darragh knows property. He knew roughly the value of a house on that road and when he went to see it – when he saw the road frontage it had – he was gobsmacked.' She took a deep breath and let it out on a shuddering sigh. 'It didn't take him long to sus out his relationship to Doris, then he was around in a flash to introduce himself. He can be very charming, especially–' a sour expression twisted her mouth, '–when he wants something.'

'Was the charade his idea?' West asked.

Lynda's eyes flicked to her solicitor. When he said nothing, she pressed her lips together for a few seconds. 'Yes, it was,' she said finally as if deciding that the truth was the best option. 'I called around to see Doris about once a week. I liked her but she was an eccentric woman.' Lynda gave a sad smile. 'Maybe that was *why* I liked her. She was a recluse, you know, rarely went out, then only to the local shops. Emotionally, she seemed quite fragile and she had this weird hoarding disorder – I don't think she ever threw anything out. Over the years, stuff was piled high in towers almost as tall as she was, leaving narrow paths through them. I never understood why they didn't fall, but when I voiced my concern she laughed and waved it away. It's a huge house, but she used only a small part of it. The only room I'd been into before she died was the kitchen.'

'And that was where you found her?'

Bradshaw laid a hand on her arm. 'I don't think you should answer that, Lynda.'

She looked at him. 'You're a good man, Xavier, but you haven't a clue.' She turned back to West, her face set. 'Darragh had convinced her to give us a key in case anything ever happened... like one of those blasted piles of rubbish falling on her and trapping her. When I called that day, she didn't answer, so I went home to get the key.' Her eyes clouded over. 'She was sitting in the kitchen as if she were waiting to have coffee with me. At first, I thought I'd made a mistake. I started to apologise for barging in on her but then I saw I'd been right.' Lynda stopped. She swallowed, held a hand over her mouth and shut her eyes. When she opened them again, they were tear-filled.

'I'd never seen a dead body before. I felt for a pulse in her wrist but there was nothing. Her skin–' the memory made her shiver, '–it was so cold I knew she must have been dead for a while.'

'You didn't ring an ambulance?'

She shook her head slowly. 'No. I wasn't really sure what to do, so I rang Darragh. He came over straight away, but when he arrived he had a grin on his face. I knew he was up to something, then he told me his idea.'

'You could have refused to go along with it,' Andrews said.

'You don't know him. He's like a tidal wave, pushing you along, pulling you under. You fight a bit but after a while it's simply easier to go the same direction.'

'You put her body in a freezer. In her house?'

Lynda looked at West. 'Yes, she has one of those old-fashioned chest things. Didn't keep much in it so it wasn't hard to clear it out.'

'And you dumped the poor old dear inside.' Andrews voice was scathing.

Lynda looked at him without saying a word, then she started to laugh, an unpleasant sound without even a whisper of humour. 'The poor old dear,' she mimicked Andrews. 'You have no idea.'

'Why don't you tell us?' West said calmly, wondering where this was going. There was something in her expression that worried him.

To his surprise, she shook her head. 'No. There aren't enough words in my vocabulary... in anyone's really... to explain.' She got to her feet so abruptly that she startled everyone. 'It's better if we go there.'

Bradshaw reached for her hand and tried to pull her down but she shook him off. 'This is the best way, honestly.' She put a hand on his shoulder. 'Thank you, I know you're trying to do the best for me, but actually this is the best way forward. You'll see what I mean when we get there.'

The solicitor looked across the room to where both West and Andrews had got to their feet. 'I've no idea what is going on but I suppose it's no harm to go along with it.'

It took only a couple of minutes to organise their departure but several for West to pacify Darragh Checkley's irate solicitor.

She was waiting in the corridor when he came out. 'About time,' she said and turned to walk back to her client.'

'One moment,' West said. 'Unfortunately, you'll be waiting a while longer.'

If the solicitor was irate before, she was apoplectic at this, her eyes on stalks as she came back and stood so close to West he could feel the warmth of her breath on his face. 'This is unbelievable.' Her voice was almost trembling with anger. 'My client has been dragged in here on the flimsiest of pretexts and is now expected to hang around waiting till you see fit to speak to him. Unbelievable.'

'There's nothing I can do.' West held up a hand to stop her as she opened her mouth to continue her litany of complaints. 'Information we've received from Lynda Checkley has brought us in a direction we hadn't expected. Mr Checkley will have to remain until our return. If you need to leave, so be it, I'm sure there will be a duty solicitor available when we need one.'

'That's not good enough,' she said. 'I'm taking this to your superior officer.'

West pointed to the stairway behind. 'First floor, second door on your right. Inspector Morrison, I'm sure, would be delighted to listen to you.'

West was smiling as he left the station and sat into Andrews' car in the car park.

'She backed down, did she?' Andrews asked, starting the engine.

'No, she didn't. She's off to complain to the inspector.'

Andrews was still chuckling when they pulled up on the driveway of Doris Whitaker's house.

40

D oris Whitaker's house was an early twentieth-century two-storey building with little charm. The windows, two down and three up, were small and the front door, set back in a darkened porchway, looked uninviting. Gardens spread each way from the central gravelled drive, giving that long road frontage which had added so much value to the property.

West got out of the car and looked around. There was a pervading air of neglect about it all that said no care had been given or money spent on it for a long time. The gardens were a dense tangle of briars and bindweed; paint was peeling off the wooden windows, darker areas hinting at rot.

'They'll simply knock the house down and develop the site,' he said as he and Andrews crossed to join Baxter, Edwards and a subdued Lynda Checkley who were waiting by the front door.

'Did Doris keep the windows shuttered or is that your work?' West asked her.

'Every window is shuttered, and there also heavy curtains. You'll see why when we go in.'

Andrews, rolling his eyes, stepped closer to West, and muttered, 'I bet this turns out to be the biggest anticlimax ever.

Doris probably stole underwear from the neighbours' clothes lines or something equally trivial.'

'Not that we would ever consider the theft of any items to be trivial, of course, but I think you're wrong, Pete. Whatever she's seen inside, it's thrown her.'

'Underwear or something along those lines. I bet you a pint.'

'It's a bet.' West checked his watch. 'Where's that blasted solicitor?'

It was another five minutes before Bradshaw's highly polished BMW pulled into the driveway. 'I apologise,' he said, getting out. 'I got caught up with a client who doesn't understand the meaning of *I can't speak now*.'

'You shouldn't have answered your phone,' Andrews said bluntly. 'I find that works for me.'

West saw irritation flare in the solicitor's face and held up a hand. 'You're here now, so perhaps we should get on with whatever this is.' He looked at Lynda. 'You have the key?'

She reached into her jacket pocket, pulled out a small set of keys and handed them over. 'It's the gold-coloured one.'

West singled out the correct key, stepped into the dark, uninviting, covered porchway and slid it into the lock. It turned easily and he pushed the door open. Meeting resistance, he turned to Lynda. 'Is there stuff piled behind?'

'No, but she has a daily newspaper delivered. I haven't cancelled it.'

The papers had collected on the floor catching on the bottom of the door as West pushed. 'Can you squeeze through?'

'Probably.' She wriggled through the space and a moment later, the door opened fully and she stood there clutching a pile of newspapers.

The hallway behind her was wide and spacious, but tall stacks of newspapers, boxes and other paraphernalia filled it on either side leaving only a narrow passageway through it into the house. Lynda reached to place the newspapers she was holding on top of the nearest pile and waved a hand around. 'I did tell you.'

She hadn't told them about the heat. It came at them in wafts; hot stale air that settled heavily and instantly squeezed out beads of sweat. When they were all inside, West reluctantly shut the front door. 'You left the heating on full?'

'Doris always kept the house like an oven. I thought it was because she was old and didn't have much flesh on her, you know. I used to wear a T-shirt when I came to visit and I'd still be melting.'

West felt beads of perspiration ping on his forehead. 'But why didn't you turn it off since?'

Her face tightened. 'You'll see why.'

Edel would probably have enjoyed the mysteriousness of Lynda's replies but he was quickly tiring of it. Perhaps Andrews was right and it would be much ado about nothing. West peered down the narrow passage. Even on a sunny day, little light would have found its way from the small window above the front door and that day it was dull and cloudy. 'Is there a light?'

'Yes, hang on.' Lynda's hand slid along the wall. The click of the light switch was loud but the response was dismal. A single unshaded bulb hanging halfway down the hallway did little to brighten the gloom.

Baxter and Edwards were quick to take out their mobiles and switch on the torch apps and soon beams of light criss-crossed the hallway. 'I've heard of people hoarding,' Baxter said, awestruck. He shone the light over the clutter. 'But this is surreal.'

'Okay,' West said to Lynda. 'Which way?'

'The kitchen where we used to sit is down on the right. But you need to see the dining room. It's at the back of the house.' She pointed forward, angling her hand to the left like a flight attendant pointing out emergency doors. 'This way, but be careful, some of the piles are very unstable.'

'Can't we turn off that damn heating?' Bradshaw was holding a white handkerchief to his face and patting it.

'Not a good idea,' she said. 'You'll see why soon.'

They moved off, a single file snaking through the shoulder-high towers of rubbish. The passageway was narrow, designed to accommodate the slighter frame of Doris Whitaker, not the bulky frames of the men. They hadn't moved far when Edwards yelled out in alarm as a stalagmite of empty Tetra packs keeled over. Baxter brought his torch around to see his partner flailing about. 'You okay?'

'No, I'm not bloody well okay,' Edwards said, kicking the flattened cartons out of his way and looking up in alarm as another pile moved ominously.

'We're nearly there,' Lynda said, proving her point by stopping in front of a door a few seconds later. 'This is it.' She turned her head to look at them. 'I know you all think I'm being a drama queen, making a big fuss about nothing.' She laid a hand on the door, red nails splayed across the unpainted pine. 'But what we saw in here... what we had to do... it's haunting me.' Her hand slid down to the doorknob. With a loud, indrawn breath, she twisted it and flung the door open.

41

After the overwhelming clutter they'd gone through to get there, West's first thought was that even in the dim light the room appeared remarkably tidy.

It was dominated by a huge table; three high-backed chairs to each side, a matching carver at each end. The windows, as Lynda had warned them, were obscured by heavy floor-to-ceiling curtains. Only the light from the two mobiles broke through the darkness, the beams sliding around the room, showing little, hiding more.

'It all looks unremarkable,' West said. But despite the heat he felt a chill crawl through him to tighten his gut and narrow his eyes. Something very bad had taken place in this room.

Lynda's laugh bordered on the hysterical. 'Oh yes, it all looks very innocent in the dark!' She slid a hand along the wall to feel for the light switch. 'But what about now?'

A gasp of disbelief can be surprisingly loud when it comes from five men simultaneously.

'I can't...' Bradshaw tried to speak, then gagged. Holding his hand over his mouth he made a swift return down the hallway. They heard him yell out as he stumbled on the fallen Tetra packs, and the clearly spoken and surprisingly colourful invectives he used as he made his way from the building.

'That was my reaction the first time,' Lynda said. 'It's amazing how quickly the mind adapts.'

Four of the eight chairs were occupied. The ends of shrivelled arms poked from shirtsleeves to rest on the dust-covered table and dried, twisted fingers gripped dull silver cutlery. Over the years, shrinking tendons and ligaments had tightened their grip, raising the cutlery so that some pointed towards the ceiling. As if they were all anticipating a good meal.

None of the bodies had heads.

'Bloody hell. There.' Baxter pointed to the far side of the room where four skulls sat on the mantelpiece of an elaborate fireplace.

Usually, West's first thought would be to preserve the crime scene. But the crimes that had been committed in this room had happened a long time ago. 'I assume this is where the four bodies you dumped in the recycling centre came from.'

Lynda looked at him in surprise. 'You found them?' She barked a laugh. 'Yes, this is where we found them. I told Darragh that it was a crazy idea but he wouldn't listen and insisted it was the safest place to get rid of them.' She waved a hand around the macabre scene. 'What do you think of your sweet little old lady now, gentlemen?'

West walked around the table. There was a certain ghoulish fascination about the display. He looked across to Lynda. 'The bodies you found were in the other chairs?'

'Two were sitting in the same way as these. The other two were on that.' She pointed to a chaise longue against the far wall. 'They were posed.'

'Posed?'

'Yes.' Her mouth twisted as she tried to deal with the memory. 'Each had an arm around the other as if they'd been embracing and that would have been okay, maybe even a little sweet. But the man's hand was on her breast, and her hand was resting on his genital area so that the overall impression was of something tawdry.'

West met Andrews' eyes. 'Lovers? Maybe that's why their skulls were left beside St Valentine.'

'I found a diary in Doris's bedroom,' Lynda said. 'It doesn't explain why she did this but it does reference her husband having an affair. He wanted to leave Doris and take the children with him. She was distraught.'

'Looks like she got her revenge,' Edwards said, dragging his eyes away from the scene. 'We know the bodies we have are her husband and two children and we can probably assume now that the woman was the one he was having the affair with but...' He waved a hand around the dusty table. 'Who are they?'

Baxter was the first to notice something strange. 'Look at their clothes,' he said, pointing to one of the bodies. 'That's a Foo Fighters T-shirt. They weren't formed until 1994.'

Edwards, standing near the carver chair at the end, looked down at the occupant. A flash of colour on the shrivelled wrist caught his eye. 'What year did Pandora bracelets become fashionable?'

It was Lynda who answered. '2001... or around about then.'

West looked around the table with a sinking feeling. Had they stumbled upon the oldest serial killer in history?

He tried to gather his scrambled thoughts. 'Okay, so this might be more of an active crime scene that we'd first thought.' He looked to Baxter and Edwards. 'Call it in. We'll need the usual suspects, the garda technical team and the state pathologist.'

'Why didn't you report this?' Andrews asked Lynda.

'Because Darragh has creditors snapping at his heels and he needed to get this place sold. All this–' she waved a hand around the room, '–it might have delayed things for weeks, months even. He didn't want to risk it.'

'So, you chopped the bodies up and disposed of them like rubbish.' Andrews' voice was caustic. 'You didn't think they were entitled to a proper burial.' He pointed to what were likely to be more recent bodies. 'That the families of those poor people wouldn't want to know what happened to their loved ones.'

'We were in shock,' she said, her voice a whisper. 'It made us act out of character.'

West looked at her. Which was the real Lynda, the hard-faced and manipulative woman or the vulnerable and easily dominated one? He guessed whichever would get her out of this mess. 'You'd better come up with a more convincing argument, Mrs Checkley. There'll be no place for your diamonds in Mountjoy jail.'

Her expression tightened, flint in the glance she threw at West. 'It was Darragh's idea.' She jabbed a finger at him. 'All of it. He pressured me to go along with it.'

Taking advantage of her sudden desire to pin everything on her husband, West asked, 'And the murder of Muriel Hennessy?'

Murder was a word that brought even the toughest down to reality and Lynda Checkley may have been self-obsessed and manipulative but she wasn't tough. She flinched. 'Murder... I...'

'Premeditated murder,' Andrews added with a certain amount of enjoyment. 'You'll get used to things in Mountjoy... after a few years.'

Her eyes flicked between them, horror dawning at the implication.

West thought he could see the exact moment when she'd decided she'd sacrifice anything... anyone... to prevent spending time in prison.

'That was Darragh's idea too. I was to drive along Torquay Road at a specific time and identify the body I'd find there as

Doris and tell the guards that it had been a hit-and-run.' Lynda wrapped her arms about herself. 'It was all his doing. I have no idea where he found the woman, or how he killed her.' She dropped her chin to her chest and muttered, 'I never asked.'

Baxter arrived back. 'The pathologist and the tech team will be here within the hour.'

'Good. Okay, take Mrs Checkley back to the station.' West turned to Lynda. 'We'll need you to write a statement about what you've told us and your part in all of this.'

'It will help, if I do, won't it? You know, if I stand witness against Darragh, they'll take that into account, won't they?' Desperation added a hint of pleading to her words. If she realised, she didn't care. She'd seen the future as Andrews had painted it and she was going to do anything not to face it.

West fought to keep the contempt from his voice. 'Your solicitor is outside; I'd advise you speak to him. We're not in the position to make promises.'

42

'She is some piece of work,' Andrews said when they were alone.

'Two of a kind, her and her husband.' West pulled off his jacket and loosened his tie. 'We've had some weird cases, Peter, but this one... it beats them all.'

'Lynda was right about leaving the heat on though. I guess if the temperature dropped, these mummies might start to disintegrate.' He did a circle of the table, stopping to stare at each of the remaining four bodies. 'How did Doris get away with it?' He glanced down at the bracelet Edwards had noticed. 'If Lynda is right about the date those bracelets came out, then Doris would have been around seventy when she killed this woman.'

'She had a good disguise. Little old ladies aren't generally murderers.' West walked across to the chaise longue where Lynda had said Doris had posed her husband and his lover. 'I wonder, did her husband want to leave Doris because she'd shown psychopathic tendencies or did his affair tip her over the edge?' He felt in his jacket for his mobile. 'That Checkley woman was right about one thing though, this is impossible to explain. It's something Inspector Morrison needs to see to believe.'

He was put through to the inspector almost immediately. 'I think you need to see for yourself,' he said when he'd given a brief explanation. He listened, then hung up. 'He's on his way. Seemed a bit stuck for words.'

Andrews laughed. 'We're never going to live this down, you know. Morrison will tell this story for years.'

'So he might.' West indicated the door with a tilt of his head. 'Let's wait for him outside where we can breathe.'

They negotiated the passageway back, Andrews grunting in annoyance when he came upon the mess of Tetra packs. 'I'll clear this away before anyone else comes.'

They did it together, piling the cartons on top of some of the more stable piles. 'I don't envy the person who has to empty this lot out,' Andrews said as they finished and made their way outside. 'But I guess it won't be the Checkleys.'

'Unlikely.' West took a deep breath of the chilly air. A minute later, he shivered and pulled his jacket on. 'If those four bodies have been reported missing, there might be DNA somewhere. We might be able to find out who they are, put a family out of its misery.'

'We haven't identified the other woman as yet,' Andrews pointed out.

'But we will. We'll do what we're good at, keep looking until we find out who they are.'

'You know, that will be several cases solved in one fell swoop. Morrison will be happy with that.'

'He won't be so happy when the press get wind of a ninety-year-old serial killer.' West pointed towards the tangled, overgrown garden. 'Doris killed eight people over the last fifty years that we know of, but our sweet little old lady may not have mummified all her victims. They're going to have to bring in the cadaver dogs and search the entire area.'

'Darragh Checkley was right about that anyway,' Andrews said. 'It's going to take weeks to clear this.'

Morrison's car pulled into the driveway. He was wearing an understandably bemused expression as he climbed from the car. 'I know it's bad when Garda Baxter is stuck for words.'

'This case has left us all a bit speechless,' West said. 'You'll understand when you see inside.' He eyed the heavy coat the inspector was wearing. 'I'd advise leaving your coat in the car, Inspector, it's hot inside.' He saw the inspector hesitate and added, 'Hot enough to mummify the bodies.'

Morrison grimaced, shrugged off his coat and threw it into the car. 'Right, let's see what all the fuss is about.' He made no comment about the piles that edged the hallway as he followed West and Andrews but when they reached the door of the dining room his eyebrows had unified in one dark criticism.

West had shut the door behind them when they left. He opened it now, resisting the temptation to sing out ta-dah as he unveiled the macabre scene of the headless diners.

No amount of explanation could prepare someone for the reality so he wasn't surprised when Morrison swore softly under his breath. 'Now you understand,' West said.

'Yes.' Morrison walked around the table, stopping to examine each body. 'You think some of these poor unfortunates are later than the original dismembered bodies?'

West pointed to the man on the far side of the table. 'Baxter recognised the name of the band on the T-shirt. No earlier than 1994.' He joined the inspector and indicated the next body. 'Edwards spotted the bracelet. According to the Checkley woman, it wouldn't be earlier than 2001. There's nothing obvious on the other two but forensics might be able to pinpoint a time frame for us.'

'A serial killer working without suspicion for the last fifty years or thereabouts.' Morrison took a handkerchief from his pocket and wiped it over his face. 'Unbelievable.'

The distant sound of voices broke into the silence. 'The tech team,' Andrews said. 'I'll go and fill them in.'

'Of the eight bodies, you've identified three,' Morrison said.

'Yes. The Checkleys disposed of four of the bodies in the recycling centre. DNA gave us the two children. Lynda Checkley stated that the other two were posed in a sexual way on the chaise longue. It appears that the husband had been having an affair and Doris found out, so I think it's logical to assume the male body we found is the husband and the unidentified woman his lover.' He looked around the table. 'These four might be in our missing persons file. We'll do our best to return them to their families and allow them to have a proper funeral.'

'Like you did for Abasiama.'

West looked at him, surprised and pleased the inspector had remembered the child's name. 'Yes. It's the least we can do.'

43

West heard footsteps in the hallway, the muttered imprecations of someone who was stunned by the amount of clutter. He waited in the doorway and raised a hand in greeting when the technical team manager appeared.

Detective Sergeant Maddison dropped a bulging kitbag at his feet and rubbed a hand over his grey buzz cut. 'The team got some garbled message about headless mummified bodies.'

'We're all struggling to find words for this crime scene. It's simpler to show it, which is why Inspector Morrison is here.'

Maddison looked impressed. 'The message wasn't so garbled?'

'Not even exaggerated,' West said and waved him into the room.

The inspector was at the end of the room, peering between the heavy curtains. He turned when Maddison entered. 'I think this one might even surprise you.'

'I've seen some weird carry-on, Inspector, but this...' Maddison looked around. 'Yes, it probably beats them all.' He spent several minutes staring at each of the four bodies from every angle, then stepped back.

'Two male, two female. You've already spotted the T-shirt and the bracelet which give a good time frame. The other female is wearing a wedding, engagement, and eternity ring. You might get lucky and find they're engraved. The second male is wearing a necktie around what's left of his neck – if you look closer you can see there's a logo on the front of it. A bee to be precise. The bee logo was designed for Dior Homme. I'd need to check but I think the earliest date was 2000. But it's still used to this day so...'

'He could be the most recent.' West walked over to the corpse and leaned forward to examine the tie. 'Okay, so that's two of them somewhere in the last twenty years.'

'No doubt the state pathologist will be able to help pinpoint a closer date.' Maddison tilted his head. 'If I'm not mistaken that's his cheery voice now.'

The voice grew louder as it approached then stopped abruptly when Dr Kennedy appeared in the doorway and took in the scene. 'Bloody hell!' Ignoring the three men at the window, he walked around the table, eyes wide. 'Never in all my days...' With a shake of his head, he joined the others.

West drew his attention to the mantelpiece. 'Their skulls are there.'

'Making an interesting addition to the macabre décor. It will be good to reunite them with their bodies.' Kennedy rubbed his arm over his forehead.

'You'll be looking for information to try to identify these poor souls. From clothes and personal items, at least two are dead less than twenty years, a third around twenty-five years. The fourth...' he see-sawed a hand. 'Hopefully, we'll get lucky.'

'It's going to take some manoeuvring to get them out,' Maddison said. 'There's not much space in the hallways.'

West met the inspector's eye. They'd be better out of the way if Maddison and Kennedy were going to get into a conversation about the best way to move and transport the bodies.

Outside, both men took a deep breath.

'What now?' Morrison asked.

'Now, I'm going back to the station to try and get both Lynda and Darragh Checkley locked away.'

Morrison looked back to the house. 'Doris Whitaker will never be held to account for her crimes.'

'No, but if we do our job and find the families of the people she killed, maybe they'll be able to get some compensation from her estate. It's worth around five million. I'd far prefer to see the money going to them than ever lining either of the Checkleys' pockets.'

Morrison turned back to him. 'Let's get that done, Mike.'

44

'Let's see what Darragh Checkley has to say for himself,' West said as he and Andrews walked into Foxrock Station.

They were waylaid in reception by Sergeant Blunt who asked in his usual blunt style, 'Is it true?'

Guessing he'd have heard all the details from Baxter and Edwards, West simply nodded. It was enough for the desk sergeant who mouthed *wow* but said nothing more.

'What are the chances of this being a nine-day wonder?' West asked Andrews as they walked towards the interview rooms.

Andrews laughed. 'The ninety-year-old serial killer would have been enough to keep this story spinning for a while. But a little old lady who slit open the corpses of her victims, removed their organs and stuffed them with straw and rags? Mummified headless corpses? This one will be told for years to come.'

It wasn't what Darragh Checkley's solicitor Emily Gallagher wanted to talk about though. She was far more concerned with the amount of time she'd been kept waiting and let loose with her complaints as soon as the door was opened.

West held up a hand. 'I'm sure Inspector Morrison addressed

your complaints. Now, to prevent any further delay, shall we get on?'

Gallagher was caught between wanting to continue her diatribe and the truth of his statement. 'Very well then,' she conceded and took her seat behind the table beside her client.

'That might be okay for you, but it's not bloody well acceptable from my point of view.' Darragh Checkley's face was an unhealthy shade of plum as he vented his own brand of fury at the gardaí. 'So now,' he finished, 'I want to know exactly what I'm being charged with.'

West looked at Andrews. 'Shall we tell the gentleman, Detective Garda Andrews?'

'Oh, I think we should, Detective Garda Sergeant West.'

'Oh, please,' Gallagher said with a sharp glance for each. 'Can we just get on with it?'

'Fair enough,' West said. 'Mr Checkley, we had a long and remarkably interesting conversation with your wife earlier, following which we checked out a house on Torquay Road. Your cousin Doris Whitaker's house to be exact.' He watched as a flicker of disbelief dampened Checkley's aggressively hostile expression. 'Of course, you'll know what we found there.'

'More games,' Gallagher said. 'If you've found something damaging to my client's case, it would be helpful if you'd spit it out.'

'Okay. In the dining room of Doris Whitaker's house, we found four corpses.' He met the solicitor's eyes. 'Mummified corpses.'

'Headless mummified corpses,' Andrews corrected him.

The solicitor's bark of disbelieving laughter died quickly when she realised they were serious. She looked from them to her client. 'You know about this?'

'Not only does your client know about it, Ms Gallagher, but

he was involved in the dismemberment and dumping of a further four bodies.'

'Four... there were eight bodies?'

'That's correct. We have identified three of them as being the husband and children of Doris Whitaker. The other five bodies have not yet been identified.' He hesitated. 'Some of the bodies are less than twenty years old.'

Checkley's eyes widened at this. 'Is this true?'

'Yes, two of the bodies were wearing items only available in the last twenty years. Their murder could have occurred any time since then.'

Gallagher looked at Checkley in horror. 'Your cousin was a serial killer?'

Checkley gulped. 'I didn't know.' He met West's sceptical gaze. 'I swear! We found her diary. It said she was devastated when she found out her husband was having an affair and planning to leave her. It didn't say, but we assumed she went a bit crazy and killed everyone who was there that day.'

'That's not the case,' West said. 'Now, we're not in a position to charge your cousin with murder but we are in the fortunate position of being able to charge you.'

'What?' Gallagher and Checkley said simultaneously.

Checkley's mouth opened and closed soundlessly as he fought to get the words out. 'Charge me... murder... who?'

'Muriel Hennessy. The woman your wife identified as Doris Whitaker.'

'What!' Checkley turned to his solicitor, panic in his eyes. He gripped her arm painfully enough to have her cry out and pull away. 'Do something! They're trying to stitch me up!'

Gallagher pushed him away and rubbed her arm. 'Sit back and shut up.' Only when he had done so, did she turn to West. 'You're charging my client with the murder of this woman, Muriel... Muriel?'

'Hennessy. Lynda Checkley identified her as being Doris Whitaker at the request of your client. Lynda states that she was told that there would be a body on the side of the road that day, at that time. Your client told her to drive past and to, as it were, accidentally come upon it. She was then to identify this body as being Mrs Whitaker.'

'No!' The one word came out on a howl. Darragh Checkley looked at his solicitor, then across the table to the two detectives as if not sure who best to plead with. 'That bitch... she's setting me up!'

This wasn't going quite as West had expected. He had assumed Checkley would deny any involvement in the murder of Muriel Hennessy but this... this was more than denial. 'Okay,' he said, sitting back and folding his arms. 'Why don't you tell us what happened?'

Checkley ran a shaking hand over his face. 'Lynda rang me to say she'd found Doris lying on the side of the road. A victim of a hit-and-run, she said. She sounded shocked.'

'And you never saw your cousin's body?'

Checkley squirmed in his chair. 'Lynda said her face was scraped and bruised. I have a thing about blood. I didn't want to see her like that.'

West's thoughts were a tangle. 'You really believe your cousin was the victim of a hit-and-run?'

'Why wouldn't I?' Checkley glared at the two detectives. 'Lynda told me she had! Why would she have lied? And why would I have been pestering you lot to find the driver if I didn't believe it, eh?' Then, as if a penny had dropped with a loud clunk, his expression changed. 'Are you telling me Doris is still alive?'

'No, she died, but not in a hit-and-run.' West held up his hand when it looked as if Checkley was going to ask more questions. 'Early last month, you went with Lynda to see your cousin's solicitor, is that correct?'

With obvious reluctance, Checkley replied, 'Sounds like you already know we did so there's no point in my lying, is there?'

Gallagher tapped the pen she was holding on the desk to get attention, a long-suffering expression on her face. 'What is this about?'

'Your client acquired a lifelike mask to enable Lynda to disguise herself as an older woman, as Doris Whitaker, to be exact. And in this disguise, she visited the solicitor and Doris Whitaker's will was changed in Mr Checkley's favour.'

Gallagher turned to look down her nose at Checkley as if he were a particularly loathsome bug. 'Is this correct?'

He shrugged. 'She was going to leave it to some damn charity. She'd never have known about it.'

West leaned forward. 'Of course she wouldn't have known anything about it, because she was already dead.'

45

Darragh Checkley looked confused. 'What?'

Either he was a very good actor, or he genuinely didn't know what West was talking about. 'Whose idea was it for Lynda to impersonate your cousin?'

'Hers. Some friend had had a mask made for a fancy dress, she'd seen it and thought it was so lifelike that it would fool anyone.' He glanced at his solicitor, then with a shake of his head continued. 'I'd tried to persuade Doris to change her will in my favour but wasn't having much luck.' His expression was sour. 'Lynda is a great believer in making her own luck. Doris didn't have much time for me, but Lynda called around most weeks to keep an eye on her. A few weeks ago, she said Doris wasn't looking too well... a bit blue around the gills, you know... and she was afraid the old bat would pop her clogs before I could persuade her to change her will and we'd get nothing. That's when she came up with the idea.'

Gallagher, who was struggling to keep up with the twists and turns this was taking, suddenly remembered her role. 'My client, however, was unaware at this time that his cousin was already dead.'

Checkley looked at her in horror. 'Of course I was.' He wiped his shirtsleeve over his face. 'I don't understand, when did she die?'

West was fast coming to an understanding that Lynda Checkley wasn't simply manipulative, she was incredibly cunning.

'Doris Whitaker's body was found last Friday. We're not a hundred per cent sure when she died... her body had been frozen.'

It was Gallagher, looking like she'd been caught in the headlights, who spoke first. 'Frozen?'

'Yes, then thawed and dumped in the laneway where she was found. Rodents caused damage to her body and especially her face which made identification difficult. Muriel Hennessy had been reported missing a couple of days beforehand so it was assumed to be her. Because of the rodent damage, the family identified the body from a distinctive ring Muriel was known to wear.'

West waited for that information to sink in before continuing. 'During the course of our investigation we had reason to check the DNA of the body against that of Mrs Hennessy's daughter and discovered there was no match. What we did find was that there was a match between the body in the laneway and two of the dismembered bodies that had been found dumped in the recycling centre.' He saw Checkley blink as he began to understand. 'Bodies that you discovered in your cousin's house and were desperately trying to get rid of.'

Checkley's face was a sickly shade of grey. 'I'd like to speak to my solicitor. Alone.'

'We'll take a break,' West announced for the benefit of the recording and he and Andrews left the room.

The rest of the team were in the main office, Allen and Ryan agog as Baxter told them what had been uncovered in Doris

Whitaker's house. 'They wouldn't believe us at first, thought we were making it up,' Baxter said as West and Andrews joined them.

'It's so unbelievable,' Allen said.

West pulled a chair from behind a desk and sat. 'More unbelievable is that Lynda Checkley is blaming her husband whereas he's doing a fairly good impression of a man who is clueless about much of what went on.' He filled them in on the earlier interview with Lynda and the more recent one with Darragh.

Edwards perched on the side of a desk. 'Wow, that is a tangle.'

Allen moved to the Wall and flicked through some of the reports. 'I've been thinking about Muriel Hennessy and wondering how she got to where she was supposedly knocked down. Lynda's statement indicated that Darragh dumped her body there for her to find.' He looked back to West for confirmation and when he agreed, Allen went on. 'But if Darragh isn't involved, maybe Lynda did it herself.'

'Knocked her down? But that still doesn't explain how Muriel Hennessy got to Torquay Road,' Baxter said.

'Maybe she didn't knock her down.' Allen crossed to the road map of the area and pointed to where Muriel Hennessy lived. 'Maybe, Lynda saw this little old lady walking along the street and an idea came to her. Or maybe she was actively looking for the right candidate. She stopped to offer her a lift and when she got to where she wanted to be, she pushed Muriel out of the door, maybe even with the car still moving. Then–' he tapped the map, '–Lynda got out and rushed over to bash the woman's head off the kerb to make sure she was dead. Only then did she ring for help.'

The silence that followed lasted so long that Allen shuffled from foot to foot. 'It's just an idea.'

'We've all the CCTV footage from when we were looking for Mrs Hennessy,' Edwards said, walking over to the road map. 'We never saw her but then, we weren't looking at the cars. If we go back to the Wednesday, before the hit-and-run, we might be able to see Mrs Checkley's car going through this junction.' He pointed to the junction at the end of Mrs Hennessy's road.

West stood and joined Edwards, his eyes following the road between where Muriel Hennessy lived and where she died. 'Well done, Mick,' he said, turning to Allen. 'I think your idea might be exactly what happened. Now we need to prove it. Check out the CCTV footage.' He pointed to the junction of Westminster Road and the Stillorgan Road. 'Did we get footage from the cameras here?'

'No, but we will,' Edwards said. 'If we all work on it, we should get through it quickly, it's a narrow time frame.'

'Good, get me something.'

46

West headed into his office. Andrews, surprised, trailed behind. 'We're not heading back to the interview room?'

'Let them stew for a bit,' West said, sitting and running a hand over his face. 'If this case gets any more complicated...'

'I'll get us some coffee,' Andrews said, heading away. He returned moments later and placed an overfilled mug on the desk in front of West. 'Sorry, I was thinking. Not a good idea when you're pouring coffee.'

'I hope you thought of something solid.'

'Not really, but I was wondering if we'd let our dislike of Darragh Checkley cloud our judgement.'

West lifted the mug carefully, swigged a mouthful to lower the level, then sat back with it cupped in his hand. 'Yes, we did, I suppose. But that Lynda woman, what a piece of work. She killed Muriel Hennessy–'

'And I bet she killed Doris Whitaker too.' Andrews held a hand up. 'Yes, I know Kennedy said she probably had a heart attack, but he couldn't be sure it was before or after she was put in the freezer, could he?'

West held the mug to his lips, then put it down. 'I wonder...' he said and picked up the phone. 'Maybe Maddison will be able to help us.'

It was a few minutes before he managed to get through to the garda technical team manager. 'David, sorry to bother you but this case is growing tentacles. We need to find the freezer where we think Doris Whitaker was kept. I know the house is a nightmare but could you make it a priority.' He listened for a moment. 'Yes, I know it's a complex crime scene but we think that Doris may have been put into the freezer while she was still alive.' He gave a quick laugh. 'Yes, very Edgar Allen Poe indeed. You will? Much appreciated.' He hung up. 'He's going to assign a couple of his team to search for the freezer.'

'*The Fall of the House of Usher*,' Andrews said. 'I looked it up, something about a woman being buried alive in a tomb.'

'Yes, she broke her fingernails trying to get out. If Doris was alive, maybe we'll get lucky.' He realised the implications of what he'd said and groaned. 'Not that I'd have wanted her to die in that way.'

'Wouldn't matter, it's unlikely anyway.' Andrews was being his usual practical self. 'The inside of those freezers are smooth. There'd be nowhere for her to break a nail on.'

'A delightful thought.' West drained his coffee. 'Right, we'd better go and see what Checkley and his solicitor have cooked up between them.'

Both Gallagher and Checkley looked up with set resigned expressions when they went back into the interview room.

'Interview is resumed,' West said. 'Right, do you have anything more to say, Mr Checkley.'

'I admit I went along with Lynda's plan to have the will changed. I also admit that I panicked when we found those corpses and furthermore admit to having...' he swallowed noisily, '...cut up four of the bodies we found and disposed of them in the rubbish bins in the recycling centre.' He lifted his chin. 'But I know nothing about the death of that woman, Muriel whatshername, or about the death of my cousin.'

'If you didn't kill Muriel Hennessy, who did?'

To the detectives' surprise, Darragh Checkley wasn't hurrying to take the leap to blame his wife. 'It was some unknown hit-and-run driver, wasn't it?'

Andrews wasn't letting him off the hook that easily. 'Muriel Hennessy had mobility issues. She wouldn't have been able to walk to where her body was found and identified by your wife as being Doris. Somebody brought her there... the same person is probably responsible for her death. Your wife insists that person is you, Mr Checkley. If it wasn't you... it had to have been her.'

Checkley looked at him without saying a word.

'Okay, let me put it another way... do you think your wife is capable of murder?'

Checkley grunted. 'Up till now, I thought our marriage was okay. Good as most. Then I discover my wife is happily fitting me up for murder. I wouldn't have thought she were capable of that... so how do I know what more she is capable of. All I can do, is repeat that I didn't have anything to do with the death of that woman or the death of my cousin.'

West got to his feet. 'Interview suspended. Sit tight,' he said, and he and Andrews left the room again.

'I'm not going into the wife without something to pin her down,' West said as they walked back into the main detective office. 'It would sink to a game of *he said, she said* and drive us crazy.'

The team were all glued to computer screens. Eureka moments rarely happened when they needed them.

There was nothing they could do except sit, go over everything again and wait for a breakthrough.

The first came twenty minutes later. 'I have her,' Gemma Ryan yelled, and punched the air in her excitement.

Within seconds, everyone else was crowded around. 'With everyone checking the traffic cameras, I thought I'd try something else,' she said, trying hard to sound calm. 'After the murder in St Monica's, I knew they'd beefed up their CCTV so I rang the sacristan and he was more than happy to send over the footage. Have a look.' She hit a key on her keyboard and the screen came to life. 'Just... there.' She pointed to Lynda Checkley's Volvo as it indicated to turn onto Kill Lane from Beech Park Road where Muriel Hennessy had lived.

With the time frame narrowed down to minutes, it was easy then for the team to track Lynda's journey to Torquay Road. 'Well done, everyone,' West said a few minutes later. 'And good thinking, Gemma. It's not proof but it's a hell of a lot closer and might give us the leverage we need.'

Back in the Other One, Lynda Checkley looked bored but relaxed. Xavier Bradshaw had obviously used up his store of polite chit-chat. He had a small laptop out, his fingers flying with speed across the keys. It wasn't until West said, 'Interview resumed,' that he stopped and shut it.

West rested his arms on the table and joined his hands together. 'We've had a long conversation with your husband, Mrs Checkley.'

'I'm sure that was informative. I hope he told you the truth.' She shrugged. 'I've learned over the years that he tends to be a little shy about that.'

Just as West had expected, a nasty game of *he said, she said*. 'On the day of the hit-and-run where were you beforehand?'

She gave the question some thought. 'At home. I work from home Wednesday to Friday.'

'And your route to Torquay Road?'

'Straightforward. Up Stillorgan Road, down Westminster Road and onto Torquay Road.'

'Sounds very straightforward,' West agreed. 'You didn't need to make any detours?'

Lynda's eyes narrowed. It was a full minute before she answered and when she did she proved herself to be a worthy opponent. 'Not a detour, as such, but I did call into St Monica's. I often do, to say a prayer and light a candle.'

West had to give her credit. She was good. And believable. He could feel his advantage slipping away. 'You parked in the church car park?'

'Lord no, it's a nightmare to get out of there,' she said, sure of herself again. 'I'm certain it annoys the residents, but I parked on Beech Park Road.'

West felt a dart of anger mixed with frustration. She was too damn clever.

The door opened behind him. 'Sorry,' Allen said, peering around the edge of the door and meeting West's eye. 'Can I have a quick word?'

It was several minutes before West returned. He gave a slight nod to Andrews who was sitting silently with his arms folded.

'My apologies,' West said, taking his seat. He put a slim folder on the desk in front of him. 'Now, as I said, we've had a long conversation with your husband. He seems, unfortunately, to have no recollection of you ringing him to say his cousin had died. In fact, he was under the impression that the hit-and-run victim *was* his cousin.'

Lynda laughed as if he'd made a joke, the sound fading quickly. 'You're serious?' She looked to her solicitor, a hand reaching towards him... pleading. 'Oh God, Xavier, Darragh is trying to pin it all on me!'

Ignoring the dramatics, West said, 'You stated, Mrs Checkley, that Doris was dead when you found her.'

'Yes, she was. It was a terrible shock.'

'And that was why you rang your husband rather than an ambulance.'

'Yes.'

'And it was your husband's idea to put his cousin into the freezer.'

'That's right.'

'After she was dead.'

Lynda looked to her solicitor with a raised eyebrow.

'I think my client has already explained that Mrs Whitaker was dead, Sergeant West, so perhaps we could get to the point.'

'The point, ah yes, good idea.' West looked at Lynda. 'Tell me, Mrs Checkley... how did a dead woman write her name in the ice inside the freezer?'

47

West sat back and folded his arms, not bothering to hide his satisfaction. Lynda Checkley was good, he gave her credit for being one of the more clever, devious and manipulative women he'd met. She was good... but they were better and there was a lot of pride to be had in that.

'That's impossible,' Lynda said with a sneer. 'I know this is a set-up. She was dead when I arrived. Stone-cold dead. Dead when we put her in the freezer.'

'We,' West said. 'Interesting, the only fingerprints found on the freezer, apart from Mrs Whitaker's, were yours.'

'Darragh was wearing gloves,' Lynda said quickly. 'He always wears gloves when he's driving and hadn't taken them off.'

West was almost impressed. 'Think carefully, Mrs Checkley... could it have been that Doris was merely unconscious and the shock of being put into the freezer brought her around?' He watched her carefully, could almost see the cogs and wheels rolling before she came to the decision to stick with her story.

'Absolutely not. Honestly, her skin was ice-cold. I think she'd been dead for a long while by the time I'd found her.' She turned to Bradshaw. 'They're trying to set me up but there's no way Doris was alive. And absolutely no way they could have found anything scratched into the ice since I defrosted the freezer after we moved her body. There didn't seem to be any point in leaving it on.'

'You heard my client, sergeant,' the solicitor said. 'So, unless you have proof of any of these allegations...'

West opened the file on the desk, took out a photograph and looked at it before putting it on the desk and sliding it across. 'You wanted proof. It's not the best resolution, but we wanted to show you as soon as we could. This is a photograph of the name scratched into the ice of the freezer in Doris Whitaker's home. It was taken by the garda technical team less than an hour ago.' He reached over and followed the line of the letters with his fingers. 'They're roughly done but then she was probably in a certain amount of shock having been tipped into a freezer. I think she may have been trying to write the date after her name.' He pointed to a few squiggles after the jaggedly-written *Doris*. 'Her fingers were probably too cold to do any more. Then, of course, she had the heart attack that finally killed her.'

Lynda snorted. 'This has to be a fake.' She turned to her solicitor. 'They're trying to stitch me up here. There would have been no ice. The freezer was unplugged.'

West opened the file again for another photograph. 'Yes, you unplugged it here.' The photocopy showed a single socket, the plug lying on the floor nearby.

'Exactly. I had to reach behind a pile of junk to get access.'

'Yes, your fingerprint was found on this plug.' West put the photo back into the file and took out the final one, a photograph of a plug in a socket. 'It wasn't, however, found on this one. And this one, is the plug for the freezer. What you unplugged was a vacuum cleaner hidden behind some clutter.'

He almost laughed at her shocked expression of disbelief.

'You really should have checked to make sure. If you had, you'd have seen the evidence.' He shook his head. 'It's always the little details that catch people out.'

West tapped the photograph of Doris's name in the ice. 'It looks like she managed to get her revenge even after her death.' He looked at Bradshaw. 'Among other things, we'll be requesting that the Director of Public Prosecutions charge your client with the premeditated murder of Doris Whitaker.'

48

The hard work was done. Now it was a matter of presenting the book of evidence to the DPP and letting her decide what charges to bring. West had met the current director and knew her to be an intelligent, clever woman who would handle the complexities of this case the way she did every other. He thought of the headless corpses sitting around the table and hoped she wasn't squeamish.

'We did good,' Andrews said as they went back to the main office where the rest of the team were already back-slapping and congratulating one another.

'We certainly did.' West looked around the room. 'We did very well indeed to tie up three messy, complicated cases into one incredibly complex one. They'll be talking about this for a while.'

'I rang Jarvis,' Baxter said. 'He's bummed that he missed it all.'

'It won't be our last complicated case,' Edwards said with a laugh. 'We do seem to attract them.'

'Good,' Gemma Ryan said, her eyes gleaming. 'Who wants a straightforward murder?'

Allen shook his head. 'It scrambles my brain working here, but I wouldn't want it any other way.'

'And I'll second that.' Inspector Morrison stood in the doorway. 'I wanted to come and offer my congratulations to you all. This,' he shook his head, 'has to have been the weirdest case I've seen in all my years. As Garda Allen has put it so eloquently, it scrambles my brain sometimes but I'm never bored.' He looked at West. 'Job very well done, Mike. Very well done indeed.'

It took another few hours' work to get the loose ends tied up and the book of evidence sent to the DPP.

Darragh Checkley was released on bail but a grim-faced, silent Lynda was led away to spend that night and many nights to come in Mountjoy jail.

'She won't be bothering us for a few years,' Andrews said. He was sitting in West's office with yet another mug of coffee in his hand.

West laced his fingers behind his head. It had been a long and exhausting day. 'What we have on her for Muriel Hennessy's death is circumstantial but Dr Kennedy is revisiting the post-mortem results. He might have something we can use.'

'She'll be put away for Doris anyway.'

'Doris Whitaker. I'll never look at a little old lady in the same way again.' West dropped his hands to the desk. 'Monday, we'll start trying to find who her victims were. I've asked them to rush the DNA.'

'We'll get there,' Andrews said. He got to his feet and checked his watch. 'This day feels like it's gone on forever.'

West glanced at the time on the corner of his computer screen. 'Damn,' he said. 'I hadn't realised it was so late.' He shut down his computer and jumped to his feet.

'7pm.' Andrews stood aside as West grabbed his jacket from the back of the door. 'I thought we'd go for a pint to celebrate.'

West smacked him on the shoulder. 'Not tonight, have to fly. Monday. We'll celebrate then.'

He was gone before Andrews could answer. Sergeant Blunt looked as if he were going to stop West for a chat but he stopped him with a raised hand. 'Fill you in on Monday, have to dash.'

Then he was in the car and swerving out onto the road, his eyes flicking to the time, swearing softly under his breath as he was stopped at every traffic light on the way. Usually a careful driver, he sped through amber lights and broke the speed limit most of the way home. Despite this, it was still 7.30pm as he pulled up outside his house.

'I'm sorry,' he said, pushing open the front door.

Edel came from the kitchen. She was wearing a tight-fitting black dress he didn't remember seeing before, her feet bare, hair loose around her shoulders. 'Bad day?'

'A long day,' he said. 'You look beautiful.'

Her smile melted all the stress of the day away. 'We don't need to go out. There's pizza in the freezer, we could have that.'

'No, we're going out,' West insisted. He pulled off his tie and hung it over the bannisters. 'There, casual gear, I'm ready to go.'

It drew a chuckle from her. 'Right, let me put on shoes and grab my coat.'

'We'll drive,' West said. 'We can leave the car in the car park and get a taxi home. I'll pick it up tomorrow.'

'I don't mind not drinking,' Edel said. Dropping her shoes to the floor, she slipped her feet in. 'Ready.'

'We'll see,' he said and opened the front door.

'How is the investigation going?' Edel asked as he drove the short distance to the restaurant.

'I'll tell you all about it over dinner,' he said. 'It had Peter talking about Edgar Allen Poe, put it that way.'

'Quoting Arthur Conan Doyle and now talking about Poe! What have you done with the Peter Andrews I know and love?'

The restaurant car park was busy but West squeezed his car into a tight spot in the corner. 'Here we go,' he said, putting an arm around Edel's shoulder. 'We're only twenty minutes late.'

'I hope we get the table in the window.'

'Oh, that's been organised.'

'Really?' Edel squeezed his arm. 'Clever man. I never remember to ask.'

In fact, not only did they have a table at the large bay window overlooking the marina but theirs was the only one there. Edel sat on the chair the waiter pulled out for her and looked around in surprise. 'I wonder why they moved the other table away.'

'It's nice to have more privacy,' West said. He met the eye of the owner who was standing behind and gave a silent prearranged signal. Almost immediately, an ice bucket holding a bottle of champagne arrived and two waiters appeared, tall candleholders in each hand that they placed between their table and the other diners. Then they lit the candles.

Edel's eyes flicked from the candles to the champagne. 'What is going on?'

'Wait and see,' West said with a grin. He held up a hand and suddenly the background music that had been playing stopped and into the silence fell the heart-warming sounds of a violin. The violinist drew closer and stood on the far side of the candlelight.

The stage was set. West got to his feet, moved closer to Edel and dropped to one knee. 'The first time wasn't very romantic. I thought, this time, I'd do it better.' He reached into his pocket for the ring box. 'Will you marry me, Edel?' He opened the box and watched as her eyes widened.

She shook her head, then laughed, pulled the fake ring from her finger and tossed it onto the table. 'Yes, Mike, I'll marry you.'

West stood to a chorus of whoops and cheers from the other

diners and because it seemed to be expected, he pulled Edel into his arms and kissed her. There were more cheers and some bawdy suggestions but once West took his seat and there wasn't more excitement, the other diners' attention returned to their own companions and dinners.

The violinist played once more, then he too, left them alone. Edel held her hand out, the diamond sparkling in the light from the candles, and asked, 'How did you know?'

He wanted to tell her that he loved her so much that her slightest worry was clear to him, that he would go to any lengths to keep her from being hurt, do anything to make her happy. Instead, he reached for her hand, lifted it to his lips and kissed it. *'You know my method. It is founded upon the observation of trifles.'*

She narrowed her eyes. 'Poe?'

West laughed. 'Sherlock Homes.' He quickly filled her in on Andrews' role in getting her ring back.

'I owe him,' she said, tilting her hand to admire it.

'We both do. But now,' West said, putting down his glass, 'wait till you hear about our latest case. The Case of the Headless Bodies.' He laughed at her expression and reached for her hand, brushing his thumb against the back of it. Then, in the romantic candlelight, he told her the details of the grim tale with her eyes sparkling as much as the ring on her finger.

Crime – it had brought them together and had nearly broken them apart. He'd keep chasing the criminals, she'd keep writing her crime stories and maybe together they'd solve the puzzles of the strange crimes that were sure to come in the future.

Because they'd come... of that he was certain.

THE END

ACKNOWLEDGEMENTS

Details are often adjusted for the sake of a story – the Mater Hospital, where I trained as a nurse years ago, has many departments and probably far more than were there in my day – but as far as I'm aware it doesn't have a department of anaplastology.

Grateful thanks to all at Bloodhound Books, especially Betsy Reavley, Fred Freeman, Tara Lyons, Heather Fitt, Clare Law, Ian Skewis, and the wonderful cover design team.

As usual, a big thank you to my brother-in-law, retired Detective Garda Gerry Doyle for assisting me with some of the details of the Garda Síochána – as ever, mistakes are mine alone.

Thanks to Lynda Checkley for the use of her name – I hope she enjoys being the 'baddie'!

A huge thanks to the writer Jenny O'Brien who is generous with both her time and support and who helped me pull this book into shape.

To other writers in the writing community who make this such a fun job – all of my fellow Bloodhound writers, plus the writers Leslie Bratspis, Patricia Gitt, Mary Karpin, Pam Lecky, Catherine Kullmann and Jim Ody.

We writers would be lost without the wonderful support of readers, bloggers and reviewers, thanks to every one of you.

A big thanks to all my friends who help celebrate each new book.

And finally – the foundation of everything I do... my amazing, wonderful family – husband, sisters, brothers, in-laws, nieces, nephews, grand-nieces, grand-nephews, and cousins.

I love to hear from readers – you can find me here:
Facebook: www.facebook.com/valeriekeoghnovels
Twitter: @ValerieKeogh1
Instagram: valeriekeogh2

A NOTE FROM THE PUBLISHER

Thank you for reading this book. If you enjoyed it please do consider leaving a review on Amazon to help others find it too.

We hate typos. All of our books have been rigorously edited and proofread, but sometimes mistakes do slip through. If you have spotted a typo, please do let us know and we can get it amended within hours.

info@bloodhoundbooks.com